MUR...
IN THE H...
GRAN...

SPIN

Bob Judd

BERKLEY PRIME CRIME, NEW YORK

SPIN

A Berkley Prime Crime Book / published by arrangement with the author

PRINTING HISTORY
Berkley Prime Crime edition / April 1994

ISBN: 0-425-14179-9

Berkley Prime Crime Books are published
by The Berkley Publishing Group,
200 Madison Avenue, New York, New York 10016.
The name BERKLEY PRIME CRIME and the
BERKLEY PRIME CRIME
design are trademarks belonging to Berkley Publishing Corporation.

PRINTED IN THE UNITED STATES OF AMERICA

10   9   8   7   6   5   4   3   2   1

Acknowledgments

Fake Space Labs is copyrighted by and used with the kind permission of Fake Space Labs, Menlo Park, California.

I'd like to thank Damon Hill for the laps around Silverstone.
And Martin Brundle for Magny Cours.
And Russell Bulgin, who caught some of my high-tech goofs and added a bit of his own impeccable style.

"God writes a lot of comedy.
Only trouble is he gets these terrible actors who keep
trying to play it as tragedy."

—GARRISON KEILLOR

Chapter 1

When I was seven I wanted to drive racing cars.

When I was sixteen my parents pointed out from their separate continents that being a racing driver was not a realistic goal. It was an escape, my father said, from real life.

By the time I was nineteen I had to admit they were right, so naturally I loved it. I loved turning the wheel, all the bets down, doing that pumping dance on the pedals and soaring into the corner. Racers call it "committed." You roll yourself and your car into an arc and you bet, as you enter, that you will come out whole on the other side. Commit too little and you are too slow. Commit too much and you fall off the track. Either way, once you are committed, there is nothing you can do to change your path.

Commitment has never been easy for me in what most people call "real life." On the track I am superb at weighing the balance, the grip, the curve of the track around a blind corner, and of course the speed.

I could ease onto the brake pedal in a motion as fluid as any dancer, bringing my thousand-pound projectile down from 195 miles an hour to a mere 145 in a slice of time so thin it is transparent, load the weight of the car onto the outside wheels, slip down a gear into fifth, kiss the curb on the inside of the curve, roll back on the power and feel four times the force of gravity drain my blood from my right side to my left as I brought my car out the edge of the track at 180, a half inch from the edge, accelerating hard.

But of course I wasn't thinking of commitment then. All

1

I wanted, I thought, was to drive.

I am in my London flat five stories up, looking out over Holland Park. The first snow hangs in the air and turns the trees to wet black and white in the fading early afternoon light. A taxi hisses by below, making tracks in the slush. I'd like to think it will snow all night and blanket this scarred city with white but the forecasters say rain tonight will wash the snow away.

A year ago, almost to the day, I was in Paris looking for a chance to drive a Formula One car again. Looking, to use the word in a different way, for a commitment. Meaning the money. You can have all the talent in the world in Formula One. But if you don't have the money you walk.

A year ago Chantal had the money.

A year ago Panaguian, Chantal's Director of Marketing, leaned toward me and spread his hands on his glass desk, pink buffed nails at the ends of his long narrow fingers and heavy, glossy black hair shading his pale skin. His face had a sheen of after-shave and gave off a scent of animals and flowers. "What I want," he said with a French accent, "is to make you the most sexually attractive man in the world."

His heavy mouth smiled a carpet dealer's reassurance at me while his eyes roamed the room. He was dressed with the heavy expense of the modern French executive—tousled razor cut, button-down collar and a hip purple necktie with a golden King Kong waving Fay Wray, biplanes circling around. Behind him, on glass shelves, lit from underneath so that they glowed with light, were the crystal bottles of the fabulously expensive perfumes that made Parfums Chantal rich. Fix ("Just This Once," the advertising said). Luxu ("Purely Primitive"). Calm ("Before the Storm"). Climax ("The End. And the Beginning.") and of course the classic Chantal ("The Essence of Success"). Small monuments to the power of marketing and packaging. Bottled dreams. Icons of wealth and desire.

Outside, Paris was enjoying a day of brilliant sunshine and freezing cold. Inside the offices of Parfums Chantal, the light was soft, and the air was scented with flowers and sex.

"I don't drive," I said.

Panaguian waved that away with his hand and the scowl that Frenchmen make when they hear something they don't want to hear. He made a pyramid with his hairy hands to rest his chin. Amusement replaced the scowl.

"We won't call it a men's cologne. 'Men's cologne' is too swish, too feminine. Besides it's not a cologne, you can't even smell it. If our projections are right we are looking at gross figures ex-factory, year one around the world, of around four hundred and twenty-five million dollars. Do you know what pheromones are, how they work? Never mind. Just take it on board that this sexual attractor is a very important new product for us."

Obviously it was important. They had flown me from London on their corporate jet, given me a suite at the George V. The least I could do, I thought, was hear Panaguian out. Paying attention is getting harder these days. The world burns and men in suits still talk of marketing. I dragged myself from the view out the window of the industrial haze that now spreads from city to city and cruised along the erotic "Purely Primitive" Luxu nudes that lined his walls. He was still talking.

"So we don't want it macho—we don't want to hear the clank of gold chains with tasteless gold medallions. What it has to be is new, contemporary, a kind of high-tech secret weapon"—his voice lowered to the level of a secret briefing—"unnoticeable, unavoidable, and absolutely irresistible to women."

"Is it?" I said.

"Is it what?"

"Absolutely irresistible."

"Legally what we can say is that it is 'attractive.' It is definitely attractive."

He gave me a small indulgent smile. "We test-marketed all kinds of names, as you can imagine. Mucho, Hit, Balls, Errecion.—" He went on, enjoying himself. "Emphasis,

Wave Length. We got a lot of playback on Length, but we didn't take it any further.''

A short pause for me to appreciate his joke. ''Then after the Gulf War, we looked at military associations: Missile, Scud, Firepower. And they all had their possibilities. But we are just not comfortable with the idea that any of our products could be thought of as a weapon. Then we hit on the perfect name—high-tech, masculine, glamorous, sexy, competitive, with worldwide appeal, and comes with its own built-in marketing strategy. No doubt you've already guessed what it is.''

I shrugged.

He held his hands up in surrender to the power of the idea. ''We are going to call it Formula One.''

''What a good name,'' I said without enthusiasm. ''But it doesn't have anything to do with me. And I don't have anything to do with Formula One anymore. I don't drive.''

His face relaxed into the patient smile of a man who has a fully funded corporate retirement plan. ''You are dangerous, Evers. Controversial, still mildly famous. You'd be surprised at your recognition rating in the Far East as well as across the U.S. and Europe. And, thank God, you are single. You would have a high profile. And you look—if you will excuse me but it is a phrase that came out of the research—like a walking crag.''

I gave him a craggy grimace. ''You look real,'' he said, ''not like a model. We don't want a gentleman of the gay persuasion, and we don't want a Tom Cruise who is so damn good-looking he doesn't need this stuff. We need to show that it works. Please don't make that face. With a little retouching we can make you quite handsome enough. But really you are perfect, Evers. Absolutely perfect. You have a certain street cred. A little down on your luck; there is a touch of scandal hanging around you, isn't there? And yet, and even better, like every wannabe out there dreams of, you actually have a chance to be a star. And we are going to give you that chance. Not just give it to you, pay you to take it.''

He took a sip of dark, thick coffee from a small white porcelain cup, considered his sip, pursing his fleshy lips and set the cup carefully down on its fragile saucer.

"You see, we don't want to give consumers the impression that this stuff is for the sexually deprived. We want our target users to think of themselves as strong, virile men like you who attract women like a magnet, who don't really need it. We would prefer for them to feel they just splash it on for backup. Excuse me, I must learn to stop calling it 'it.' They just splash on Formula One for backup."

"So you want me to walk around wearing this stuff."

"Do what you like. Naturally as a company we would prefer you would wear Formula One every day, but that would be your personal choice. I think you might find your life more interesting. Personally," he said, waving the thought away, "I don't give a fuck whether you wear it or not.

"We have scheduled a global rollout with a sequential sixteen country launch timed to feature you in each of the sixteen countries on five continents during the week of the host country's Grand Prix. Start in South Africa in March, finish in Adelaide early November. The month prior to the week of the South African Grand Prix, we will shoot two sixty-second commercials at Kyalami for cinema and television with thirty- and ten-second pool outs. We will also do newspaper and magazine advertising in forty-eight countries, but the majority of our media mix is allocated to PR. So we will be asking you to do your share of the PR. With some of the most desirable women in the world, I might add. You'll love it, believe me. And them.

"We are talking a six-figure fee with your manager to be paid in sterling into the bank of your choice on the Monday following each Grand Prix weekend. He's asking—no doubt he tells you all this—for something on the order of a Ferrari F-40 for you, plus all travel expenses, health and retirement packages, guarantees, insurance. He's asking for rather a lot.

The F-40 is out of the question. But I am sure we can come to some agreement.''

I winced at the thought. A year spent hanging around outside the doors of Formula One had been painful enough. Playing a French version of an international playboy reeking of a "sexual attractor" was too nasty to even think about. I tried to be diplomatic but I never have had a feel for diplomacy.

I said, "It's a stunning offer, but somebody has seriously misled you. I don't know how much you know about Formula One racing, so let me tell you. A former Grand Prix driver has about as much street cred and glamour as a camel dealer."

"Jackie Stewart."

"Was World Champion three times and worth whatever they pay him."

"And is married and on the board of one of our competitors. But yes, Mr. Evers, I absolutely agree with you. We don't want a former driver, we want a driver. And we have done our homework carefully enough to know that you still have your Super-Licence and that in your last season, which was only just over a year ago, you had a chance at the World Championship. We also know that you have twice attempted to run your own Formula One team in the past year and the less said about that, I'm sure you would agree, the better."

Panaguian pushed his yellow leather executive chair back and stood up, searching for the right words. The right words, evidently, were out the window. He leaned on the sill, looking out, his back to me. "As I said, our marketing strategy calls for a man who has a chance to be a star, not one who has already made it. We will give you that chance. We don't presume to choose the team or the car; that's your field as long as you pick a team that can qualify. We assume you know far more than we do about the teams and that you will choose the best you can get."

He turned back to me, knowing he had me. "We have three months before the teams have to declare their drivers.

You go out there and get the best driver you can. We have budgeted for six million dollars to put 'Formula One' on the side of your car. On the side pods. Solus. We want the exposure.''

Chapter 2

At the far end of the pit lane the green, blue, yellow and red car, bright as a bunch of balloons, nosed out of the Benetton pits, screaming.

Monaco glitters from the air. The blue-green sea sparkles, and the sun flashes on the chrome railings of the yachts and dances on the silver trolleys as they wheel out the lobster and champagne onto the verandas by the pools. Up close condoms bob alongside the jellyfish, but why knock a city as lovely as Monaco just because she is sliding downhill? Besides, it's spring, the air is soft in the evenings and the city rises up from the sea like a jewel thief's dream. If someone else is paying the bill, there are moments when you think you could live here forever.

Drop the anchor, Brompton. Wheel on the silver trolleys, Alison. And pop a magnum of the Dom Perignon, if you would be so kind, Remington, it's time to play rich. I like playing rich and I was grinning like a crocodile, remembering the Monaco dowager who heard the scream of Formula One cars outside her villa and sniffed, "In the old days they were gentleman playing at being mechanics. Now they are mechanics playing at being gentlemen."

We were coming in over the city in Phil's jet. Phil banked the plane for another loop over the harbor before touching down at Nice. Phil's large pointed face was clamped between the earphones. "This is going to be a hell of a year, Evers. I don't know if I ever told you, but I was in the stands when you got your first win here three years ago. I'd love to see you do it again, if it's not bad luck to mention it.''

"I'm glad somebody else remembers it besides me. Best race in the world to win,'' I said, thinking of that sunny afternoon in May when I had won my first Grand Prix. Monaco is too tight and too slow for the modern Grand Prix cars. It is too dangerous, with no real run-off areas and no room for the slightest error anywhere. They should have packed up the race years ago. Half of the joy of winning Monaco, I can tell you, was the sheer relief of having it over with, not having to charge the elephant through the china shop for another lap. Even so, I was looking forward to racing through the streets again. Phil was right. This was a great year. We could win.

The Umptiemme Grand Prix d'Monaco is, among all the other things that it is, the Mardi Gras of poseurs. And of the wannabes, shouldabeens and the men named Giorgio at the discos and the bars, with their battered faces, linen trousers, aqua shirts and hooded, glittering eyes.

I was feeling a little whorish so I thought I would fit right in.

Four months before, on that cold December day in Paris, I had taken a hard look at myself and at Chantal's proposition and thought, why not? What else could I do?

Not a damn thing.

Life as an ex–racing driver might have been all right if I hadn't left in disgrace and suspicion. But the disgrace and the suspicion still clung to me, and nothing was going to change that. That crash in my last race killed my teammate and destroyed my team and my career. I was about as welcome on the Formula One celebrity circuit as a toad in a finger bowl.

Panaguian was right: I had started two Formula One teams. One in America never grew beyond an idea, and the other, in Britain, grew just enough to eat virtually all of my money before we put a wheel on a racetrack. Herein followeth Evers First Law of Grand Prix Racing: He who has, gets. He who needs, gets screwed.

I'm not complaining, just passing along a little lesson I spent two million pounds learning. You may have it for free.

On that clear day in Paris I saw a goofy, tacky and morally suspect offer. The trouble was, you never know which chance to take when you are down. Any one might be the last. Look on the bright side, I thought. It was an opportunity to redeem my reputation. A chance to rejoin the club. A chance to stop living off my capital, staring down my money well and watching it run dry. Maybe even win again. With six million dollars of sponsorship under my arm, my manager could bargain for one or maybe even two million dollars a year for me. To do what I would gladly pay to do; drive a race car sixteen weekends a year and on the forty days of practice in between. If I had to smear crushed bat balls (or whatever they made the stuff from) behind my ears, it would smell like bread and butter. Nothing comes without strings, ol' puppet. Beggers do not dance to their own tune. Always happy to meet women with their own point of view, I told myself.

So I took the money and went hunting for a team.

Motor racing always was a money sport. Now it's ten times more money than sport, and sheer talent isn't enough. If you've got a few million dollars and you can drive around a racing track without bumping into the guardrails, you too can be a Formula One driver. If you don't have the money, you don't get to wear the suit. It's not fair, but it has been years since anybody accused Formula One of being fair.

In the distance, through the confusion of mechanics and photographers, of team managers, technicians, drivers and their cars in the crowded alley of the Monaco pits, Berenson shifted the Benetton from first to second, a flick of the finger under the wheel, the engine note sliding down a notch to repeat the rising scream of 750 horses burning.

The big-money teams—McLaren, Williams, Ferrari and Benetton—had all signed their drivers. And even if they hadn't, they wouldn't have answered my phone calls. But Team Joyce did. After a year in Formula One, Team Joyce had the enthusiasm, and talent and discipline, to win a race. All they lacked was the money. So sure, they were glad to talk about it, but would I be offended if they asked me to do a wee test for them? At Estoril, where they were testing? I had, after all, been out of a car for over a year. They just needed the reassurance that I still knew how to work the pedals. Could I be in Portugal next week? Which, translated, meant that they had twenty drivers knocking on their door. They weren't so desperate for money that they would take just anybody with six million in his hand. So could I show them that after a year's sabbatical I could keep the car on the track and that, given a break or two, I was still quick enough to get on the podium? Because Team Joyce wasn't interested in just showing up. They still had that old-fashioned attitude—they wanted to win.

Estoril is ten miles from the westernmost point in Europe. Bleak and rainy days sweep in off the Atlantic in January and make you wonder why you left bleak and rainy England. But that January day was as sunny as June, and when I slid down into the Joyce for the first time and took the wheel in my hands, I felt like I had come home. Even the electric zing of adrenaline on my tongue tasted familiar as I rumbled out of the pits and squeezed into a cockpit too small for me, my shins and elbows banging against the tub. I drove around easily for four laps, taking my time, learning the track again.

An empty track is a playground for a driver, a place to wail and dance, sing and charge. Nobody holds you up and nobody breathes down your neck as you soar down the black ribbon at a speed that erases the past and the future; there is only the one bright pinpoint of focus—the microsecond of time up ahead on the outside edge of the track where you will ease the vicious monster into another direction, keeping it on the edge of breaking loose, feeling the heat, and the strain of turning the wheel with four times the car's normal weight, as you load on the brakes and the downforce of the aerodynamics squashes the car onto the track. Two more laps, leaning into it, and it felt as if I'd never left. The concentration, the intensity grooves the brain so deep you never forget.

Soaring up and down those soft curves, charging out to the red-and-white curbs, the car was stiffer, faster and rougher than the Team Arundel car I remembered. And it took a while to use the extra speed, to wait the extra flicker of time before getting on the brakes. But I felt at ease with all that power, gradually unreeling the car out, onto the limit of that slippery moving crest just before the wave breaks, and holding it there, taking my time, feeling the car underneath the furnace blast of vibration and noise, feeling the unease in the car, the edgy uncertainty as the left front wheel begins to let go, in the first part of a thousandth of a second, into chaos and oblivion, and turning the wheel a fraction to the outside, loading a little more weight on that tire and willing the car back in control before the thousandth of a second had passed.

There was, as Jackie Stewart used to say, plenty of time. It was understeering too much for my taste, there was a strange vibration at 13,000 rpm that seemed to come from the left rear of the car, there was no room to move my feet, and my thighs and shins banged against the lumps of cables and the fire extinguisher, and I was grinning ear to ear. It was far and away the sweetest race car I had ever driven.

It took fifteen laps to get down to 1m.565s on race tires, fast enough to have put me second on last year's grid. And two-tenths of a second down on my new teammate, Russell Simpson, a twenty-three-year-old kid from the East End of London who had won the British Formula Two championship and had enough natural talent for both of us. Russell had had his session in the morning, and he stood in the pits, in T-shirt and jeans, his stopwatch in his hand, watching me. This afternoon the car and the track were all mine.

When I came back into the pits, Phil said, "So what is this stuff?"

"What stuff? I thought I was pretty quick for a man who was just having fun."

"Not you, for Chrissake," he said. "There's plenty of room for improvement, Evers. I can hear you braking too late for the esses on the back of the track, so you're a little wild coming into them, but you've got the ride. What I mean is what's this stuff you want to put on the side of my cars? This 'Formula One' concoction."

"It's a sexual attractor. What a man like you badly needs."

Phil grinned the stiff smile of confidence that team managers learn to wear. "I have enough trouble peeling them away. If I wore the stuff, I'd never get a lick of work done. I mean what's it made of? How's it work?" I wasn't even out of the car yet, and he wanted to know if the Chantal stuff would improve his sex life.

"You know those ads," I said, "in the back of *Autosport* that say, 'Do you attract Women?' It's like that. It doesn't smell like anything, but it's supposed to draw them like flies. Even to old spiders like you."

"I'm not having that on the side of my car."

"Six million dollars for the season, Phil."

"It really works?"

"They say it has a range of five miles," I lied. I had no idea whether the stuff "worked" or not. If it did, it was a trick. If it didn't, it was a waste of time. Either way, I had no intention of wearing it. Suppose it did work, suppose it was fantastically effective—after I had sorted all of the deluded women who were attracted by the stuff and found the one that I liked, how would I know if she was attracted to me or a fluke of industrial chemistry?

Phil stood up and stepped back, looking at his car with the pride of a father. "Well, I think it's atrocious," he said. "Can you get me some?"

Phil had driven in Formula Three, running his own team and winning the European championship. Then he retired from driving and started a Formula Two team. His Team Joyce won the European Championship after two seasons, and now he was determined to win the World Championship in Formula One. Phil was small, slim, had a large bald head with a large nose and deep-set eyes, and he wore a toupee. "It's only for the warmth," he said through clenched teeth.

Formula One team managers tend to talk through clenched teeth, and walk with the upright walk of tightened sphincters. It's a sign of being retentive, essential for running a business where detail is everything and nothing counts as much as money. But Phil also had spirit. And laughter. And Susan.

His wife Susan did most of the thankless work—luring sponsors and keeping them happy. She organized the sponsor and the media presentations and made the marketing men and women feel glad to be a part of such an outrageous and happy team in such a successful, glamorous sport. She looked "cute" in the sense that she had short and soft brown hair and a turned-up nose and wide soft mouth, and dimples. One eye was just slightly askew, as if there were something else, something playful and sensual in what she said. So it sometimes took a little while before you realized she had pinned your wings to the wall. The first time I met her she smiled that delicious smile and said if I crashed one of "her" cars, I needn't bother to get out. Later she told me that she and Phil had fought over whether I should join the team. As far as she was concerned, she had lost the argument. And for the first two weeks after I joined Team Joyce, I had the feeling that anything I did right proved her wrong.

Team Joyce's headquarters were in Pury End, a tiny village six miles from Silverstone; one winding street of stone cottages, two pubs, a little shop and post office and from time to time, one of the Great Sounds of Great Britain—along with Big Ben and steam trains—the sound of a Formula One engine starting up, idling, screaming and dying abruptly.

For his entry into Formula One, Phil bought a two-hundred-acre farm with a big farmhouse and got planning permission to convert the farm buildings into a modern Formula One complex. From a distance it looked like it was still a sheep farm. Inside the big sheds Team Joyce was out of the space program with a 12,000-degree autoclave for cooking the carbon-fiber tub and a machine shop that British Aerospace would have been proud of.

In a real way the Team Joyce farm was a mirror of Phil. Homely and down to earth on the outside; efficient, high-tech and single-minded inside. "The whole point of Formula One," Susan said, "is to win. If you win the races, the rest will follow."

Pury End was two hours from my flat in London. Just far enough that after a long day of testing at Silverstone it was all too easy to stay on for the evening, to talk about what we were going to do, and how. After a month of dinners, Susan and I had made peace. I had my own room in their rambling farmhouse, and with Susan's blessing, I was part of the family.

There were two running jokes on Team Joyce. One was Phil's toupee. "Just something for the birds to scrape their feet on," he said.

"He has to give it back to the raccoon in the winter," Susan said.

And the other joke was what he called his "incredible sex appeal." "I'm blessed with it, the way the sea has waves. Susan never had a chance, poor lass. None of them do."

"Oh, I have plenty of chances," she said over a gin and tonic one night. "You never see them because I push your hairpiece over your eyes."

Berenson's rear wheels kicked out to the left, toward the pit wall, and back toward the crowd in pit lane as his wheels spun, accelerating, 0–60 in 1.7 seconds. 60–100 in a heartbeat.

I went down to South Africa a week early for the Chantal shoot—two commercials for Formula One directed by Lane Hackmeyer, who, as everybody from the agency breathlessly told me, had won the Golden Crow at Cannes last year. His commercials have a lot of mist and fog. You may have seen the one we shot . . . It's dawn, the sun just coming over the hills, the track is deserted, and I walk into the pit garage at the empty Kyalami racetrack. Shots of mist and empty track and grandstands so you know there is nobody around for miles. Then half a dozen stunning women virtually materialize out of the mist. They stand around in the pit garage watching me, and I climb into my Formula One car and drive off down the track.

The tallest woman, the stunningly beautiful Margot, who has cheekbones like elbows and enormous innocent eyes, and who has been on the cover of *The Face, Vogue, Harper's, Elle, Vanity Fair, Cosmo*, etc., says, looking after my car disappearing in the distance, "He'll be back. He'd better." A logo at the end shows a bottle of Formula One for Men and a line underneath that reads, "The secret of attraction."

I thought it was a stupid commercial and said so. It seemed about twenty years out of date, the old *Playboy* women-revolve-around-my-cock dream. There were six people from the agency, four from the client, Hackmeyer the director and a crew of twelve. They listened patiently, and they all said, in the nicest possible way, "Shut up and drive."

Evidently there are plenty of good-looking teenage wannabe models in South Africa willing to work for almost nothing and the chance to be discovered and go to Paris and London. They squealed, read comic books and asked me to teach them what I knew about acting. They made me feel about forty years old.

But I liked Margot. Maggie Clanahan, if you want to know her real name, was six feet two inches tall, bony as a cart horse, wore no bra under a sweatshirt she didn't change for a week and read the *Wall Street Journal* ("I'm sorry, Forrest, did you say something?") to keep track of her investments. She was thoroughly professional ("Can we shoot it again, Lane? I didn't feel right about my hand move."). She was bright, had no sense of humor about her passion for animals ("A dog has just as much right as anybody") or anything else that I could see. Conversation was not her strong point but I liked her because she was considerate, worked hard and took her work seriously. For what it's worth I thought she was about as sexy as a hat rack. No doubt she thought the same about me.

For four mornings in a row, we got up at four A.M. to catch that just-over-the-horizon, horizontal golden light that looks so good on film, and then sat around for ninety-eight percent of the rest of the day while they set up shots. ("We're still seeing Margot taller than Forrest in the camera. Can you get something for Mr. Evers to stand on, Martin?") Hours and hours of waiting and then the camera goes hummmmmm for twenty seconds and then you wait for hours again.

After four days of the tv shoot ("Lift your chin, Forrest, that's it. A little more to the side. Good. A little more. Now smile. Can you put a little more sincerity into the smile, Forrest? Good. Very Good. Just a little more. Brilliant. I like that. Hold that while we take a peek at you through the other lens.") After four days of the TV shoot Maggie and I did the still shots for the press and PR. Margot and Formula One racing driver Forrest Evers getting in and out of limos, whooping it up at a discotheque, staring into each other's eyes at a café, going for walks together, rolling around on a sandpile in a photographer's studio. Cliché after cliché. The PR story was that one of the world's most desirable women had met me at the Grand Prix and fallen in love. Some of the outtakes of Maggie—sorry, Margot—they used for the Luxu advertising, but most of the shots of the two of us were distributed to men's magazines and newspapers around the world the week of the South African Grand Prix, with the bogus story building up the fiction of a hot romance, and of the power of the magical potion called Formula One. The best shots went into the advertising campaign that broke in the newspapers the week of the Grand Prix.

After a week of being pushed, prodded, directed and shot, I was glad to meet Team Joyce at the airport. "What's it like to make love to a taller woman, Forrest? Does she get on top or do you stand on a stool?" Susan asked sweetly.

Phil and Susan were followed off the plane by a shy man

with a pencil neck and long hair, wearing a wild and rumpled Hawaiian shirt. Phil introduced Alistair Benkins as their new aerodynamicist. I thought he was another pleasant twenty-five-year-old technoid who looked like he had been sleeping in doorways and standing in high winds. Formula One is always turning up weird refugees from the far shores of computer science and theoretical physics. I liked him. He was shy but rock solid when he started talking about his aero-dynamic theories.

Phil, facing me with his back to pit lane, looks at me in surprise, his mouth falling open and his eyes opening wide. He steps back.

Neither car finished at Kyalami. The good news was that we were competitive. I worked my way up to fifth before the gearbox started choosing its own gears. We did better in Brazil—Russell finished fourth and I came in seventh. Yes, there really was a reason I finished behind Russell. And if you'd like to hear about my leaking front monoshock, I'll tell you all about what it's like to have a front wheel go bounding up and down at 170 miles an hour. Unless you'd rather hear about Lalia.

Lalia was my next make-believe heartthrob, this time for the Brazilian Press, and she was outrageous, a cartoon of noise and lips, pushed-up boobs, a fog of tropical perfume, flashing eyelashes and thick black hair hanging down to her round little rump. Women's liberation to Lalia meant a willingness to try any position, anywhere, she told me on the first day of the shoot. They next day they were shooting the two of us in an un-air-conditioned studio, and we were sweating heavily in the backseat of a taxi that had been sawn in half to let in the camera and the lights. The photographer had Lalia throw her leg over me and had me bury my face in the boiled onion smell of the lovely Lalia's armpit, which also sported a large brown mole and the white caked glue of yesterday's deodorant. "Jesus, that's so sexy I think I'm coming," the photographer said.

While the photographer's assistants were arranging the

lights, Lalia bent her head down and whispered in my ear, "You like my ass, Forreeest? Señor Clemendez, the minister of culture, fucked me there, and he said I had the best ass in South America. You should try me. You'll never forget."

I declined that dark honor by telling her armpit that while I was sure she had a perfect asshole, I was, alas, in love with my fiancée back in England. A little white lie. And she said, "So what? You wear a strong rubber, nobody is going to know. You pay in dollars, I only charge you three hundred. You have cash?"

In Mexico we just didn't have the power to keep up with the faster teams. I finished seventh and Russell eighth, running nose-to-tail for the distance the way teammates sometimes do, trying hard to show who is faster and getting in each other's way.

My Mexican PR love that weekend was Maria Theresa Santa Caravaca, a law student from the University of Mexico who was openly contemptuous of me and of the whole process. She was only doing this, she wanted me to know, to piss off her father. "It will cause him terrible embarrassment at the bank," she said. The photographs show her beaming the same fixed smile in all of the pictures. They show me looking like I've bitten into a lemon. Panaguian rang me at my hotel in Mexico to say he thought they were the best pictures by far. He liked my look of "disdain," as he called it.

By the time we got to Italy for the San Marino GP and the start of the European season, Benkins and his laptop computer had given the cars a new triple rear wing and raised the nose three millimeters. I didn't think little aerodynamic tweaks were going to help much. What we needed was more power. "I'm working on that," Benkins said in his deep soft voice.

Phil looks at me in horror and takes another step back and I reach out for him, trying to grab his shirt to pull him back, and he takes two more quick steps back into the path of the Benetton, not hearing it, staring at me. Berenson has time to lift off the throttle—I can hear him lift—but not in time to get on the brakes—there is no time, and the front wing slices into Phil's ankles, knocking him sideways, the wing exploding in a cloud of fiberglass, throwing Phil back into the car, his head smashing against the roll bar and cartwheeling up over the rear wing, his big yellow earphones lazily looping through the blue Monaco sky, followed, at a distance, by his toupee.

Chapter 3

The limousine crept forward a few feet and stopped. Rain drummed the roof and on either side the green fields rose up and down in lush waves that faded to watery gray in the distance. Ahead of us and behind, a slow-moving stream of funeral cars—Porsches, Ferraris, Minis, Mercedes, Jaguars, Bentleys, Range Rovers and Rent-a-cars—wound their way, single file up the narrow lane.

We were meant to go first, but the lanes were already blocked with cars on their way to the cemetery, so we crept along in the middle of our own sad parade. Susan sat alongside me in a long black dress and a plastic rain hat someone had given her. Josh, her nine-year-old son, and Sue Two, her three-year-old daughter sat on the jump seats facing us, hair freshly combed, dressed up for church.

"Why do we live in this wretched country?" Susan said, staring out at the rain.

Sue Two wriggled off her seat and hugged her mother's leg. "Mummy, you love our house."

Susan bent forward and pulled the child up to her, gave her a hug and sat Sue Two on her lap. "You bet your bippy I love our house."

"And you like the neighbors," Josh said. "Except for those shits, the Younts." The man of the family now. Straight back and brave face. He had Phil's nose, but he would be taller.

"Don't call them that, Josh."

"You always do."

"Not today," Susan said.

We drove in silence for a few yards that felt like ten minutes.

"I had no idea there would be so many people," Susan said to the window. "No idea so many people would feel that they were his friends. I thought I knew them, but I'd swear that half the faces I've seen this morning, I've never seen before. I'm glad you are here, Forrest. I know I have to get used to it, but I don't want to face them alone."

"They are your friends too," I said, wanting to say something comforting and missing.

Stop.

Crawl.

Stop.

The church in Towcester had filled to overflowing, and when we came out of the funeral service, the TV lights were in our eyes. It took a few moments to realize that two or three hundred mourners had been standing outside the church, making a small field of umbrellas spreading out into the town, with black, maroon and yellow funeral flowers slick and shining in the rain and the TV lights.

The funeral procession consumed an hour crawling five miles to the cemetery. It didn't matter. No one was in a hurry, and the earth would wait.

The cemetery was on the side of a hill, facing south. A marching band stood shivering under a tarpaulin, and several hundred souls stood huddled against the driving rain. As the coffin was lowered, the vicar commended Phil's soul to God and the band played a stately, honking version of "The Monkey Wrapped His Tail Around the Flagpole" several times.

I hadn't heard it in twenty years, but the little nonsense ditty kept running through my head with the tune: "Oh, the monkey wrapped his tail around the flagpole, around the flagpole. And he pulled it down." The tubas and the saxophones, the bass drum and the clarinets squeaked and boomed, giving Phil an absurd joke of a send-off, a kind of jaunty, don't-give-a-damn shove to the funeral barge.

It was his choice. Susan said they had discussed what they would do if one of them died, and his instructions had been specific.

We threw dirt on the casket, and stood for a moment, watching the clumps turning to mud in the rain, dirty little rivulets running down the polished oak. The band came to an uneven halt, and we made our way back to the car, squelching through the long grass. Anxious faces bent forward, streaked with rain, saying how sorry they were, what a shame it was.

No one knows what to say in the face of death. And even if we did, it wouldn't ring true, it would only be a phrase, something to pass the awkward and painful moment. We are alive and he is not, and nothing we say will change a thing. So we mumble what we can and wander away from the grave knowing the earth waits with an open mouth for our return.

Susan smiled and shook their proffered hands and dove into the limousine, glad for the refuge.

On the way back, in the car, Josh roughly wiped a streak of tears off Sue Two's cheek with his sleeve and we were quiet for a while.

Susan took my hand and said, "When I first met Phil, at an abandoned sand pit outside our village in the Midlands, it must have been, oh, twenty years ago. He was three years ahead of me at school, so I knew who he was, but I had never actually met him.

"That day he was racing some bigger kids down the steep side of the sand pit, and the bet was who could get down the quickest on their bicycle. He was the only one who made it down to the bottom. I think he won around a pound, and I hung around out of sight for a while after the other boys went home. And when he started pulling up the boards that he'd hidden under the sand so his bike didn't sink in, I thought, That's interesting. He's tricky, but he's a winner. I mean he always took risks, Forrest. But only when he knew what the odds were."

It had been on my mind too. The press had said that it was an accident that had been waiting to happen. That the Monaco pits were far too small and too crowded for even thinking about a Formula One race. If the pits had been in any other track in the world, the race never would have been allowed to take place. The Monaco pits fell short of FISA requirements in every dimension. All of that was true. But Phil wasn't pushed. He didn't trip. I saw him step back, one, two, three steps into the path of Berenson's Benetton. His hands were up, as if he were suddenly afraid of me, and his face looked as if something terrified him.

At the last moment he started to look toward the car that was coming at him at something like 125 miles an hour, but by then it was too late. Until then, he was looking straight through me, at something. I wished I'd had the presence of mind to turn around, because I had no idea what had frightened Phil.

Something.

"Was there anything he was frightened of?" I asked Sue.

"Sometimes I think he was frightened of me," Sue said with a small smile, remembering.

"He was scared of dogs," Josh said. "That was the whole thing why we couldn't have a dog. He said they were a nuisance, but he was scared of them, wasn't he?"

"Only the big ones, Josh." Susan turned to me to explain. "He was chased off the grounds of the manor house when he was a boy by some Alsatians and got his leg bitten in the bargain. He liked to tell the story how they nearly chewed him to death, but I always thought it was mostly just a story. He didn't have any scars from it."

I searched the crowd in my memory. The usual mixture of photographers, mechanics, poseurs, movie stars and starlets and a stunning girl in hot pants and roller blades, but there weren't any dogs that I could remember. Dogs were never allowed in the pits. If there had been a dog and Phil had reacted to it, the dog would have shown up on the videos. "If there was a dog, it was invisible," I said, thinking of Phil stepping back, arms up; thinking of the gruesome scene after the accident. The ambulances, the crowds pushing in and Phil lying broken and soft on the hot track like a pile of dirty laundry in his own blood.

We withdrew from the race and began the sad business of ushering Phil's body through the Monasque bureaucracy. Susan was incredibly strong for the first two days. Then on Sunday, with the scream of the cars outside her hotel window, she collapsed and wept until a doctor gave her a sedative. My co-driver Russell Simpson and his wife, Judy, flew back with Susan to London. I had to stay on anyway for the Chantal shoot. I tried to get out of it, but there was no way. I was committed by contract and Chantal pointed out that there was a nasty penalty clause if I defaulted. If I didn't show up for the shoot, they could cancel their sponsorship of Team Joyce. Which meant I would lose my drive and Susan would loose her sponsorship money when she needed it. Besides, they said, the PR was terrific.

My Monaco passion flower was a nice, pretty teenage American model from California with clear blue eyes who called herself Mia and said "outstanding" almost as often as she said "awesome." In my fractured state her bright, happy, impersonal friendliness filled me with despair. They shot us groping each other at the Monaco Casino, on a yacht and embracing on the harbor wall. If that sounds just swell to you, let me point out that faking passion with a pretty, energetic and cheerful sixteen-year-old can give you the longest afternoons of your life. In between shots I was on the phone arranging for shipping Phil's body. I got back to my flat in London the day before the funeral, and there was a message from Susan on my answering machine asking me to come up as soon as I could, stay at the house and help her "face the music," as she put it.

The driver of our funeral limo let us off at the end of the drive leading to the Joyce house and Formula One team headquarters. I gathered up Sue Two, Susan took Josh by the hand and we ran a hundred yards in the rain, past the cars that were jammed into the Joyce driveway, and burst into the front door streaming and panting. Nobody paid much attention. The party was going full swing. Like the band at the cemetery, the party was Phil's idea. "I want it to be like an Irish wake," he'd said. "Only put me in the ground first, then I'll buy the last round."

Everyone in Formula One from the journalists to the drivers has taken risks and sacrificed what most people would call normal life to be in the sport. They are all driven by the conviction that on any given day they are the best in the world. And because they have given up home and in many cases family and are on the road from March to November, the Formula One crowd are as tight a community as any other circus. Put them together in one house, put drinks in their hands, and within minutes the place will be roaring with gossip and laughter. Which was, no doubt, what Phil wanted—for his house to echo with the warmth and jokes of his friends.

Alistair Benkins was the first to greet us, looking sheepish in a baggy designer suit he probably bought without trying on and carried home from Harvey Nichols in a shopping bag. The shoulders were creased and the sleeves were too short and his long neck rose out of a shirt that circled it at a distance. Susan gave him a kiss, and he gave her a kiss and held her to him as if they were falling through the sky together. Susan looked up at him for a moment and put her hand on his cheek before sweeping the kids away.

Alistair watched her go and drew me over to one side. "Did you talk to her? She won't talk to me. I've been going crazy. Did she tell you what she is going to do with the team?" he said, his long hand gripping my arm. "You don't think she'll sell it, do you? We're so close to breaking through now and it would take me a half a year to transfer the software to another car. It would kill me."

"It won't kill you," I said, feeling affection for this earnest kid. "Whatever happens, you will be fine." I had no idea what Susan was going to do. It had been on everybody's mind, but it seemed an insult to Phil to ask Susan about her plans before he was buried. I liked Alistair. He was an aerodynamicist and race-car designer and he had a kind of cautious solemnity. He had his own company, which, through a special arrangement, was working full-time for Phil. Which meant that he was always around. I was glad for his gloomy company.

Someone was tapping a spoon on a glass in the other room. Speech.

We crowded through the doorway and into the main room of the house with its high cathedral ceilings and tall windows overlooking the fields. In the near corner, looking solemn in their dark suits, I recognized the stubby figure of Jeremy Buckingham, the marketing manager of Emron, the multinational investment group that was our major sponsor.

Next to him was the tall slim figure of Sam Naughton, chairman and CEO of Emron. I'd seen Sam's photograph in the business magazines that crossed my desk along with the offers for platinum credit cards. And from time to time he was in the gossip columns, dating some new outrageous beauty with a low neckline and high ambitions. His long mild face, with the silver hair too long to be conventional, had been on the cover of *Fortune* a year or so ago. I didn't remember the article in detail; it had been one of those will-the-controversial-executive-hang-onto-his-empire pieces that business magazines like to run. But I did remember a nasty undercurrent. A suggestion that Emron's construction and arms companies were operating with the protection and guidance of the CIA in the Middle East.

Emron looked plausible on the surface, an important independent international investment organization, its advertisements said. But its public front covered a dungeon of holding companies, subsidiaries, affiliates, nonintegrated autonomous financial directorates, insider dealings, shell corporations, designated unnamed board members, front men, buy-back arrangements, divided corporate structures and split audits. The flimflam of modern corporate snake oil and tax evasion.

I hadn't seen Naughton in person before. He had the tan that rich businessmen like to wear in the winter, and he gave me the slightest of nods, appropriate to the solemnity of the occasion. Just enough to let me know he recognized me and small enough to let me know I worked for him.

The rest of the stories about him in the business press were mixed. Lately the rumors had been that Emron was overextended and in trouble. He was, according to *Forbes*, one of the "young pirates" who thrived on danger and ran at high speed in shallow waters. *Barrons* coined the phrase "Vampire Capitalist" to fit the vanishing breed of quick-rich junk-bond-takeover titans of the eighties and named Naughton one of the breed. He had grown rich buying large companies out of their future receipts and selling them off piece by piece. When the boom ended, he was left owing money on a dozen empty companies with no revenue.

Through the heads and bodies we could see Susan at the other end of the room, her hair down and her back straight, holding up her hands, asking for silence. Next to me, a journalist had taken a notebook out of his jacket pocket.

"I wanted to say thank you, all of you," she said her voice strained but clear, "for coming to our home, it will always be *our* home, and thank you for being such good friends to Phil. There are just too many people and too many things to say, so forgive me if I stand up and make a fool of myself, but thought I'd better do it now before I do something really silly and unprofessional like burst into tears." Susan took a deep breath, bit her lip and gave us a quickie smile.

"Phil was a part of my life for twenty-one years this September. I loved him and I will always love him. Which is why I am so glad you are here this afternoon. Phil died doing exactly what he loved to do, and I think, before we all go around wearing long faces, it helps to remember that. He had a great time. And so did I with him.

"It still doesn't seem possible to me. I'm not sure what's

happened has really sunk in. But as you know, you can't wait for the right time in Formula One. Decisions that Phil would have made still have to be made, and I have made some. I have tried to keep to what I think he would have done, and I thought you might like to know what that is so there is no misunderstanding.

"So," she said, drawing another breath, "of course Team Joyce will go on. No one, least of all me, could possibly underestimate what Phil gave to the team. Energy, direction, motivation, laughter—that's just part of a very long list. I really don't know how we can begin to replace any of what Phil gave to the team.

"But we have an obligation to our sponsors that goes beyond contracts. I look around the room here and I see faces from Texon and Goodyear, Marlboro, Emron Investments, Launceton Sportswear, The National Bank of Quatar, Hozuki Industries, Wriston Home Tools and Phelps Security. These people have been our friends and supported us and we can not let them down. And I think we have an even bigger obligation to Phil to carry on. He'd be terribly disappointed if we didn't, and so would I. I dread to think how lonely this house will be when you've all gone, and I don't think I could bear staying here if it weren't for my children and the team.

"Several friends have suggested that we skip the next race, in Canada Sunday week. We need to regroup. You probably know we have some new technical developments on the car we need to work on here. And we need to mourn Phil," she said, closing her eyes. "We need to catch our breath and understand how much we have lost and need to replace. So maybe Team Joyce should skip the Canadian Grand Prix. I think, under the circumstances, you and FISA will understand. But I am a businesswoman who has run the business side of this team. And I have to take the tough business decisions. Which I'll do the way I've always taken the tough decisions. I'll ask Phil. And when I ask myself what Phil would have done, if he were here, there is no question. Of course we'll race. I see several friends from the other teams and I want to reassure you that we will drive you off the track.''

There was laughter and applause at that, and Susan had to raise her voice to be heard, standing on tiptoe. ''In the meantime, thank you for coming, and for celebrating the wonderful man I love. Here's to the old sexpot.'' And she reached out and took a champagne glass from the table in front of her and held it up in a toast. And unless you knew her well, you would not have known that it was taking a powerful effort for her to keep from weeping. You would have thought that she was smiling.

When Susan came up to me later, in the kitchen, there were a couple of streaks down her cheeks and her mascara was smudged, but her voice was steady. ''Forrest,'' she said, holding my hand and giving it a maternal squeeze, ''could you possibly bear to stay on just for a bit after they've all left? There is something I need to say to you.''

Hours later, after the guests had gone and the catering staff was trudging in and out carting the glasses and trays out to their van, Susan and I were sitting in the front room. The rain was still coming down, streaming down the leaded windows. Outside there was just enough light to see the outline of the hill behind the house with the one oak tree throwing its branches against the sky. Sue had kicked her shoes off and her head was resting against the cushion and I was struck again how soft and pretty she looked, almost cuddly, with soft cheeks and dimples—and by how tough she was. ''Tomorrow,'' she said, ''I'll bawl like a baby. But first there is one more thing I have to do. I can't do this alone.''

''There's no reason why you should,'' I said. ''Jim Barton, Phil's assistant, could run the team for a while at least.''

''Jim's never made a decision in his life. He's a wonderful number two, and that's very rare and worth having, but he is not a team leader.''

''Well what about Tony Farnham? He's run both Dallara and March, and he knows the business inside out.''

''He knows how to finish in the back of the field. Look,

Forrest, I don't mean to be unkind. Tony is a lovely man. But I know exactly who I want to run this time. I want you to run it.''

I'd had a suspicion she might ask me, and I didn't want to do it. Ask any driver, driving is a full-time job. Jack Brabham had won the world championship with his own team in the days before sponsors, television and teams the size of small corporations. Ask Emerson Fittipaldi, who was World Champion, how running your own team can break your heart and your bank. No, I didn't want to run a team, I wanted to drive. I said, "I've tried to run a team, and it didn't work. And I don't want to be filling Phil's shoes.''

"You were trying to start a Formula One team from scratch. This one is up and running, and it is a damn good one. Besides, you won't be doing it alone. I'll retain full ownership, but I will have my lawyers draw up a contract that will give stock options over your current agreement and a substantial raise in your income. You'll have to work for it, but I know you could do it. I don't want some stranger coming in and putting his hands all over our team. I want somebody I know and trust. I want you to do it.''

"Susan, I like you, and I like this team. But I am a driver. It doesn't feel right to me.''

"I'm not asking you to give up driving. I just need somebody to help fend off the dragons. Give the team direction. I've always handled the business side, and Phil handled the racing side. And you could do it. Won't you do it, please? As Phil's friend?'' she said, taking my hand for the second time that day. "I will give you a substantial guarantee, put it in writing that you will manage the team for a year or I'll have to pay you something even more ridiculous than what we pay you now. So you won't have the pressure of trying to please me or anybody. You will have complete freedom.''

She gave my hand back to me and looked at me, tears starting down her face. "Forrest, please? Won't you do it? For me?''

Chapter 4

"I want to feel your big wide warm jimmy inside me," she whispered. "I want to suck . . ."

"Who is this?" I said. *Jimmy?*

"Wanda, Wanda Humph . . ."

"Wanda, I'm sorry to interrupt you, but I have herpes, AIDS and a boyfriend."

"Couldn't we just talk?"

I'd been getting two or three of these goofy calls a day since *Vogue* ran the article. I don't know how or where they got my phone number, but they were not shy. One woman wanted to know if I liked "doing it doggy style."

"Love it," I told her. "Rottweilers, corgis."

You never knew. Any one of them could have been a gentleman in a housedress. Or a lady with an ice pick. Or more likely the seriously bewildered, lonely and emotionally deprived. They were out there calling me because of that damn article, and there was nothing I could do about it until British Telecom got around to changing my number.

Vogue had called their article "The Race for Summer." The photos started on page 147 in the July issue and ran for six pages. They were all there—Maggie, Lalia, Maria Theresa, Mia, and Claudia from the San Marino shoot, rolling on the beach with "virile racing driver, Forrest Evers," leaning up against him, kissing him, feeling his rump. Supposedly the article was about the clothes (or lack of them) of summer but nearly every page mentioned that my "wardrobe" included a few drops of the new and irresistible For-

mula One by Chantal. The article was one of those multi
tie-in deals that *Vogue* does: designers, shops and prices for
the clothes, shots of the Formula One bottle on a dresser or
discreetly tucked in among the close-ups of writhing limbs.
I looked at the pictures, and I remembered the dirt grinding
in my back, the hot lights in my eyes and fifteen people
pushing, pulling, primping, telling me to raise my knee ''just
a notch, now lower the other one, hold it, and can we have
that faraway look again, Forrest? More passion, please, Mia.
Wait a minute; we're getting too much perspiration on Forrest. Martin, can you wipe Forrest for me please? No, no,
just his tummy, Martin; it's looking good on his chest. Forrest, you're squinting again.''

And yet, I had to admit, the pictures looked sexy. I didn't
think the half-naked poser in them looked much like me, but
strange and deluded women were calling me in the night and
first thing in the morning.

I was already late. I was due to see Jeremy Buckingham
in his office at Emron Investments in Berkeley Square at
eight-thirty for breakfast. Breakfast, in the code of today's
business world, means a tepid cup of chemical coffee in
somebody else's office and a silver platter of juicy problems.
The taxi was chugging outside, waiting.

I had four cars in the basement, none of which I'd paid
for. Car manufacturers pass out new cars to Formula One
drivers like candy. They think that if the public sees a hero
driver driving a Flogmobile, the public will rush out and buy
Flogmobiles. It must work, because they keep calling from
Germany, France, Italy and the Midlands to ask if I'd like
another one, when the kindest thing I could do for the
clogged drain of London would be to leave my cars in the
garage.

The last time I'd driven in from my flat in Holland Park
to the middle of the West End, some teenager with braces
on her teeth recognized my Aston Martin and planted three
lipstick-pink mouthprints on my window. A pretty and flat-
tering little gesture, but still, knowing they were out there,

thinking I was fair game, made me wary, and when I had a choice, I took a taxi. Riding in the back of a cab gave me time to think.

As we crept along Knightsbridge toward the gridlock of Hyde Park Corner, my disciplined mind cut through the agenda for my Emron meeting, glided right past the forty-seven things that absolutely must be done this morning for Team Joyce and landed softly between the perfumed breasts of Claudia, the Italian actress Chantal had chosen for my San Marino Grand Prix leading lady. It was a well-worn path. I could still smell her perfume.

For the first shot, taken in a bedroom at a hotel in Bologna, Claudia was wearing a black slip and I was in trousers with no shirt and no socks or shoes. Behind us the bed was tou-sled. And I came into the shot thinking I was a pro now, I knew how to do this, where were my marks on the floor? Thinking she was quite pretty in a dark, bosomy, Italian way.

They positioned us standing at the foot of the bed, with Claudia's arms around me, me looking off into the distance as if I am interested in a sea gull or, as the photographer put it, "Give us that far-off look of intensity, if you would please, Forrest. Think of the rain in Spain." And as they were checking their light meters, arranging the rumpled sheets, I felt her hand slide up my back, and her body, warm and soft, moved into me. Her hand moved up to my neck, pulling me into her and her soft thighs, and the warm, soft (sorry to keep using those same two words, but I hadn't really looked at her yet and all my impressions were warm and soft) mound in between her thighs moved against my leg and squished around. I looked down, and I was staring into the loveliest brown eyes I had ever seen, and I didn't even stop to think—I fell in.

Claudia was looking up at me with longing, lust, adoration and love, and the next thing I knew we were kissing and the photographer was going crazy, leaping around us, taking shots with his hand-held Hasselblad.

Then he said, "OK, stop. I've got to reload. Let's take a break for a minute."

And Claudia's tongue withdrew and she was away, on the other side of the room, talking to her hairdresser. I had ceased to exist.

We were shot on the floor, sitting on the bed, lying, rolling, writhing, she's on top, now me, on the bed, and each time it was the same. This incredibly beautiful, voluptuous woman would be crazed in heat for me, and looking in her eyes, I could see she was in love with me. She was so much in love with me I couldn't help but return the favor. Delicious, delectable woman. And then the photographer would say take a break, and I would be left there with my tongue hanging out and a hard-on. The second time, after going through thirty seconds of feeling rejected, I realized that she was an actress and she was doing her job extremely well and I might as well do the same. Claudia's recovery time was much quicker than mine, though. It was all I could do to keep from lunging after her when she got up from the bed.

The busses were stacked up six deep, blocking Hyde Park Corner like red elephants. Eight-fifteen A.M. Plenty of time to walk if I wanted. I looked out the window at the traffic— five lanes abreast straining forward, fumes rising into the gray sky. I pictured Phil's startled, frightened face, stepping away from me, into the path of the oncoming car. The car knocking his feet out of his shoes, his Fila running shoes standing on the tarmac, empty and unmarked as if his ghost were still in them. I tried to tell the Monaco police that something had frightened him and made him step back, and they were interested, but there was nothing more to tell them.

Several hundred other people had seen the accident, several million if you count television, and nobody else noticed that he was frightened. And even if he was frightened by something, I didn't know what it was. They called it "accidental" death and left it at that. It was possible that Phil had had enemies. You can't run a twenty-five million-dollar business as competitive as Formula One without stepping on some toes. But I couldn't think of a soul who knew Phil and didn't like him, and neither could Susan.

I asked the driver to let me out at the bottom of Berkeley Square, a perfect miniature of a perfect park. The great trees of Berkeley Square were planted in 1790, when the far western frontier of America was in Connecticut. They rise high overhead, making a green and leafy canopy over an oval island circled by traffic. Trees so tall and ancient that when you walk among them and think of the time that they have been there, the clutter of everyday hassles fades along with the growl of the traffic. The lawn is green and the light comes down in golden shafts and still, in this island of calm, Phil's terrified face stayed with me. What was I doing, running his team?

Going to hold the hand of his major sponsor for a start.

Emron's London office is a five-storey town house on the east side of Berkeley Square with enough mahogany, walnut paneling, spiral marble staircases and crystal chandeliers to furnish an American billionaire's fantasy of a London gentleman's town house.

"Forrest Evers to see Mr. Buckingham," I told the receptionist. She looked at me as if she expected me to deliver a package. Maybe I should have worn a suit. Maybe I'll buy one someday. Dark blue with the racy pinstripes of fast-track banking. Would I please take a seat? Mr. Buckingham was "engaged" at the moment.

I cruised through the financial magazines—"Don't Count GM Out" "Will Gold Bounce Back?"—and presently a woman in a black-and-white checked suit with natural shoulders and a skirt the length of a belt led me up the marble stairs, through the library stacked high with leather-bound books, and through a small door in the paneling that led into Buckingham's office.

It was like being led into the servant's quarters. Except for the view over Berkeley Square it might have been any middle manager's office. Flat green walls with calendars and charts tacked on, plain beige carpet on the floor, a large wood desk with three computer monitors, three chairs and a sofa. Buckingham peered around a monitor with a phone crooked in his ear and waved me to a chair.

Would I care for cream in my coffee? the woman with the oval face and exceptional leg length wanted to know.

Black, I said, would be fine.

As she handed me a porcelain cup and saucer, she bent close to me with her back to Buckingham and sniffed. She looked at me as if I were a filing cabinet.

"It only affects the sensually gifted," I said. Which may or may not have been true. I'd never tried the stuff. But I didn't like being sniffed at like a dog.

Buckingham put the phone down. "Thanks for coming in, Evers. I've got some concerns I want to share with you."

"These are uneasy times," I said. Buckingham was about twenty-six, going on forty-five. His accent said British public school, with a graduate degree from an American business college for the final twist of you-bet-your-ass efficiency. His late hours in the chair behind his desk had added pounds to his face and pouches under his eyes.

"I got a lot on my plate this morning, Evers; I don't want to drag this out. You probably know I'm a financial guy. I look at marketing as profit and loss. And I look at our involvement with Joyce, and I have to wonder what the hell are we doing? Why motor racing? Why go with a team like yours that isn't even in the top six? Turn on the TV and I can see a dozen sports that have more visual impact on the viewer than motor racing. You guys don't even pass each other anymore. We have a responsibility to our investors, we're reviewing all of our budgets, and I can't understand what the hell you are doing in our marketing mix."

"I don't know a marketing mix from a cake mix," I said, wishing I hadn't. They controlled half our budget. Be nice, Forrest, to the hand that feeds you. Remember the young hotshots hit you first, then they shake your hand. Try. "I'm sorry Susan can't be here," I said. "This is really her field. It's a little soon for her."

"She's a nice lady, and she's very good. Don't worry about it. I'm just telling you what I think. I don't run this company. This is Naughton's personal thing, so whether I like it or not, I have to make the best of it. So what are your plans?"

Plans. What were my plans? I said, "The only reason to race is to win. And if you can't do that, the only reason to race is to prepare to win. And right now—"

"No, no, no." He cut me off, waving his hands. "Marketing plans. I don't give a damn how you run your team. I'm looking for ways to market Emron. OK, you're new, Evers. Maybe you haven't had time to do your homework. Emron is a large international corporate investment group that retains active ownership in a number of large corporations. We are heavily invested in construction companies like Charter Corporation, which is rebuilding half of Kuwait; we own Phelps Security, world's largest security agency, and a number of offshore banks and holding companies, and if you read the financial press, you will know that we are under a small cloud after BCCI. So we are looking to shift a percentage of our financial resources out of finance and into high-tech areas. OK? That is the official line, and that is the one reason and the only reason we are investing twelve million dollars a year in Team Joyce. What we want is a high-tech presence around the world, like TAG with McLaren. OK? Because off the record, between you and me, Evers, if the interest rates come back up, we are going to start lunching off your budget."

I nodded, appropriately serious.

"So what I want to know is what you are going to do for us. I have to say this for Phil—he did make some great connections for us. Like Soft Air. That's one that Naughton is especially interested in following up. The one with that kook, the airhead, Alistair whatsisname—Benson—who does your aerodynamics for you."

"Benkins," I corrected him. "Why don't you just call him up?"

"Sure. We could do that. But what Phil did was find ways to put us together. Like the way he put that promotion together for the Japanese Grand Prix, between us and Sumoto Bank. That was great. In any case Soft Air say they are not looking for investment now and I think they are a little scared by the size of us. We don't want to go where we're not wanted but we like to know what our fellow investors in Team Joyce are up to. We value the cross-fertilization and the opportunity to share marketing exercises. A kind of corporate symbiosis, you might say. Mr. Naughton finds these relationships very useful, he says. I'm sorry, has your coffee gone cold? Sylvia, bring Mr. Evers another cup," he shouted into the air.

He leaned close to me. Man to man, lowering his voice. "She's a tiger," he said, "an absolute sexual tiger."

Chapter 5

Anoint yourself a Formula One team manager (a dab of lithium grease on the forehead should do it), and ZAPPO, you will be tailed by a conga line of designers, mechanics, accountants, businessmen, physicists, drivers, PR people, press, sponsors, marketing promoters and, so help me, the tea lady. The length of the line will vary, but the moment you step inside the premises, they will follow you, hopping with impatience, demanding your decision on every issue and every detail. You will wish they didn't because you'll know there is no way you can make every decision. And even if you could, you know the chances of your making the right decision about, say, how many liters of backup lightweight water-substitute coolant you should ship to Mexico are remote. But still they wait for you to make the decisions because they know you will tear their heads off if they don't. Delegation, I was learning, is a learned skill.

It was Alistair's turn and he was walking backward in front of me, pulling at his Hawaiian shirt, the red one with the green-and-gold palm trees and the blue sea swarming with grinning purple sharks. He looked like a starving surfer with a stretched neck. His walrus mustache drooped in gloom as he went through the sixteen reasons why he wanted whatever it was he wanted. Where, I wondered idly, does a man as thin as Alistair hide the mammoth echo chambers that make his voice sound like it comes from the bottom of a cave? I wasn't really listening because I knew what he was saying and I didn't want to hear it. Phrases like ''vectors interstice'' and ''multivalued logic 9'' stuck out of his conversational flow like dark, impenetrable islands. Not that Alistair was hard to understand. He wanted money. He wanted more money for some more time on the Cray computer, and I didn't have it. It didn't make any difference if he was right or wrong—Team Joyce didn't have any money. We were broke. Permanently stained with red ink.

The most common word used by team managers with small budgets, I was learning, is ''no.'' We were in the workshop, with the mechanics and technicians who were prepping the cars for shipping. The floor was bright white and so shining clean you could see the blue-and-green reflection of the three Joyce Team cars like Technicolor shadows on the surface. The cars were on the narrow alloy setup wheels that looked like the wheels of Ben Hur's chariot. Archaeological curios for the future.

''OK, if you won't listen to me,'' Alistair said, knowing he had lost my attention, ''look at this. I hate to be the first one to show it to you, but it's not going to go away. And you are going to need some news to deflect the shit that is flying your way.''

He handed me a copy of *The Eclipse*, a newspaper that alternates gossip about the Royals with nudes and murders. We had six hours to finish getting the three cars (two race cars and a spare), tools, spares, computers and radio equipment—just over five tons of racing team—ready for shipping and loaded on the transporters, get the transporters over to Heathrow, off-loaded and loaded onto the two jet freighters bound for Montreal with a manifest of 32,543 items on 347 pages. Every item had to be checked, checked again and rechecked.

I had been working flat out and I hadn't seen a newspaper in a week, so I assumed that *The Eclipse* was running some suggestive out-takes from a Chantal shoot. The paper was folded back to page five, lower half. A glimpse of the grainy figures in the picture and I knew it was something much sleazier. I could feel the shop go quiet around me, the faces turned to me.

"I wasn't going to show it to you," Alistair said. "But the thought occurred to me that you better see it before we leave because the hacks are going to be all over you."

The fuzzed face was definitely mine. It must have been taken from half a mile away.

I remembered the morning. We were in the main office, a converted dining room with a high oak-beamed ceiling. At one end of the room Karen, our business manager, shared a scarred pine table with a printer, a copier. Jilly and Charles, our two secretaries, had desks along the wall, Susan had a desk in front of one window overlooking the farm fields, and I had a beat-up old oak desk where Phil's had been.

Susan was on the phone to Launceton Sportswear, telling the managing director's secretary that their tickets were opposite the pits. "Not *in* the pits," she said patiently into the phone, "*opposite* the pits are the *good* seats." There was a pause, and Susan looked over at me with her eyebrows arched, putting a smile in her voice, saying she knew the expression "the pits," and if the managing director's son's friends wanted other seats, she could probably arrange it, but "pits" in racing were where they stopped to change the tires and work on the cars, and their seats were opposite the start/finish line. "Where they start the race," she said.

I was going through Phil's accounts on the computer screen. Susan had said she handled the business and Phil handled the racing, but it wasn't that simple. Large amounts of money were floating around in separate accounts. Susan's general account said we were spending more than we were taking in. But if you counted two of Phil's subaccounts— one for incidental revenue and one for "management"— there seemed to be plenty of money. "Seemed" is the key word because the money in Phil's accounts had been transferred to some codes that I didn't understand. In other words the team was operating at a loss, and somebody was making a profit. I was going down the receivables in the management account and finding that several drivers, two in Formula One, had been paying Phil several thousand pounds a month. One of the Formula One drivers was my teammate Russell Simpson. Something to ask Russell about. If, as the team account showed, Phil had paid Russell to drive, why did Russell kick back a third of his driver's fee to Phil? And where did the money go after it went to Phil? Into his pocket, into some secret account in Switzerland?

I was making a mental note to ask Russell about Phil's management fees when Sue Two came running in the office, tears running down her cheeks. She didn't make a sound, just ran to her mother's leg and hung on. Susan patted her daughter on the bottom and told the phone, "I'll have to ring you back." She put down the receiver, said, "Come on, Princess, let's attend to your toilette," swept her daughter up in her arms and went off to change her.

Since Phil's funeral Sue Two had been wetting herself. While she didn't fuss about it, she was old enough to be embarrassed. A few minutes later I heard Susan shout from upstairs, "Come back here." I heard the stomping feet of a three-year-old in full flight, and Sue Two, wearing nothing but a big grin came charging into the office straight at me. I caught her, as she knew I would, and had her in my arms going out the front door when Susan came down the stairs. "Do you mind," she said, "just for a little while?"

"I'll take Sue Two over accounts receivable anytime," I said, and holding the child in the crook of my arm, I went out into the sunny day to see what was happening in the garden. And that must have been when they shot the picture. The headline read "Evers's New Nudie"

"**Bed-hopping Formula One driver Forrest Evers, famous for lapping faster off the track than on, has yet another new playmate. The wee lass is Susan Joyce, daughter of Team Owner Phil Joyce, who died violently two weeks ago in Monaco. Evers's overnight pit stops with little Suzie's knockout sexy mum, Joyce's widow**

Susan, in the 2.2-million-pound Joyce Northampton-
shire home, has the neighbors buzzing."

It was mean, nasty, despicable and true. Of course I had
been spending the nights. Susan had insisted. She'd said that
she'd feel better, safer, and that there was no point in my
spending hours a day pounding up and down the motorway
when we had so much to do. I slept in another part of the
house, on another floor, in the room I'd always slept in. But
that detail had been Eclipsed.

"Has Susan seen this?" I asked.

"Doubt it," Alistair said. "I don't think *The Eclipse* is on
the top of Susan's reading list."

"I'll be right back," I said, heading for the door.

"Calm down, Forrest. Give me two minutes before you
go. I've got to show you this. Believe me, it's more
important."

"I'll be back in two minutes," I said.

Susan was at her desk in the office, bent over the word
processor. "Just a tic, Forrest," she said. "I'm trying to get
our newsletter finished and off to the printer before we go.
I want to write something about Phil, but it all sounds like
our brave departed leader. I don't know whether to laugh or
cry."

"Before you laugh, you better read this," I said.

She arched an eyebrow and took the paper. Bending over
her desk, her brown hair had just a touch of gold in it from
the afternoon sun coming in the window, falling over the
side of her face so I couldn't see her expression until she
looked up smiling happily.

"Isn't that cute," she said.

"Cute, Susan? We should sue their ass off. It's what the
tabloids call news these days, twist the facts to keep their
circulation up. Keep their advertisers happy. Those bastards
are smearing us to sell their goddamn rag. So no, I don't
think it's cute."

"Forrest, you're such an old prig. Of course we'll sue the
ass off them. Don't be so glum. OK, this is not going to be

a joke to our friends at the Bank of Quatar. But I can handle them. And I promise you we are going to take this little gift horse and run. You can't buy PR like this. We'll have *The Eclipse* buying us a dozen engines and a lifetime supply of roses, before I'm through. Phil would have loved that nasty phrase, 'knockout sexy.' And he would have run with it. Oohhh, wait a minute. I've got an idea. What's your shirt size?''

I was going out the door and Susan called after me, "Forrest. Is it true? Do you really sleep around that much?''

I found Alistair in his design office, peering into a detailed schematic drawing of our car on his computer screen. He didn't look up. Punching buttons, he said, "Here's our car, OK? This is the latest configuration from Bill and Cathy's CAD/CAM design.'' The car was accurate in detail and yet still looked weird, a three-dimensional cartoon with the flat, shadowless colors of a computer. As he punched the buttons, the wheels started to rotate. The wheels moved up and down, and the car acted as if it were going around a track, loading up on the suspension on one side, then the other, changing attitude as if it were going up and down hills.

"This is the Barcelona circuit from last year," he said, "taken from the data we picked up in our own computers: gradient, acceleration, lateral and deceleration forces. Plus I can punch in ambient temperature, atmospheric pressure, humidity, altitude. And, of course, since we already have a record of it, the exact speed on any given part of the course. I can show you Canada, but they've changed the course so much from last year . . . ''

"Looks like it would make a hell of a game," I said.

Alistair gave me a look of disgust and pity and turned back to the screen. "Let me make it simple, so even you can understand, Forrest. With the Chaos theory airflow software from Fake Space Labs in Palo Alto, and a satellite hookup with the Cray computer at Stanford, what we have here is a virtual-reality wind tunnel.''

"As opposed to real reality.''

"Right. The big teams like McLaren and Williams spend five to ten million dollars on their own wind tunnels, and teams like us have to beg, borrow and steal time on whatever wind tunnels we can find. But real wind tunnels have a lot of problems. They don't use real cars, they use scale models, which are expensive and take at least two weeks to a month to make. Williams spends around a million and a half a year just on models. Besides the expense and time, even a min-uscule variation from the full-size car can give you the wrong picture.

"A real wind tunnel is a tube with a big fan sucking the air through a tube. Put a model in the middle and you get all kinds of eddies and swirls that you don't get out on the open air of a racetrack. Plus you've got the wind sheer at the edge of the rolling road, so there's another bunch of curls in the airstream to screw up your results. Your ten-million-dollar wind tunnels can't get your fat Goodyears spinning around, and they can't give you the bow wave you get when a car accelerates from 85 to 165 in three seconds. The virtual-reality wind tunnel can do all of that."

"Don't see how we can get along without a bow wave," I said, hoping to deflect him, but I don't think he heard me.

"See what we do is provide an interface between the to-pology of the exterior surface from our CAD/CAM with the Fake Space Labs software, and we can dial in any damn situation we like. And even better, when I plug into the Cray in Palo Alto, we can hook up Clarence, Bill and Cathy's stations, and they can redesign any part of the car on CAD/CAM, and we can see the effect right now. We can dial in any design changes we like, and you don't have to build a model and wait a couple of weeks. You see what I'm saying? You can test a mathematically exact design in ten minutes, change it, and test the difference ten minutes later. You know as well as I do, Forrest, that most races are won before a car gets to the race these days. This could give us a hell of an advantage. For sure it will piss off teams like Williams who have just spent ten million on a new wind tunnel."

I tried to break in again, but Alistair was flying, waving his hands in the air like a large bird. "Like right now. You could take the cars with you to Montreal, and if we find a better wing configuration, we can try it on the computer, have our guys build it overnight, and you could have it at the track the next day, see how it works."

He paused for breath, and I said, "What's it cost for time on your super computer in California?"

"Well, with the time differential we're really in an excellent position to take advantage of their late-night downtime rates and a special deal that this Wilbur at Fake Space Labs has . . ."

"The bottom line," I said. "How much are you asking for?"

"Two hundred twenty-five thousand dollars for a primary exploration and to work out the bugs. There are always bugs," he said.

"Spend it," I said.

Chapter 6

The Hotel Gran Caique hangs over the St. Lawrence Seaway, pointing south, like the prow of a ship that has backed into the man-made Isle de France. It was built for Expo years ago, and there's not much reason to stay there unless it's the week of the Canadian Grand Prix. The front entrance of the Gran Caique is a five-minute walk from the track.

Big Cock, as Russell called it, was Susan's choice. She said we were going to be up front. That if you want to be successful, you have to act like you are a success. One of those paperback self-help phrases that comes from thinking all achievement takes is wishful thinking. But I kept my mouth shut. It was her money and she'd had, and was going to have, a tough time.

Team Joyce pulled up front in a flotilla of taxis. In the clutter of people going up and down the steps, a TV news team was peering inside the taxis, looking to see who we were.

No, they didn't want to talk to me or to Russell. Forget the drivers, where was Knockout Sexy Mum? The One Who Owned a Formula One Team. Recently Widowed. Mixed Up in a Sex Scandal. TV news teams travel light these days. This one had one blond female with an on-and-off smile, wearing a spiffy red suit, reporting live from the Isle de Notre Dame; one longhair cameraman with baggy pants, squinting into his lens; and one shapeless bored and balding sound man draped with a battery pack and a tape recorder, holding a long pole with a mike dangling on the end. His T-shirt said,

"Sound Men Do It in Your Ear." A lanky producer in jeans and a leather motorcycle jacket, with a clipboard in her hand, told Susan as we got out of the cab, "Let's do it now, sweetheart 'cause we only got time for one take, and we'd like to make the five o'clock."

Knockout Sexy was running up the steps and into the lobby and back out again, followed by three hotel bellboys carrying boxes, and a large, scowling woman in high heels and a print dress who had to run to keep up. "Forrest," Susan said, putting her hand on my arm, "I want you to meet Sallye Babaneau, our PR contact in Montreal."

Sallye had a face like an eel—smooth, sleek, with beady eyes, and shiny black hair drawn back in a ponytail. She looked over the milling crowd and spotted the crew while I said hello. She nodded, not looking at me. Susan was saying, "Did you check them, the jackets? Where's ESPN? I don't see ESPN."

Sallye Babaneau said, as if Susan should know this, "ESPN said they don't have the airtime. And their crew won't be here until Friday anyway. I talked to their producer, Mel Skulnik. Do you know Mel? He's a darling. Very influential at ESPN." Her eel face went into smile mode for a moment at the one-up of knowing Mel. "Mel said he'll see how it goes. Maybe they'll do a studio one-on-one on Saturday for a race insert if the story's still current."

Susan said, "Shit. OK, let's get those jackets out and get this done. Have you got my press release?" Sally handed Susan a typed piece of paper. Susan glanced at it and said, "Can you give me a hand, Forrest? We have to get these jackets on everybody."

The jackets were purple satin, with all our sponsors' logos in patches except for the Bank of Quatar. In its place in bright red letters were the words "Knockout Sexy."

Susan was talking to the TV news team—where they wanted her to stand, who she thought should be covered, how long her statement would take. Ms. Babaneau wanted to be sure they did an establishing shot of the Hotel Gran Caique. "Part of the deal," she said.

I took Susan by the arm. "If you have a minute."

"I don't have a minute."

"Make one," I said, pulling her away. "Whatever you are up to, Susan, you are out of your gourd."

"Let's get a few things straight, Forrest. The next time you pull me away like that I will slug you. Second, I run the business of this team. You win the races. If you can."

"Fine. You run the team. But I think you could use a little perspective here, Susan. We are three weeks away from Phil's funeral. The papers—"

"What do you think I should do? Wear a veil and weep?" She gave me a quick, false smile. No more conventional emotions. "I am not going to sit still for that stinking story in *The Eclipse*. Maybe you think a woman's place is by her husband's grave, but I don't and Phil wouldn't either. In fact, Phil would have loved this. So you watch me, Evers," she said, putting her hand on my chest, dropping her voice so I had to bend to listen. "I am going to take this team further than he ever dreamed. There are two ways to win in Formula One. One is to win the race, because that gets you the exposure and that is what the sponsors want. The other is to go out and get the exposure anyway."

The camera crew were waving. They had a satellite uplink with the UK and a tight production schedule. "Cheer up, for God's sake, Forrest. If you can't stand the heat, stay out of the bedroom. I mean kitchen. Wherever."

Susan went up on the steps in front of the hotel, put on one of the purple satin jackets and held the piece of paper in front of her. The wind was fluttering her hair, and with the hotel's grand entrance rising above her, she looked vulnerable and frail. "My husband died three weeks ago today," she said to the camera. "And I am sure he would be glad for me to tell you that I am now suing the *Eclipse* newspaper for 100 million pounds. That is the value of a team that depends on the goodwill and esteem of its sponsors for its survival. The only reason our sponsors are associated with us is our reputation. The fact that we have lost the Royal Bank of Quatar as one of our sponsors indicates the damage this vicious slander has cost us. A slander whose only statement I do not absolutely reject as unfounded and untrue was that I am," she paused for a moment, " 'knockout sexy.' I mean that is typical of the sexist level of *The Eclipse*, but I am not going to contest that particular statement legally. Just everything else that they have printed about me. Phil's death is painful and difficult enough without being preyed on by scandal sheets. I think I have a right to my privacy and to my family, both of which have been invaded and degraded by this wretched paper. A woman's life is not over when her husband dies, and I am not going to take this gross insult lying down. I am going to hit back." Susan clenched her fist and swung at the camera.

No doubt the camera zoomed in on the Knockout Sexy logo to close. The cameraman took his camera off his shoulder, and Susan turned to Sallye. "I can't say that."

Sallye's nose rose up a notch. "Of course you can. You just did."

"Not the part about taking it lying down. This isn't a joke."

Sallye looked down at Susan from a higher step. "You don't understand," she said. "That is just the sort of thing the newspapers will pick up on. 'Knockout Sexy Mum Won't Take It Lying Down.' Super headline. We'll get a load of mileage out of it."

Susan said, "Does the word 'bullshit' mean anything to you?"

Sallye said, "OK. I don't know if we have the time to reshoot, but we could cut to another angle for a voice-over if I can get them to do an outtake."

A bellman put his hand on my sleeve, "Excuse me? You are Forrest Evers?" I nodded, automatically reaching for my pen, thinking he wanted an autograph. "There's a call for you from Paris."

At the concierge's desk, the bell captain looked over the crowd of heads and said, "Booth seven. Wait for the ring."

The phone rang and went, "Forrest, my friend, I've been reading about you in the English papers. How does it feel to be a superstud?"

"What a joy to hear from you, Panaguian. There is nothing to that story."

"*Au contraire, mon ami.* I mean do not misunderstand me. What you do on your own time does not really concern me. She is a very attractive woman."

"What are you calling about?"

"We have done some sweep telephone surveys in Britain where the story appeared, and the bottom line is positive."

"I don't care what the reactions are. That story is a lie. Nothing to it. End of story."

"It's not that simple. I mean, we have been getting some mixed reactions to our marketing strategy. You know, the different woman in every port. Especially among women, but it seems to be making some men uneasy too. This is not the ideal time to be seen having multiple partners."

"Panaguian, this is your strategy."

"Of course, of course. We're not talking about a major shift here, just a small adjustment."

"What do you mean a small adjustment. You want me to sleep with Susan? You think that's a smart marketing move?"

"Calm down, Evers. No, no. The interesting thing was that of the men who are aware of Formula One in our target audience, the majority reacted positively to the concept of permanence. They don't want so much to seduce a lot of women, they want to find the right one. The idea that you might be settling down was what they liked. The idea that you might be screwing Mrs. Joyce, most of them found off-putting. From a marketing standpoint I wouldn't recommend it."

"I'm so glad for your guidance here."

"Why are you so touchy this afternoon, my friend? Just

listen to me for a moment, if you would please. What I am talking about is that we are no longer going to link you up with a series of women. For the balance of the campaign—and let's see, we have a marketing rollout in some seventy countries to go—but for the remainder of the year we are going to link you romantically with just one woman. The perfect woman. Do you know Virgin?''

"The over-the-hill pop star?''

"Her last disc went platinum. She's very excited about meeting you, Forrest.''

"Her last disc was five years ago. Virgin is a piranha.''

"She's a very sweet girl. O.K., her career has leveled off. And she was never that big in Europe. But it's a great chance for her to break into Europe. And she has a new record coming out.''

"Muscle Tits.''

"I beg your pardon?''

"It's what the kids call her.''

"The album is called *Ready for You,* and it is going to be very big. We're bicycling our new product intro with coupons in Western Europe with Olympia Records. She's a lovely, lovely person, Evers, and you are going to enjoy working with her. You can't buy this kind of exposure.''

There is a fine simplicity about a dot on the horizon. The sharp point on the blurred cone of vision at 195 miles an hour. A mathematical certainty that you will arrive at the point at almost the same time that you can see it. There are no sexual distractions; there is no moral wrestling with the ethics of what you do or why you do it. There are no reporters or confused teenage girls angling for a feel. And no directors asking you to do it one more time with a little more smile this time so we'll have it in the can. There is only one chance and one question. As simple as any question can be. A question not of the laws of human nature or of the wandering throb of desire, but of the laws of physics, of velocity, adhesion, slip angles, temperature, aerodynamics and momentum. The question is, Will you turn? Or will you lose control?

I was halfway through Friday morning's untimed practice session, leaning on it. Pushing hard to get somewhere near a competitive time. Marlboro, McLaren, Ferrari, Williams and Lotus had active suspension, sensors that noted the irregularities of the track and reported them back to an electronic brain that set each wheel with a rise in the spring rate in time to greet the rise of the wheel over a bump. I was strapped to the chassis and bounced like a bean in a tin can. We didn't have an automatic transmission or fly-by-wire technology that let the driver keep his hands on the wheel and his mind on the strategy of the race. We didn't have the outer-space electronic technology of the front runners, and we didn't have a chance of running in front. What we did have a chance for was one or two points for finishing fifth or sixth. If some of the front teams broke or bumped into one another, and we had a lucky break or two, and Russell or I drove the car to the absolute edge of its possibility, we could finish in the points, win some of the prize money, stay out of the horrors of prequalifying and possibly attract enough sponsorship to buy some of the go-faster technology. That was our dot on the horizon that we were racing toward—more money to move up into the front rank.

So I stayed on the throttle for an extra microsecond, easing off and onto the brake, coming into the corner a shade quicker, using a little more of the curb on the outside, hitting the inside of the curb a little harder and getting hard on the throttle just a moment quicker—and the car spun.

There are great drivers who can make a car, any car, go faster than anybody else can. Jimmy Clark, for example, once stepped into a vintage Formula One Aston-Martin at Silverstone and broke the car's track record. On his first lap. From a standing start. But there are no drivers who can make a car go faster than it will go. Not that this little Evers's law of race driver physics mattered. I wasn't a race driver anymore; I was just a passenger. It took a long time for the car to spin all the way around, cross the track, nose across the soft green grass on the outside of the turn, bound across the gravel packed down with rain from the night before, shed its wings in the plume of stones rising from the front of the car and the wheels and hit the barrier. Plenty of time to think that Phil would be really pissed off. And time to think, of course, that he wasn't the team manager, he was dead. I was the team manager. And I said what the airline pilots say on the voice recorder when they find the nose of the stretch 747 pointing straight down, 387 screaming passengers on board, the little dot of a suburban roof coming up fast to fill the screen. I said what they always say just before the impact.

"Oh fuck."

Chapter 7

"How is my diffuser?" Alistair's deep, resonant voice sounded like he was in the hotel basement instead of bouncing off a satellite from Pury End. Outside my window an ore freighter was gliding past. It was noon, and my half-acre bed had been turned down and a chocolate truffle, foil-wrapped, sat on my pillow like the dropping from some exotic bird. No sweets for the hero driver lest he gain an ounce. No sweet young woman to swirl the sheets and cloud the mind with kindness and desire. First qualifying session started in an hour, and the mechanics had a good chance of having the car ready. No scent of perfume in the air or clutter of lotions and potions in the double-sink bathroom with the wall to wall mirrors. Being a Formula One driver must be glamorous, because it is wall-to-wall denial. How do you feel if you can see a long ways and you cannot share the view? "My diffuser isn't damaged, is it?" Alistair continued in my ear.

His diffuser. If you are one of the truly weird who enjoy looking up the backside of a racing car, you know that a diffuser looks something like the channels on a hair dryer. And that a diffuser speeds up and disperses the air as it exits, creating more vacuum underneath the car, dispelling the vacuum behind the car. Formula One aerodynamicists can talk for six hours straight about diffusers. My limit is around six seconds.

"It's fine. I didn't hit the back of the car at all. The front wings came off along with the nose cone and the front wheels."

"Good. How's the driver?"

"The driver is embarrassed, but he'll get over it," I said. There was a young woman on the deck of the freighter. She looked in my direction, seeing, perhaps, her ship reflected in the faceless slab of a modern hotel. Then she opened a door and disappeared. "Speaking as the team manager, it was the dummy driver. He was trying too hard too soon. What do you mean, 'good'?"

"I mean we've been getting some interesting results on our linkup with the artificial wind tunnel. And it will be a few weeks before we have the new configuration on the diffuser sorted out, because it takes so damn long to make up the carbon fiber. But the new end plates on the front wing are just about ready to go. Might help keep you on the track and off the wall."

Aerodynamic designers like to think of themselves as free spirits who dwell in the rarefied air of unexplored physics. They are gliding there, lest you get carried away with the romance of these soaring intellects, looking for a free lunch.

Basically, you can either tilt the wings for more downforce to hold you on the track while you go around corners, or trim them for speed down the straights. Anybody can turn a wing up for more downforce or down for more speed—the trick is to turn it up and down at the same time. Ferrari found a gap in the front wing rules in 1991, and since then the aerodynamic engineers had been coming up with all sorts of shapes on the front wing end plates to add to the downforce on the front end of the car.

"We're crawling down the straight as it is," I said. "I don't need more drag, I need more power."

Alistair was patient, explaining the facts of life to an unruly child. "We'll give you more speed. What we're playing with is curving the end plates on the front wings, turning them into lateral vortex generators, to channel the air out of the way of the wheels and under the car, give it a better seal. At the same time we're accelerating the air through the underwing so you get better suction without more drag. And we're getting rid of a lot of the turbulence from the front wheels. Isn't that just superb? Are you listening to me, Forrest?''

''Partially.''

''I mean, it's all numbers, all we get out of this satellite linkup are numbers, but the way I read them, they look very good. We can play around with vector interstices any way we like, in 3D. For a while there we were messing around with compound curves on the upsweep. We've just about finished making up the new front wings, and we'll have them on a plane tonight so you'll have them in time for practice in the morning. See how it goes. What's all this shit about Susan?''

''Susan's fine.''

''Yeah, she definitely looks great. On all the channels. She just doesn't sound like the sweet little lady I used to know.''

''She's not.''

''Is she really serious about that lawsuit? A hundred million pounds and we could really do some aero.''

''Don't spend it yet.''

''You are a barrel of fun to talk to this evening, Forrest. I'm flying over with the wing tonight, so I'll see you first thing tomorrow morning. Cheer up.''

''Take the plane.''

''What?''

''That's a joke.''

''Right. Joke. Try to keep your ass aboveground until I get there, Forrest.''

''I'll try. You sound pretty cocky for a twenty-six-year-old aerodynamic physicist. Is this new underwing that good?''

''Yeah, and I've just had another phone call from Emron.''

''When I saw them in Berkeley Square, they told me they want to buy a piece of your company.''

''They want to buy all of it. I told them to go fuck themselves. Felt great.'' There was a pause. ''Is there anything between you and Susan?''

"About eight floors of luxury hotel. Do you play with yourself more than twice a day, Alistair?"

"What the hell are you talking about?"

"I thought, as long as we're getting personal . . . Susan is in mourning. And it may be hard for you to appreciate without the software to back it up, but different people react in different ways. I think Susan is extremely angry about Phil's death, and suing the newspaper gives her a chance to let off some steam."

"You have any new ideas about what happened to Phil?"

"I wish I did. I think about it all the time, but nothing fresh turns up."

"There is one thing I just thought of. I would have said something, but I just forgot about it. I mean it happens—uh, used to happen—all the time. Probably doesn't mean anything."

"What are you talking about, Alistair?"

"He was wearing my earphones. I mean we are all plugged into the same channel, so I can't see that it would make any difference. But you know, they were lying on the pit wall, and I just picked up a set, and Phil grabbed a set, and it was only later that I saw my earphones had his name on them."

"Those little dymo sticker tags. You mention this to anybody?"

"No. I didn't think of it. You think there might be something in it?"

"Well, if you were as paranoid as I am, the thought might come up that if somebody did engineer Phil's accident, maybe they weren't after Phil."

"You're just pissed off I was sounding so cocky."

I couldn't sleep. The afternoon qualifying session had not gone well. There was nothing wrong with the car. It just wasn't fast enough. Russell and I had tried everything, bounding off the curbs, getting on the accelerator that microsecond quicker. But the readouts said it all. We were fifteen miles an hour slower down the straights than Williams and the McLarens. We backed off the wings, gained a couple of miles an hour down the straights and slid like penguins in the corners. No active suspension. No automatic transmission. No supertrick engine from the engineering prowess of a thousand engineers linked together at a major motor manufacturer. We were driving a Stone-Age device in the age of hypertech. Russell was nineteenth and I was twenty-first. Somewhere below nowhere.

Russell said he could nimble up on the McLarens in the corners, but they just disappeared on the straights. He was driving well, taking huge risks and making them look easy, and if he had had a decent car, he could have been on the podium at the end of the race. But he was glad to be there. Glad to have a chance at twenty-three to drive a Formula One car in a Formula One race. He was on the way up, and unless we picked up serious speed, Team Joyce was just a stepping stone for him. He was cocky and had a lot to learn, but he was not a problem.

Did I really say, "not a problem"? Being a team manager was getting to me. I wasn't in as good shape as I should have been. I just didn't have the time to work out three hours a day as I used to. And I was taking mental shortcuts, simplifying. With so many things to deal with, a handsome kid, with a sharp jaw and curly blond hair, who walked with a bounce and drove like an angel was "not a problem." I was learning why team managers walk around looking like they have lockjaw. Because the things you think about are the "problems."

One of the problems was the press cluttering up the pits, standing around, taking pictures. Asking for interviews. The team was wearing the Knockout Sexy jackets. I told Susan I thought they were juvenile and in bad taste. Susan said, "When did you get to be such a boring old fart?"

"Ever since the twenty-third TV journalist asked if she could do an interview on our 'relationship.' " I said.

"Well, make up something. Something I can deny. This

won't last more than a few days.''

What was making me uncomfortable was the nasty implication that lay like a leak under the carpet, the implication
that I had jumped into Phil Joyce's bed and taken over his
team. That I had taken advantage of his death. Susan didn't
seem to mind. But who knows what she would feel tomorrow? Or the next day.

It was a bad odor that would last as long as I was connected to Team Joyce. Which would be at least for the rest
of the season, because there was no other team I could go
to. All my sponsor money was tied up with Joyce. And even
if I changed teams, it wouldn't end. Not as long as Phil's
death was unexplained. Something fishy about Evers.

Still not sleeping.

It wasn't late, just a little past midnight. So I pulled on
some blue jeans, slipped on a pair of loafers and a T-shirt
and headed for the lobby to get a book to take my mind
away from being nowhere on the grid and feeling vaguely
guilty about Susan. Even though there was nothing to feel
guilty about—was there? As I stepped into the hall, closing
the door to my room, Russell was coming down the hall in
his shorts, carrying an ice bucket.

He grinned when he saw me. "Forrest, my man. Whatcher
up to, creeping around this time of night? Goin' trollin' down
in the pub, pick up a few groupies? Give the ladies a sniff?''
Just behind him, a door was open to his room.

"Children your age should be in beddy bye," I said. "Do
you know if Alistair has checked in? He was coming over
with the new front wing."

"Didn't see him. You know those aero guys they go
shhhhhhhh." He made a plane motion with his hand, big
grin on his face. "You never hear them. Tell you who did
check in, though. Virgin. Did you see her? She looks pretty
good for an old bag."

"She's thirty-eight."

"Yeah, well. Have you heard from Rick Morrall?'' I

shook my head no. "He's my new manager, You know I had that deal with Phil."

"I meant to ask you about that. Phil got thirty percent of your income?"

"Yeah, bummer. I was just starting out." His quick blue driver's eyes were taking me in, thinking of several things, looking at the open door just behind me. "We'd only been married for a bit; Cathy had the kid. I would have cleaned the gorilla cage, you know, let the zoo keep the change. But I was stupid. It was for life and for everything. You know, wherever I went, Phil was going to get thirty percent. Coulda been millions." The grin never left his face, and I thought of his wife with a baby and seven months pregnant back in London.

"Bummer," I said.

Behind him, a voice came out of the bedroom door, "Russsellll."

"Gotta run," he said.

I went down to the lobby, got Steven Hawking's new book as a surefire sleep inducer and when I got back to my room there was a note slipped under the door signed, Susan. "Twenty-first is nowhere," it said.

Chapter 8

"I heard you have the biggest prick in racing. Izzat true, or were they just talking about your personality?"

I was flywheeling. After two hours of pushing, shoving, whipping and cursing 700 horsepower to stay on the track and on the limit, my muscles were numb. The aches would come later. I was dehydrated, and my mind wanted to let go, slow down and rest but it wouldn't stop spinning. Takes a while to slow down after a race.

My mind was still out on the track, thinking of that corner, six laps from the finish, trying to get past Patrese, who was having suspension problems on the inside of the long, sweeping left-hander at Sainte Marie, before the chicane, trying to get inside him and getting off the line, feeling the car begin to get away, the back end starting to come around, and turning into it, getting in front of Patrese, the car sliding in front of him as he got on the brakes to keep from hitting me. And I thought, Maybe I can go over the curb. I gave the car its head, accelerating into the curb, as in the next instant I hit the curb hard and the front wheels launched the car up in the air, banging my shins on the bulkhead. I hung onto the steering wheel, the back wheels hit the curb not quite together for a crooked takeoff, launched the whole car up clear of the gravel trap and flying free through the warm afternoon air, before the aerodynamics pointed the nose sharply down and the right wheel touched the track just beyond the curb on the inside of the next turn, and the car bounced, the front end lifting up just for a moment as the back end slammed down, and a flick of the wrist and it is pointed straight ahead, lined up for the straight, and I have gained six car lengths on Patrese and I am accelerating away. He had to back off, not knowing, any more than I did, what the hell was going to happen next. A fluke, a lucky break. I had half wished it and half hung on, and I couldn't have done it again if I tried.

On the other hand, if a track makes it impossible to pass, you have to try to do the impossible to pass. And I was reliving that incredible quarter of a second of free flight, the car free of vibration and then the crashing return to the tarmac, slamming me hard on my backbone, knocking the wind out of me. I was thinking of that while they were unbuckling me, hot, sweating, and the sun seemed too bright, shining in my eyes, and I realized it was not the sun, it was a TV light to compensate for the gloom. Which doesn't make sense. Because I have finished sixth, and while I am profoundly glad to have gotten the one all-important point in the championship, it is unlikely that anybody else, least of all the media, will give a damn. Just taking my oil-stained helmet off, peeling off the sopping Nomex sweat sock I wear over my head, pulling off my gloves and feeling the cool breeze coming in off the Seaway, about to get out, shower, change and go to sleep back in my hotel. And there is a bleach-blond woman whose head is too large for her body, saying this to me.

She was thin, a mop of bleached blond hair, wearing what looked like artificial eyebrows over intense blue eyes and a pasty white face, as if she hadn't been outdoors in a year, and raw-liver lipstick. A lot of neck cords showing in the neck. I put my hands on the side of the car and pushed myself up, standing, and was about to step out when she reached out and took, through my Nomex driving suit and three layers of fireproof underwear, firm hold of my balls. Not squeezing hard, but holding and not letting go. A clenched fist.

She was wearing a gauzy crisscross yellow scarf over her boobs, showing a lot of breast and pale white stomach, and baggy yellow shorts with red birds on them. And she was going in a false little-girl voice, "Is it true all racing drivers have big round ones?" She wore a pleasant smile. "Or izzat macho bullshit?"

The human male sexual response is immediate. And careless of surroundings and social decor. Something every teenage boy, crouched at an intersection, embarrassed about a boner that just sprang up from a passing thought, knows all about.

All right, it had been a while, and some primitive part of my brain was getting out the drums and the guitars, jumping up and down, saying that feels goooooooood. But it was an insult and a cheap publicity trick, and I do not enjoy being the object of somebody else's control, least of all in front of TV cameras. She was just a little thing, not much more than sinew and bone. And short. I reached down and grabbed her silver-buckle cowboy belt and lifted her up. She couldn't have weighed much over ninety pounds. I lifted her straight over my head, taking both hands to do it. She tried to keep her cool for a moment, while I held her overhead; she arched her back. The tapes they played on the network news showed her smiling above my head, like an Olympic ice skater, arms spread out.

She said, through the smile, just loud enough for me to hear, "Put me down, you dumb shit." Then I let her drop forward, and she screamed. I caught her feet so she was dangling headfirst over the ground. Then I let her slowly down.

Her head touched the tarmac, I let go of her feet, she rolled and was up, her blond hair smudged with oil from brushing the tarmac in the pit lane, her face red, mouth open, her fist swinging at me, aiming for my crotch. She was screaming, "Asshole."

I caught her hand. "I'm sorry," I said. "What did you say your name was?"

Chapter 9

I dove under the incoming wave of photographers. As I worked my way out to the other side, one of them, cameras hanging from his neck, holding a 300-mm zoom lens, his dark eyes bright with the possibility of selling a pic said, "What's it all about, Forrest?"

"I came in sixth," I said. He looked at me, puzzled for a moment, and then pushed in shoulder-first, holding his camera high to see if he could get a shot of whatever it was.

Fans had broken through the fencing and were running onto the track from several directions. Down pit lane, drivers were climbing out of their cars and Baurenbaur was on his way up to the podium to celebrate his first Grand Prix win. At the base of the podium a group of photographers clustered with their lenses pointed upward like baby birds, waiting for their champagne shower. There were only half as many as usual because the podium was not where the action was.

Lord knows what she was telling them. There were four reporters tagging along with me, and three photographers backpeddling in front of me, as I pushed through the crowd to our garage in the pits. The reporters went, "How long you know her, Forrest?" "Hey, Forrest, you and Virgin bonking or what?" "What's she like, Forrest? She give head?" I didn't answer them. I'd had enough of somebody else's charade.

Maybe the need to be famous comes from being an outcast at six or having a mother who died before you felt safe in her arms or from knowing too soon that you too will die—

maybe there are no reasons. Maybe it's just the vibrations of the electric media that make certain people buzz a certain way, makes the stars shine bright and the wannabes think all they have to do is wear the right clothes, buy the right brands, mouth the hip phrases, hum the notes and life could be a glide, man. Not knowing how backbreaking the famous business is. Because the surest deadly sin of being famous is to let the effort show. Just happened to wander out on the stage tonight. Where the bright light burns holes in your soul. When the effort shows, the lights go out and the fans click the dial to the new girl with the new rap. When the bright lights go out, here, take these pills, darling, to turn the watts back up, and pour the wine to ease the pain as the friends and promoters slip out the side door. The suicide rate among the young superstars runs high because from where they are, all directions are down and the effort of staying up is a killer.

But what the hell, maybe I was just jealous. I'd done my acrobatic act, flat out in a blender for two hours, defying death for the entertainment of myself and the public, and she stole my thunder as easily as a brass band taking over the stage from a boy with a toy trombone.

As I ducked under the cordon into the darkness of the garage, a man with a notebook, baggy chocolate slacks, dark green shirt with BOSS on the pocket, in case you missed that it was expensive, and neatly combed hip haircut, short on the sides, long in the back, was saying, "What's the story with the new wing, Forrest?"

"Talk to Alistair, over there," I said, nodding toward the gaunt figure bent over the monitor in the corner of the garage. "He's the aero guy. He can tell you more than I can." I wasn't being rude, but I was tired and I did want to get out of my hot, wet suit and into a shower. At least he was asking me about the race.

"You changed the end plates," he said, "before Saturday's qualifying and you were a whole second a lap faster."

I looked at him. That kind of scrutiny is not unusual in Formula One. There are fans who care about end plates and,

God bless them, journalists who report on the dynamic implications of the inverted topology of diffusers. A FISA media pass hung around his neck. His face was pudgy but fit. And he was very neat. Most reporters look as if somebody else has slept on them. "Bill Hoshower," he said, "*Road and Track*. You guys been doing a lot of wind tunnel work?"

Something wasn't quite right, but it was refreshing to talk about the car. "We have a new program that Alistair is working on. I really can't tell you much about it because what I know about aerodynamics would blow away in a high wind."

"Sure," holding his pen over his notebook. "But you must have noticed a difference in the car."

"You're right, the car had a lot more grip in the corners, and we picked up three to four hundred rpm on the main straight. But Alistair is the guy you want to talk to."

He clicked off his tape recorder. "No, that's OK," he said. "That's all I need."

"Forrest?" Susan was just behind me. I turned around, and she threw her arms around my neck and gave me a big sisterly kiss on the cheek. "Congratulations," she said. "You had to go cross-country to do it, but you brought us home a big fat beautiful point."

"Hey, be careful," I said. "I've gotten filthy racing driver all over your sexy purple satin jacket."

"This old rag," she said, smiling, tossing her head. "It was just a one-race stunt. What was all that commotion outside?"

"Just a pop star," I said, "popping off. You sure seem relaxed compared to your Monster Mum, Queen of PR."

"Not relaxed, exhausted," she said, smiling and brushing a strand of hair away from her face. Her face was leaner now, the high cheekbones showing. She had dark circles under her eyes and she looked as if she needed protection. It was her best weapon, that vulnerable look. "We won a point, which is good for our sponsors, good for our income. And I'm going home to Josh and Sue Two. Which may be hell for them but it will be wonderful for me.''

"So you are happy," I said.

"Don't be ridiculous," she said.

Later, when I was talking to Alistair, going over the race and my reactions to the new wing, he asked me who I had been talking to when I came into the garage. I told him it was a reporter from the American magazine *Road & Track*.

He said, "*Road and Track* stopped covering Formula One races when they stopped having Formula One races in the U.S. What did you tell him, Forrest?"

Maybe it's just the contrast. But the day after the race the Hotel Gran Caique is one of the quieter places in the world. Some fans and sponsors were quietly checking out, a few older couples and a couple of honeymooners were in the breakfast lounge, but most of tables were empty. As I was walking across the atrium lobby with its clear dome fifteen stories overhead, I had the feeling that in a day or two I would be the only person left on this sunken ship. A hand touched my shoulder. "Mr. Evers? A call for you."

I took it by the front desk, watching the steady stream of departures. The voice of honey and oil had a touch of vinegar. "I want you to apologize, Forrest. Call her up and apologize."

"Panaguian, she grabbed my balls. In public. You want me to go kiss and make up?"

"She's a very sensitive girl and she's crying her eyes out. And she's threatening to walk. Plus I have a lawsuit pending from her lawyers for public humiliation. You probably got one too. So you go be nice to her. It was good PR but we need the follow-up. We're on a tight schedule."

"Let her break the contract. Save yourself a pile of money. She's about as sexy as a boa constrictor. But not as much fun to kiss."

"You kissed her?"

"Have you seen her?"

"Of course I've seen her. The whole world has seen her."

"Recently, I mean. I saw her yesterday and she is not aging well."

"That's not your problem. That's what I hired Scatuzzi for. Scatuzzi can make a snapping turtle look sexy. I want you to call her up and tell her you were exhausted after the race but you are much better now and looking forward to working with her."

"That's horseshit. You haven't got enough money to make me do that."

"I was thinking more in terms of not terminating your contract."

"If you want to terminate my contract, I'll be the happiest man on the plane to London this afternoon." This was pure bluff. If he terminated my contract, I would go back to my flat in Holland Park and do what I did before—stare out the window and howl at the moon.

A half hour later I was coming down the hall, considering calling the woman, and I heard the phone ringing in my room. I took my time opening the door, crossing the room and looking out the window. The phone kept ringing, so I picked it up.

"I'm sorry I was such an asshole," she said, her voice quiet, shy as a new girl in school.

"Who is this?" I said.

"You already did that joke. Are you stupid or just pretending?"

"Both."

"Couldn't you tell me you are sorry too?"

"Sorry? That was a vulgar, cheap and nasty trick at my expense. So sure, I'm sorry it happened."

"I thought that since we have to work together, maybe we could be friends and stuff. You want me to promise not to grab you by the balls anymore?"

"No," I said. "I don't want you to promise anything. But if you grab my balls again, I won't let you down so easy."

"See?" she laughed. "I knew we could work together."

Chapter 10

The bedroom was a ten on the Robber Baron scale, with ornate high ceilings, a white marble fireplace and French doors leading to a balcony overlooking the lake. There was no furniture in the room, just the red lacquer bed. A small bronze plaque at the foot of the bed confessed that it had been brought over piece by piece from Shanghai as part of the British Empire's loot from the opium wars. Its sides were swarming with a frieze of dragons, tigers and flowers. Up close, a Chinese fat man, possibly the original owner, waved, stroked and inserted a cock that would have choked a hippo. This heavily veined prong was also licked, sucked and engulfed by a large number of bending, spreading and prone ladies in different sizes and shapes, and states of undress who shared the same look of boredom. Or bliss. It was hard to know what the artist had in mind. Maybe the carver was just following orders from Cheung Hung Lee the Great Warlord, for whom the bed was built (according to the small bronze plaque). No doubt known to his friends as Old Donkey Cock. Like most pornography, it was repetitious.

I padded in velvet slippers across the inlaid floor, honeyed with generations of wax, to the French doors and the balcony overlooking the gardens and a lawn that rolled down to a small lake. The air was fresh and scented with pine and the sun was just coming up over the trees. Mummy and Daddy Canada Goose were out on the lake, cruising the shore, with their brood paddling along behind, pulling up tender shoots. The youngsters were squabbling over who got the biggest stalk. Family breakfast. I went back into the bedroom, hung my robe on a dragon's nose, kicked off the vulgar slippers, climbed up into the vast Chinese playpen, lay back on the pillows and waited.

Not long. Just long enough to close my eyes and I heard the door open and shut. I propped myself up on one elbow and watched. She had that presence—you had to watch. She was wearing silver hair, a silver satin robe with a sash and 1940s movie-star silver shoes. She had a bright red cupid mouth that spread wide in a grin when she saw me. She pirouetted once, stopped with her back to me and let the robe fall, looking over her shoulder to be sure I was watching. Of course I was watching. I was watching the Ginger Rogers spike heel shoes, the long slim ankles, the backs of her calves, the blue vein pumping in the back of her knee, the silver satin teddy shimmering with the wobbles of warm woman underneath. She pursed her lips in a little camp kiss, turned around again, kicked off her shoes, pulled back the sheet and snuggled in alongside.

Up close you could see the outlines of her real mouth, the large pores around her nose and the lines and dark circles showing through the makeup under her eyes. She closed those big blue eyes and switched off, a trick she had, I was later to learn, of tuning out the world and grabbing a few seconds' rest.

Instantly a hairdresser and her assistant were bending over her and pulling and coiling her silver hair with their hands and combs, finishing off with a few deft puffs of hairspray.

"OK," Scatuzzi said from behind his Hassleblad on a tripod, "bend over Virgin, why don't you, Forrest, and let's see how it looks—the Prince wakes Sleeping Beauty with a kiss."

Virgin said, her eyes closed, "Hi."

"You come here often?" I said.

She gave me a professional little smile. "You still pissed off?" she said, her eyes still closed.

I bent over and kissed her lightly.

Scatuzzi said, "Hold it there a sec. Forrest. Let me get another spot reading. Willard, can you move that reflector up a notch? I need more fill on Virgin's mouth."

Opening her eyes, looking up at me, the bogus lover six inches away, Virgin said, "When was the last time you were in bed with a stranger?"

"OK," Scatuzzi said. "Another little smacker, Forrest."

"It's hard to remember," I said, kissing her lightly. "A long time ago. Before we knew sex could kill you."

"I was just thinking everybody I've ever been to bed with was a stranger."

Scatuzzi called out, "Wipe the lipstick off Forrest would you please, Larry? Can we get a little more of that fill on Forrest? And move that second Dienst. I'm getting a bedpost shadow across his eyes. Don't move, Forrest."

"Including me," I said.

"Well, now that you mention it, we've known each other two days and we've had our first fight and our first kiss. In this business, that qualifies as old friends." She put her hand behind my neck and pulled me down to her.

"Great," Scatuzzi called out. "Just pretend we're not here."

It must have been like this in Hollywood years ago when they shot silent movies. The actors talking shopping lists, gossip and hip-pocket philosophy and acting passionate while a man in riding pants and a beret cranked the camera. Like "Have you seen Coop's new Hispano?" "No, but I hear it's money-green. Move your hip, honey, my arm's going to sleep. Carole says she's got Franco to buy her one just to give Clark a burn."

Except we weren't talking movie star gossip. Conversation with Virgin was like passing hand grenades back and forth. You never knew if she had pulled the pin.

"You're a nice kisser," she said.

"Is that a complaint or a compliment?"

"I'm talking to you. Talking to you is a compliment."

"Ah, she not only kisses, she speaks to me. Lucky me."

"Yeah, lucky you." Pause. "OK, it was a compliment. Call me Janice."

"Janice is a lot easier to say with a straight face than Virgin. Is that your real name?"

"Janice Corlowski. Is that real enough?" She was leaning over me now, one of those famous breasts threatening to break loose out of the silver satin, the other famous breast crowding in, trying to get a peek. "Virgin sounded great when I was nineteen, starting out. Kind of campy and cartoon, you know?"

"I remember. Your first record was, what was it? 'Try Me On.' "

"Yeah right. 'Try . . . me . . . on,' " she sang in my ear, in that mocking little girl voice she had, the three notes rising.

"I thought it was a smart marketing move."

"Everything I do is a smart marketing move. Except now Virgin sounds dumb for a thirty-two-year-old woman. But I'm stuck with it."

"I thought you were thirty-eight."

"At least Virgin's better than Janice Corlowski. When I was a kid, the kids in my class called me Louski. Like my underwear wasn't clean."

"You could call your next record 'Sniffer.' "

"Yick. You sound like an agent. Never mind. I'm rich and they're not. How does it feel to be in bed with the most desirable woman in the world?"

"I have no idea."

"Couldn't you just pretend?"

Scatuzzi had us hold a kiss while he moved around us for some hand-held shots.

When we were finally allowed to move, my mouth was numb. "And you want me to call you Janice."

"Call me anything. Just don't call me late for lunch."

"W. C. Fields."

"No it was Mae West. She wrote all the best lines."

"You're like her in a way."

"In a lot of ways. Like, we're both comediennes. You know, funny? Like, you're supposed to laugh?" She made a face. "OK, don't laugh, but call me Janice. I'm tired of being somebody else."

"Are you serious?"

"Serious?" She considered it for a moment. "Forget serious. I feel myself getting really serious, I undercut it with a joke, so be careful out there, sports fans."

"You were married too, weren't you?"

"Yeah, that started out great, then we got like serious and it was a bad joke. Did you say 'too'?"

"I was, but I was never home. You know that old line, you never know what you've got till you've lost it."

"You mean you're still looking?"

"Virgin," Scatuzzi called out. "We're seeing a little too much of Forrest in the camera. Can you shift up a bit, sweetheart? Give me just a touch more chin? Thank you. That's perfect. Harold, I'm picking up a little moisture on Virgin's chin."

There was another conversation going on under the covers. Out of sight. Unspoken. Straight face. When we rolled into another position, Virgin's hand would brush against my cock. Lightly. Almost by accident. Lingering for a beat. The silk pajama bottoms they'd given me made her touch slippery, sexy. Don't get me wrong. It didn't feel bad, it felt good. And the fact that the cameraman, the three lighting guys and two electricians, the makeup girl and the people from the Canadian advertising agency were watching us and had no idea what was going on made it even sexier. We were facing each other, and she had just held my cock for a moment, with her fingertips, under the sheets. "Just checking," she whispered in my ear.

Emily Post does not offer guidance for these situations. "Hey, cut that out," seemed like the wrong thing for a grown-up man to say. I wasn't her little plaything. And I wasn't angry, far from it. But I wasn't relaxed either. Several of the shots were no good because the male model's attempt to hide his erection cast a shadow across the bed sheets. "The great manipulator," her nickname in the record industry, took on a new meaning. Naturally my cock loved the attention. Cocks, as you have no doubt noticed, are dumber than dogs. Show the little dangler the slightest bit of attention and it's up there with its tongue hanging out, wagging its tail. The old rising cock couldn't see that this normal, gentle and loving creative act between lovers had been turned inside out into a cheap publicity trick. But you try saying that to a cock.

Then, before we broke for lunch, while Scatuzzi loomed over us on a stepladder, she grabbed my balls and squeezed. Hard. "Call me Janice," she said.

This was real pain. Maybe Virgin thought it was superstar courtship. I thought of hitting her to break her grip. I reached up with the hand tucked underneath me and pinched her nipple. "Let go, Janice," I said.

She let go. "Next time," she said, her lips just brushing my ear, "why don't you try kissing me like you mean it?"

There wasn't a next time. We did a few establishing shots: me getting into bed; Virgin in different underwear; our naked feet sticking out of the sheets, mine together pointing down, hers on either side pointing up. But that was it for sacktime under the lights with a former superstar. At the stroke of noon, Virgin was out of the bed and on her way back to Montreal to catch a plane back to the coast.

"See you in a couple of weeks, Foreplay," she said, smiling sweetly and waving to me for the benefit of the crew as she went out the door. "No hard feelings."

Two hours later, on the way to the Montreal airport, in the limo they had hired for me, the phone rang.

That little twerping electronic sound, nothing to do with the ring of bells, was reminding me of some responsibility I had forgotten, something I had left undone. I was guilty of closing my eyes for a moment, leaning back into the soft excesses of a Cadillac limousine, taking a break before the red-eye to London. Well if you go for the roses you have to expect a lot of little pricks. As soon as you see large sums of money passing through your hands, believe me, the phone will always find you with its little electric sting, reminding you that not long ago there was a time when you had time you called free and when the bells ringing on a phone was a welcome sound. I'm not complaining, just pointing out that nobody gives money away. Even inheritances come with fresh taxes and a variety of ways for softening the brain. If you want to be rich, my stern Norfolk father used to say, cancel your holidays.

"Hi."

"Hello, Susan. How'd you find me?"

"The usual way. I tell Jilly, 'Find Forrest,' and a half hour later here you are. Where have you been?"

"I spent the morning in bed. With Virgin."

"Oh goody, tell me all the details."

"For heaven's sake, Susan. There were thirty people in the room. We were shooting."

"Well, it's none of my business. Except of course that it is my business that gets neglected."

Ahead of us on the motorway there was some holdup. The limo driver moved over onto the shoulder and turned on a flashing blue light and a discreet siren suitable for dignitaries. We were doing about sixty-five, sending up a high plume of dust behind us. Move over, world, here comes Mr. Big Time in the Big Time Car.

I said, "You'll have to speak up, Susan. I can't hear you very well."

"That's my point. When Phil was running the team, he was here all the time. Twenty-four hours a day. There's a lot going on here with tire testing at Silverstone this week, and I've got my hands full with sponsors."

"I'm on my way."

"That's not good enough."

"Tell me what's happening."

"What's happening is that Sam Naughton has taken over as team manager of Team Joyce."

"*Has* taken over."

"Fiat accompli, Forrest. Look, this is not a criticism of you. I think you've done a great job. And you will be paid just the same. I don't want you to leave. I couldn't afford for you to leave, especially with your buyout option. But you've got too much to do, Forrest. You've got all your Chantal PR obligations, you've got a full-time job driving, and driving is what I would like to see you do. Without all the other distractions of trying to run a Formula One team at the same time."

Two Canadian Mounted Police patrol cars were blocking the shoulder and the limo came to a stop. A mounty was walking toward the car, the sun in his mirror sunglasses. If cops didn't go to cop movies they wouldn't look so dumb.

"Susan, I think you are panicking. We got a point in Montreal. The car is handling much better now. Alistair has some more stuff up his sleeve. And if you think I don't have enough time, what the hell do you think a man who runs twenty corporations is going to have in the way of free time?"

I was arguing, but my heart wasn't in it. In a way I felt relief. I didn't like running a team. I didn't feel that I was very good at it. And I had often longed for the days when all I had to do was put my foot down and drive. On the other hand being fired as team manager didn't feel like freedom, it felt like failure.

"What he has is thirty-five million dollars for a fifty-one percent stake in Team Joyce. If he is going to put that kind of money into the team, I think he will find the time to look after it. Look, we can get a wind tunnel, maybe do a deal for a decent engine. This could put us up into the front row. He's a wonderful man and it is a great move for the team, Forrest."

"Tell him to show you the money before you shake hands with him," I said.

"You see, Forrest, that's your problem. You're just not thinking big enough."

The mounty was rapping on the tinted window, his shades mirroring the open slit at the top. I pushed the rocker switch. The window went up a notch to shut completely. Not a good start. I pushed it the other way, and the officer leaned in, both hands on the sill. "Your driver says you are Forrest Evers."

I felt the warm flush of the privilege that goes along with being one of the privileged. "That's right," I said.

"Who the fuck is that supposed to be?" he said.

Chapter 11

My jumbo bounced into Heathrow at 6:53 A.M. in the middle of the daily herd of lumbering jumbo jets that deposit a quarter of a million tourists on Britain every summer morning.

With no suitcase to anchor me to the luggage carousel, I was out and on the M-4 by 7:30, heading for the M-25, M-40, A-43 path to Pury End, six miles past Silverstone.

It was a lovely English summer morning. The sun had been up since five, filtered by an early morning haze, and was lifting the mist from fields and forests still fresh and summer green, with rashes of yellow rape. I had a rent-a-stone from Mr. Alamo, a Cavalier with a grand total of nineteen miles on it when I picked it up and a reluctance to go over 118. On the other side of the M-40, the cars were inching along, the one-lane drains into London they call roads clogged solid as usual.

I slowed down. No need to rush. I was not in charge. Plenty of time to wonder why I was thinking of Virgin Janice when I had so much else to think about. She was spoiled, selfish, manipulative, over the hill and going down fast. She was loud and careless, inconsiderate. A coil of cable and wire wound around a soft heart. I kept going back over those staged kisses, the warmth of her and her bratlike pleading for attention and affection. A pale blue vein barely visible beneath the surface throbbed on the underside of her breast with the weight and the strain of life. A faded star.

Where had the spotlights gone? No more blazing intensity. A charred little soul. Oh Christ, Evers, you are an idiot.

There I was, veering off into being the soup-head romantic. She was strong as an ox and one of the richest women in Western civilization. How can a man talk about free will when all a woman has to do is give his cock a tug and he will follow along, wagging his tail. Still, I couldn't avoid it, I wanted to see her again. Was looking forward to seeing her again. Which surprised me. Up close, and we had certainly been up close, I hadn't felt this affection. Whatever it was that pulled me to her, she was like one of those collapsed dead stars in the far galaxies, black holes that sucked you in.

I wondered if Chantal had doused her with the female equivalent of Formula One, the stuff that was supposed to make me irresistible. It would make marketing sense. Create all the uproar and controversy with the male version the first year. Answer with the female version the next. Call it what, Formula Two? Grand Prix? The human race copulates 100 million times a day. What would happen if the whole world wore irresistible sexual attractors? Men and women making love to the limits of their physical endurance, three, four, five hundred million times a day. Goofy grins and sharp glances of desperation. No more "racial cleansing" in Yugoslavia; they'd be too busy going at it in the bushes and behind the walls. Well, I thought, I certainly had the time now to lie back and enjoy being a schoolboy out of school.

Plenty of time to stop off at a trucker's café in Brackley on the A-43. I never have an English breakfast. Nobody in England has an English breakfast. Except when you come back and a proper plate of fat brown sausages, tinned beans, a charred half tomato with its skin falling down like an old lady's skirt, two wet flat upside-down mushrooms, a curled pink bacon strip and a runny fried egg all floating in a warm pond of clear and shining fat makes you feel at home in Britain again. A couple of pieces of cold white toast to mop up the yolk, if you would please. To hell with the Evers everlasting diet of wheat chaff and springwater. I was just another driver in the café, driving to work.

A half hour later I pulled into the Joyce drive in Pury End, thinking I would slide up to the house in my usual Forrest-is-here fashion, and I had to brake hard, sending a shower of gravel over a new black BMW 850i, the one that is larger and heavier than a Ford Taurus on the outside and smaller than a Honda Civic inside. All right, I was irritated at the clod for blocking the driveway. Irritated at being reminded that I had come to think of it as my driveway and it was not mine. Never had been.

The problem of the driver of the overstuffed German isolation booth on wheels, as I squeezed by on foot, was a line of cars parked in front, blocking the way. Solid cars, nose-to-tail all the way in. The forecourt was filled with two more large black BMWs, a Ford Transit Van and a smoke-gray Bentley Continental Coupe with a plate that read S N 1. Laurel followed by Hardy came out of One Building, saw me, gave me a little wave and went back inside. Strange. Two men in pin-striped suits, shined shoes and careful haircuts came out the front door of the house, looking grim, looked my way, saw who I was, looked back down at the ground and went on looking grim, walking around the corner of the house toward the main workshop. Great to see you too.

They left the front door open and I walked in. I heard voices in the front office. "Susan," I called out.

"In here," she called from the office.

She was bent over my desk, scrolling down the screen of my computer. Three young faces were peering over her shoulder. "Hi, Forrest," she said, not looking up. "I was just taking David, Jenny and Victoria through your files." She stood up, arching her back. Letting me know what a chore it was. "We can't make head or tail of it. Can you tell them what system you used?"

"No."

Jenny, David and Victoria stood up, their faces showing mild surprise—Victoria looking gaunt, like she could have used a good feeding; Jenny pretty in an efficient, don't-even-think-about-it way.

"Oh come on, Forrest," Susan said. "Don't be petulant. We're all on the same team."

"I'm not being petulant, Susan. I just never got around to giving my system a name."

"It all seems to be under the main directory," Victoria said, showing mild amusement at my childish ways. She had straight long blond hair and a long pale face. No English breakfast for her. "You've got letters, memos, notes, orders and schedules all jumbled up in the same place."

"That's right," I said.

"You don't have separate files for receivables, current and sub accounts?" David asked.

"I wasn't really in charge of the books," I said.

"Never mind," Jenny said with a nice professional smile. "We'll sort it out. It's just a little job."

"Why don't you do that," I said. "While I chat with Susan."

"Let go," Susan said as we walked out of the office and into the cool and still front room of the house, "of my arm."

"Just making sure you're real," I said. "Nothing else around here seems to be."

"Sam doesn't believe in waiting. What do you want, Forrest?"

"Maybe somebody could say, 'Hello, Forrest, great to see you.' Or how about, 'Forrest, you old dog, we missed you.' Or 'Gee, you drove a great race there in Canada, Forrest. Let me tell you what happened while you were away.' "

"We didn't miss you a bit, if you want to know the truth."

"I don't want to know the truth, Susan. I want you to lie. Say you are delighted to see me. What's going on?"

Susan was wearing one of Phil's white shirts with the shirttails knotted in front and the sleeves rolled up, a light blue T-shirt underneath and tight and faded blue jeans. Her cleaning-house outfit, except everything was just a little too tight here and too loose there to be housewifey.

"Sam is putting in some of his corporate systems and it's about time. We're logging all our stuff onto his mainframe and we should be a lot more efficient."

"It sure looks efficient. We've only got about sixteen times more people scurrying around here than we had last week."

"At least they are here and not rolling around on the other side of the Atlantic with some old has-been bimbo."

"I'll try to keep closer to home, Susan."

"Do what you like. I didn't have a team manager before I could count on, and now I do." She was shaking, furious or exhausted or maybe both.

"Now you do," I said. "So give your old race-driver buddy a hug," I said, taking her in my arms and giving her a squeeze.

She squeezed back for a few beats. "I'm sorry, Forrest. I don't mean to be bitchy. I know I asked you to do it. But it just wasn't working out. I had to do it." Then she pushed away. "I've got to see Sam," she said. "There's a lot to do."

"You run into him, tell him I want to see him too."

"He's got you scheduled for ten-forty-five," she said over her shoulder.

"How the hell do you know that?"

She stopped in the doorway. Pushing back a wisp of hair from her high, smooth forehead, heavy breasts pushing the white shirt aside. Knockout sexy mum. "Today's schedule," she said, as if I ought to know. "It's on the bulletin board in the front hall."

"What bulletin board?"

"Or look it up on your computer. It's all there," she said, moving away. "Get Victoria to show you how," she said, slamming the door.

I thought I'd done a passable imitation of a team manager, but what the hell. To hell with the whole damn thing of running a team. I had to admit I had never been the paragon of efficiency. But I hadn't asked for the job either. "I did the best I could," says the epitaph for the Forgotten Man. I went out the door to sniff the freshness of the day and wonder at the men and women, heads down, coming out of doors and going in doors, crossing the forecourt with important frowns, on their way to doing something that really needed doing.

I smiled. There is real satisfaction in having your place taken by twenty people. And a great relief in having nothing to do but drive.

I walked around the comer of the house and back to Two Building to look at the cars. Mine would have been stripped and rebuilt, piece by piece, for the tire testing session coming up at Silverstone. I wanted to catch up with Alistair, and talk to him about setting up the car for the track we called our local.

I opened the door to Two and stepped into the brightly lit space—gleaming white floor and the skylights high above. The three cars were fully assembled, and they looked different. Looked wrong. There was something else, a noise.

Instead of the blue and green colors of Team Joyce, they were purple and gold. Block letters on the side pods said, "EMRON." On the shop wall, at the side, a large sheet of paper had been tacked up. "EFORT," it said, in large gold letters.

Upstairs, Alistair was yelling.

Chapter 12

Walking up the stairs in Two Building, along the soft gray carpet to the the back, where Alistair had his office, lab and drawing room. To where the noise was coming from. I'd never heard Alistair angry before and it was a curious sound. His deep, resonant voice louder, but not faster or higher. Almost soothing. Definitely angry.

"One hundred and twelve thousand hours," he was saying as I came through his open door into the room. Alistair had his back to his big video screen, facing Naughton, protecting his work. The room was warm from the sun coming through big skylights even though the windows were open. Clarence, Cathy and Bill, his draftsmen, had swiveled in their chairs, staring at Alistair with their mouths open, their blue screens flickering behind them.

" . . . just on the basic software and Soft Air is not just my work. There is the better part of Cambridge in there. Fifty graduate students at least. Goddammit, there are five graduate aerodynamic theses and a government grant in there. You jolly well can't own that."

Naughton heard me come in and turned to see who it was. His boyish face showed some color in the pockmarked cheeks, and he gave me the lifted Naughton eyebrows and rolled his eyes. Like "Look at what I have to put up with," giving his head a quick tilt to indicate the airhead. As in "We are superior to this," tilt of head, "looney wind freak." Naughton turned back to Alistair.

Alistair was pleading to me over Naughton's shoulder.

Naughton was six-two, so Alistair had to stretch.

"Soft Air is my company," Alistair was saying. "We lease our information to Team Joyce. Team Joyce doesn't own my stuff. I'm paid for the information. You don't own my stuff."

Naughton said, his voice low and reasonable, "Team Joyce has given me fifty-one-percent ownership and control for value, and as of this morning Team Joyce has new management, a new name and a new direction. Team Joyce's record to date, their files, their total assets, debts, contractual obligations and, believe me, the software you keep calling 'your stuff' belongs, along with the tea trolley, to Emron Formula One Racing Team."

"Hello, Sam," I said. "What's the problem, Alistair?"

Naughton didn't turn around again; he just turned his head a little to the side, holding his finger up, like this was too important for interruptions. Like he would get to me later. "Ten-forty-five," he said.

"I'll check my schedule, Sam. See if I can squeeze you in. What's the problem, Alistair?"

That turned Naughton around, facing me. He gave me a small smile to indicate even more patience. Through the smile he was explaining. "One of the things I want to determine here," Naughton said slowly, "is whether EFORT can continue to support two cars and two drivers."

"Effort?"

"Emron Formula One Racing Team. E-F-O-R-T," he spelled out, his smile widening. His idea.

"Susan told me you were pumping thirty-five million cash into the team. You thinking of cutting a car and driver, cutting the team in half to pay for your management?"

"My management, as you call it, are a few of my key people, here short term, reporting directly to me. Their assignment is to straighten out this mess you call a racing team and draw up an agenda for putting this operation on a profit-making base. Before you get too involved, Evers, I'd suggest you keep a low profile. As a number of my key people have suggested, the most attractive area for cutting cost on a team on the way up is cutting a driver who is on his way down.''

"Looked like up to me until you got here, Sam. Although I suppose if you are putting thirty-five million in that gives you the right to act like a shit.''

"No one has been talking investing cash. This team has a serious cash-flow problem and if it is going to survive it will be as a profit center for Emron. This team will have to generate its own funds.''

"What Susan did, Forrest,'' Alistair said, "was exchange Emron shares for fifty-one percent of her shares in Team Joyce. What I'm trying to tell this cretinous cowboy,'' he said in his slow, lugubrious way, "is that Phil and Sue made a deal with me. They agreed to pay me a fee for my work. But my company keeps the software. Christ, I spent half my life on this thing and this,'' he stopped for a moment, looking for the worst word, "this *executive* wants me to plug it into his mainframe.''

Naughton stuck his hands into his faded jeans and leaned back against the table. The aw shucks routine. The hip capitalist on his day away from corporate headquarters working the field. Just one of the guys. Just happens to be carrying a gun loaded with money, pointing it around. The way men fight in the corporate suites these days. With low voices, and gut-wrenching threats. "I don't mean to upset you boys. I, uh, *have* to look at every corner of this operation to see if there isn't some way to run it efficiently. That's what I'm paid to do.'' He paused, thoughtful. "And if that means I have to lose a driver and an aero-head in the process, too bad.'' He nodded and looked grim to indicate the loss. "Corporate surgery is always painful. And I don't believe in anesthetics.''

I took a half step into him. Face-to-face. Talking quietly like he did. "What is your stock worth, Sam? Last time I looked, it was dropping like a turd.''

Sam backed off a step, rolling his shoulders. "I don't know what concern that is of yours, Evers, or where you get your misinformation, but I'll answer your question. Glad to answer it.'' He rolled his shoulders, PR tape #6 for the investment analysts, slotting in, cued up and rolling. ''Yes, our shares have been leveling off. But that's nothing to be ashamed of in this market. This has been a tough period for most companies and especially difficult for those involved in construction. The construction slowdown we see in Britain reaches beyond the fall in home starts—''

''I've heard this speech,'' I said, interrupting. ''It's in the *Financial Times* every morning. Let me guess: you are going to go 'prevailing market conditions,' 'unfavorable exchange rate mechanisms' and 'global political uncertainty' and all those other flabby excuses, like 'declining consumer consumption expectations.' What I'd guess, Sam, is that all you have left are excuses. I'd guess you didn't put any cash into this team because you don't have any cash. I'd guess you are experiencing what they call in the trade a financial shortfall. Like broke.''

''A billion-dollar corporation does not go 'like broke,' Evers. You stick to the sports pages.'' A little edge in the heavy boredom of his voice.

''Well, I hate to be the one to tell you this, Sam, but these days a top professional athlete who doesn't read the financial pages before he reads the sports section has a financial advisor who does. Let me tell you what I read, Naughton, see if I've got it right. I read you were a real go-getter in the eighties, buying up companies and paying for them with promises—junk bonds that would be funded out of the hijacked company's own profits. And when the junk bonds come due there are no profits and you can't pay. You can't begin to pay and the banks and the big investors are all over you. They want their money. So you come around here to siphon off some fresh cash. So for a pile of your stock you can help yourself to Susan's little nest egg.''

''I don't know what you read, Evers, or what you smoke. You are not even close. But you are dismissed.'' The color had spread from his cheeks. ''You walk from now on, you hear me? I have one or two friends out there, and I promise you, you won't get a ride in a Go-Kart.'' The smile had gone now, but we still had the low-key voice of the control freak pretending to be laid back.

"By all means, fire me, if that is what you want to do, Sam. But I would have a think about it before you call your friends," I said. "And have your lawyers run their combs through my contract one more time. Because my contract says if I walk, I take 6 million dollars of Chantal sponsorship money with me. And I take the rest of my 1.5 million salary with me in cash, up front. Plus the 2-million-pound cash buy-out guarantee. Read it, Sam. If you hadn't been in such a rush to get your hands on this team, you would know that. If I walk, it will be in the papers in the morning for your stockholders to read. Some of those big pension funds might get the idea that you are fucking up this team the way you fucked up your Emron empire. Might get the idea that you are getting desperate. That the time has come to dump their Emron parcels."

I put my hand on his shoulder to emphasize the point and felt him stiffen. "They do that, Sam, think about how the rest of your, what do you call it now, EFORT sponsors are going to feel about being tied to a sinking ship. They'll be diving for their escape clauses left and right. Course you are new to Formula One racing so let me tell you that's the trick about sponsors, Sam. You spend five years romancing them, spend a couple of hundred thousand getting them into bed with you, and they can disappear in five minutes. And while your legal staff are doing their study of my contracts you might just take a look at Alistair's agreement. I did and I had my solicitors look at it. It doesn't say much. And one of the things it doesn't say is that anybody aside from Alistair owns his software. But nice try, Sam. Keep looking. Glad to have you aboard. And listen, do you mind if I skip the ten-forty-five with you this morning? I'd like to talk to Susan. See if there just might be a touch of fraud in the way you represented the value of those Emron shares."

"You are past your sell-by date, Evers, and you are beginning to smell. You are finished with this team."

"Sniff me, Sam," I said. "I am irresistible."

"I am out of patience and *you*," he said, with a confident little male-bond wink, "are out of here."

We listened to Sam going down the stairs. Clarence, Bill and Cathy were still staring openmouthed at us. Alistair turned to them and said, "Get on with it."

They swiveled around to bend over their screens and the blonde with the rings on her fingers and the bags under her eyes looked back at us over her shoulder. Alistair stabbed her with a stare of his own and she turned back to her screen. "Why didn't you do that before?" he said to me.

"Do what? I just got here."

"I mean act like a team manager. If you'd acted like that before, Forrest, Susan wouldn't have let Naughton in the front door. Where'd you read about him?"

"*Fortune, Barrons, FT.* The business press has another sinking junk bond pirate every week. I was guessing about him, but it sounded pretty good to me."

"Yeah, sounded great. Shame about it being wrong."

"You have a better idea?"

"What do you think a suit who runs a multibillion-dollar empire is doing here, messing with a second-division team?"

"I don't know why they like to run racing teams, but they do. Maybe they like wearing the earphones in the pits on Sunday afternoon. Show the world who's boss. Of course it's more than a game. Roger Penske doesn't do it just for fun. They do it right like Frank in Didcot, or Ron Dennis, and they can make more than ten million a year."

"Yeah, maybe, one day. But not here and now. And even if he could make a fortune, I don't think he's after the cash so much. I mean you know the books better than I do, but how much could Susan have? OK, he's a businessman and he is always after cash, but that is not the main reason he's here."

"He's in love with your software?"

"You know about that?"

"I thought I was making a joke."

"It's not a joke. Emron owns Machtel," Alistair said gloomily.

I paused.

"Machtel," he repeated. Like it was what people talk about over breakfast. "The biggest designer and builder of wind tunnels in the world. They build stuff for the American military, NASA, Aerospaciale, Boeing, Detroit, Toyota—it's a very big business. Billions. They just finished a huge one for the Saudi Air Force."

"And Machtel would love your software."

"Think about it, Forrest. The end of the cold war really hit them. Every country in the world is cutting back on their military budgets. Machtel is nosediving, and they are a big reason Emron is in such a deep financial trough."

" 'Deep financial trough.' You read the same papers I do?"

"It's in the wind mags." He went over to a desk and pawed through *Rolling Stone, Face* and a half dozen *Autosport*s to scoop up a few magazines and hand them to me. "Here, check out this month's *Transonic Flow, Vortex* and *digital air*. There's bound to be something in them. Machtel have a couple of contracts with the Americans coming up."

He peered over the shoulder of one of his designers, looked at the numbers on the screen and came back to me, resting against his drafting table. "You see part of the charm of my stuff is that as long as you have the design in CAD/CAM, in the computer, which they all do, it doesn't matter how big it is. You can run my software on a 747 and get an accurate readout at any altitude, temperature and airspeed you like. Do a wingtip or the whole damn space shuttle if you want. So if you were a U.S. senator, or let's say you were a retired Air Force general on the board of Lockheed, or in the Ministry of Defense about to approve a five-hundred-million dollar wind tunnel, and you find out you could do it on a computer for around a thousandth of the cost, and do it tomorrow instead of next year when they get the damn fan built, what would you do?''

"So your software is really worth something."

"That's what I've been trying to tell you, Forrest. If I can get it working right, it's priceless."

I thought for a moment, the buzz of summer floating in through the open windows. "Well if it's worth that much," I said, "there's a difference between our new team manager and your normal corporate captain who puts on earphones and goes racing."

"What's that?"

"Your normal guy wants to win."

When I went downstairs, my teammate Russell was sitting in his car. He had bruised his shins and shoulder in Montreal and they were remaking his seat and adjusting the padding inside the footwell to see if they could make him more comfortable. "Don't they look great," he said, looking up at me, meaning the cars.

"I liked the old colors," I said.

"Yeah, well, they're gone aren't they? I mean they were OK, but these are really ballsy, you know. Mr. Naughton explained like, you know, what he said about the colors. What they mean."

I shook my head.

"It's class, Forrest. Top of the class. He said the gold is for what we are running for. Like at the end of the rainbow. And the purple is for the passion it takes to get you there."

"So you like our new owner and team manager?"

"Yeah, he's great. He told me he's going to get me hooked up with a whole bunch of new sponsors, get me some individual sponsorship money. You know, feature me like."

"You too can be a star," I said. He was so eager, and so glad to do what he was doing, you had to feel good for him.

"Hey, yeah, I almost forgot," he said. "What's Virgin

like in bed? Is she wild or what? Did you see her tits?''

"Her tits, Russell, have their own business managers. You'll have to ask them. How was your car in Montreal? You been over the race in the computer?'' And we began what drivers do these days. Remembering the incidents, the moments, some of them fractions of seconds, when something seemed wrong or unusually right, those moments when we were faster or too slow, and looked for them in the computer printouts, looking to see which wheel was breaking loose, how the braking point compared to the other braking points, what the precise G loadings and speed were and what, if anything, stood out and made the car unstable or just a bit quicker. It is slow, precise and tedious work and if you want to be at all competitive in Formula One, it is what you do—hunt through the numbers for the smallest advantage.

By the time we had finished, it was one in the afternoon and I found Susan in the kitchen.

"Where's Naughton?'' I asked her.

"Sam's gone back to London. He's probably still in his car. You want his number?''

"What are you doing?''

"Making a sandwich, dummy. You want one?''

"I mean with this team. Alistair says you've sold it to Naughton.''

"Part of it. Sure you won't have one?''

"I had a big breakfast. Naughton said he's not putting any cash in.''

"Not now, no. But the potential is fantastic. That's the secret of a good tuna salad—squeeze of lemon.'' She put the lettuce on the tuna goop, put another slice of bread on top and took a big bite, the mayonnaise oozing out the sides.

"Glad you are enjoying it. Susan, you did this overnight. I thought we were partners. Maybe you could tell me about it instead of acting like I'm hired help.''

"You are hired help. Oh don't pull such a face. I can't help teasing you sometimes, Forrest, you are such a prickly pear. You sure you won't have one, just a bite?''

"Just a half then."

"I'll make one, and if you want the other half, it's there." Susan busied herself cutting bread and making the sandwich. "When I got back, it was about ten in the morning. I had the whole day ahead of me and I was exhausted. Sue Two had wet her pants and was screaming, and Josh had carved his initials in the dining room table. And I thought, I am not leaving these kids anymore. I am not going to let them grow up without me. And if you think I'm copping out, let me tell you running a Formula One team is a bowl of chocolate mousse compared to raising two kids. I am sick of this running around the world pretending to be something I'm not. Some big-time bitchy executive with tailored suits and a fancy leather briefcase. Raising these kids is a full-time job, and I'm going to do it until Sue Two goes to school anyway." She took a long drink of water.

"Anyway, Forrest, that's what I was thinking when I got home, and there was a message from Sam, asking me if I could come down to London to see him for lunch. And I said no, I needed a day or two up here to straighten things out. And he said that it was really important. He had a lot to show me, and if it was OK, he would come up here. He was really quite sweet. He had The Ivy cater dinner, and he put on a whole presentation in the dining room. It was really very impressive, Forrest. He had his key people with him, and they really put on a show. Video, music, lots of graphs and charts. You must get him to do it for you."

"Presentation on what?"

"Well, on Emron, mostly. What he did was lay out the future marketing potential for his company and it's huge. The reason he was doing it—he was quite clear about this—was to link the high-tech and glamour of Formula One directly with Emron and boost the value of his Emron stock. Go beyond sponsorship and actually own the team."

"Why didn't you call me?"

"Call you? Where were you? You weren't here. It wasn't your team. He needed an answer right away."

"You gave him fifty-one percent?"

"For fifty percent of his future net profits. Starting in two years."

"So you got nothing now. No cash."

"Not now, but it could be millions, hundreds of millions."

"How much is it now?"

"Is what now?"

"Emron's net profits. The ones you are going to get fifty percent of."

"I'm not sure. It's a huge company."

"From what I've seen, and you can check it out, they are making a loss."

"Now?"

"Now."

"OK. I mean that's OK. I think he told me that. We are talking a couple of years from now. That's part of Naughton's point. He wants the team to win, to build the image of Emron. What did you say to him?"

"He said I was fired. I told him that would be expensive."

"You're not fired. He can't fire you. We already agreed to that. Where are you staying tonight?"

I thought of the peace and quiet of my flat in London on the top floor of one of those old Victorian piles facing Holland Park. The mail a heap of brown envelopes with red ink saying "Urgent," "Last Notice," "Incoming Storm Troopers." The balcony on the back with the garden table facing west, to the sunset. The sitting room with its bookshelves and its old leather sofa, the room as empty as an old slipper. The answering machine glowing green with old friends and wrong numbers. "Back to London," I said. "Put out the fires."

"I turned the bed down for you," she said, "in your old room. Look, I feel kind of shaky. I'd feel better if you were in the house. Please?"

"Susan, what did you sign? Can I have my solicitor look at it?"

"Oh, look, leave it for now. Let's talk about it tomorrow.

Dinner if you like. I'm just so tired of it. The bank has it. They said it was fine."

She pushed her plate away as if the subject were closed. "When Phil proposed to me, he pulled this ring out of his pocket," she held out her finger, looking into the large diamond, "and he started to stutter. And I jumped on him. Knocked the ring out of his hand. Knocked him right over onto the bed. And he was shocked. He said 'What the hell are you doing? Does that mean yes?' And I said 'Yes, of course, you dummy.' And he said, 'I haven't finished yet. Where's the ring?' 'In the corner,' I said, 'under the dresser.' My eyes never left that ring. I knew right where it was."

And she looked up at me, her eyes calm and tired. "I knew where everything was when he was here. And I thought I was much stronger than I am. Well, I need to be home and I need to be with the kids and for once I don't give a good goddamn what the team needs. Part of it died with Phil, and maybe it's time I recognized that. Started living my own life. I need to know you are in the house tonight so I can sleep for a change. And I need to lean on you for a little while. If the deal I made with Naughton isn't right, then straighten it out. Do what you like. Finish your sandwich."

Chapter 13

"What is this, one of your intercontinental ballistic missiles?" A weird blue funnel cut in half, with dents in its throat, rotated on the screen.

"This program doesn't do ICBMs," Alistair said. "Nor does its author."

"I thought your software could do anything."

"It can't dance. And I am not into making faster bombs. Pay attention, Evers. You should recognize your own diffuser."

"I don't see my name on it, mate, but I like the color."

"Screw you," he said, suddenly angry. "Hey, look, Forrest, I'm sorry. That guy really upset me. I can't leave this project. I've got to get it sorted out first. OK, you're right, I can't do supersonic stuff yet. NASA is working on supersonic virtual reality wind tunnels at the Ames Lab in California, but I haven't seen any of their software. It would probably take me and an aerodynamics lab and a big mainframe a year to get set up. What I mean is we are set up to do this. This car, with the Cray in Stamford. It would take months, with huge funding, to adapt to aircraft. I don't know if that executive chief operating whatever the hell he is knows that. I mean maybe he has an inflated idea of the capabilities of this program."

"You said it is priceless." I wanted to draw him out. He had a kind of shy, defensive quality, rare in Formula One. Until he got going on his software. Once he got going on his software, he was a tiger.

"It is. But it needs work. I think this will work, but I've got to run it through the whole setup. What did Susan say?"

"She says we'll talk about it in the morning."

"Hey, if you are going to be here for the rest of the afternoon . . . " He punched some buttons and the funnel stopped. "Look over here," he said pointing to the screen. "Watch this."

The dimples inside the funnel moved out to become bumps. Then they moved in again.

"Very exciting," I said.

"You'll think it's exciting if it works. It could be like having another wing on the car. It could be a second a lap. Maybe even two or three on a course like Hungary or Magny Cours. The walls inside the throat of the diffuser are pressure sensitive. When you are going fast, they widen, let more air through. When you slow down, they constrict, speeding the air up. So you get more traction at slow speed if you can keep your ride height constant. And the way I read the rules, it is not a movable bit. It just happens to flex owing to the variation in thickness in the carbon fiber."

"When can I have it?"

"We'll run it through the software wind tunnel, and if it works, you'll have it for Silverstone. What's that white glob on your chin?"

The phone rang. He picked it up, I wiped the mayonnaise from my chin, and with his basset hound look he said, "It is yet another woman for you." Alistair handed me the phone and turned back to his screen, pushing buttons. I held the phone in my hand, looking at him.

"One of these nights," he said, "why don't you ask one of them along? You and Susan and I, we'll have dinner."

"We will," I said. "Although it may be just the three of us. Will that thing really work?"

"Depends on the driver," he said with his sad version of a smile.

The phone said, "Is this the first phone call you've had from a billionaire today?"

"Who is this?"

"You rat. You went to bed with me yesterday, and I just called up to say I missed you, and you don't even know who it is?"

"I'm just playing hard to get. How are you?"

"How many billionaires call you up? Maybe it's billion-airesses. I like that. Sounds sexier. I'm just getting up."

"I didn't know you were a billionaire. I thought you were a poor little rich girl from New Jersey."

"I just signed a big new contract with Warners. Huge, amazing, stupendous deal. Lots of digits for years and years. Isn't that *great*. Now do you miss me?"

"I missed you before."

"Really??"

"Really."

"How about now? Just kidding. You probably think it's dumb, but I really haven't been to bed with a man in months. You probably think I fuck all the time."

"I hadn't given it a lot of thought. What do you do all the time?"

"I work my ass off. Everybody thinks rock stars are stoned and fucking all the time. I work sixteen hours a day, and I go home and nosedive into the pillow. I liked being in bed with you."

"Yeah, me too."

"Me too? Are you with somebody?"

"I'm in a roomful of aerodynamicists." Alistair looked up from his screen. "And they are all looking at me."

"What do you do with aerodynamicists? Never mind, don't answer that. Isn't that great? About my contract?"

"Are you going to get all the money in one vault and dive in it like Scrooge McDuck?"

"Yeah. I like that. Then I'll give it all away. Some of it. To needy agents. I'm going to see you in a week."

"If I'm still driving."

"What, you're quitting?"

"The team has just been bought by a corporation. They're

talking about firing me. You ever hear of Sam Naughton?''

"Sure. I know Sam. He's cute.''

"You're kidding.''

"I am not kidding. Don't give me that shit. He put some money into a movie I made about five years ago. You remember *Virgin Velvet*?''

"No.''

"That's OK, nobody does. My first film as a director-star. *Variety* called it *A Bore Is Starred*. Anyway, he had money in it and he came out to the location in Palmdale. He was sweet.''

"I don't think he's sweet, I think he's a crook.''

"Some crooks are sweet. You better be there.''

"You mean next week?''

"Of course I mean next week. I called Chantal 'cause they had some dumb idea about you and I doing everyday things together like shopping in a supermarket. I mean bore-ing. Virgin does not do ordinary things. And I said I want a night out in Paris with you at Tour D'Argent and the best club in Paris, whatever that is, they should know. And they can take all the photographs they want and then I want to go to the Ritz or someplace like that with you and they have to wait outside. All night.''

"Are you asking me for a date?''

"It's fate. Don't fight it.''

When I hung up, Alistair said, "Who was that?''

I said, "My dinner date.''

That night after Susan put the kids to bed, she said she was sorry but did I mind if she went straight to bed because she was too tired to eat, but thanks for staying, she'd see me in the morning, good night. The phone rang in the office and I picked it up.

"Is that you, Forrest?''

"I'm on phone duty tonight.''

"I'm glad I caught you. Sam Naughton.''

"It's great to talk to you too, Sam.''

"Look, I don't have a lot of time here. I'm ringing you to apologize. I'm new at this, and I am the first to admit I've got a lot to learn. I'm sorry we got off on the wrong foot."

"You've read my contract."

"Not personally, no. But my lawyers have, and they advise me you are substantially correct. I can't afford to fire you. And since I want this to work, I want EFORT to succeed, it would be a lot easier for both of us if we were able to get along."

"It would help if we didn't have to call the team EFORT."

"All the documents are filed, the ad agency's designed the logo, and the campaign starts in the newspapers in the morning. I'm not saying it couldn't be done if you feel strongly about it, but it would be a heavy expense in a time when we need to spend money on the cars, and it means changing the name a third time, so get back to me on that one after you've had a chance to think about it. The reason I'm calling you, Forrest, is I've got to go to Tokyo this evening and I won't see you until Magny Cours."

"I will miss you too."

"Don't make this more difficult than it is, Evers. I need your help. I'm assigning Jeremy Buckingham, whom I think you met, to run the business side of the team, get the systems in place, and get the damn thing running efficiently. I'm asking him to report directly to you."

"There is something you can do if you want to help the team. Are you going to have any free time in Tokyo?"

"Not that I know of. What's on your mind?"

"You know we have a contract with Hozuki for the engines."

"Sure. I haven't read the contract . . . "

"Doesn't matter. They supply their engines at no cost to us in exchange for their name on the side pods, and I think they are losing interest. They've been promising us a new engine since Mexico. Could you call George Hozuki? He's the founder and CEO. His real name is Hashishimitu or something like that, and rather than hear the round eyes mispronounce it, he likes to be called George. He's a bear, but he's all right. He speaks English better than I do, and if you could meet him and find out what the holdup is, rattle his cage. If you came back with a new engine under your arm I might learn to love you.''

"I'll work on it. Anything else?"

"What about Alistair?"

"You tell me."

"He is a friend of mine. And the best aerodynamicist in Formula One. He stays."

"We'll see."

Chapter 14

Abbey Curve is flat. Foot-to-the-floor flat. Trying-every-thing-I-know flat. Gaining-450-pounds-sideways-mashed-against-the-side-of-the-car flat. Out flat.

Fuck.

Thinking maybe if I'd got on the throttle a tick sooner coming out of the second-gear corner at Vale and Club leading into the straight . . . But I'd already tried that. The car is clumsy at low speed, with no downforce to hold it on the track, and the back end just kicks out and the wheels spin. I wanted more speed, and the car didn't have more to give.

Flat out at 195 miles an hour going through Abbey Curve, lying on my back with the thick little steering wheel buzzing in my hands, mashed into the side of the car, my head and shoulders still pressed back from acceleration, my spine and my skull vibrating at 13,510 rpm, the engine note still rising. Just touching the inside of the curb with the edge of my tires and letting the car come out to the right edge of the track, as the car wants to fly off into the bank where the spectators would be fifty deep in two weeks. Now there is only a photographer, Bloxham, maybe, from *Autosport*, walking on the ridge, curved and lean as a comma, cameras and lenses hanging from him.

There is a stripe of cool air smelling of freshly mown lawn; they must have just cut the grass. I keep my foot down and bring the car back to the outside of the track, line up for the dive under the bridge and into Bridge, foot flat to the floor, lift just a tic to settle the car, then flat to the floor again, diving down from on high like a jet fighter, pressing for more, the car banking in the turn, feeling the car compress underneath me all the way to the bump stops. Bringing the car back across the track, the steering heavy from downforce, steer over to the right edge two beats, to where the track changes from gray to black, and precisely on that line, on the brakes hard and skipping down the gears and going hard left into the double left turn of Priory and Brooklands, all the way out to the edge of the track on the exit, get the car lined up so the back end doesn't come around, accelerating hard for a second and immediately, violently, force the car left over across the track to lead into the reverse two right turns at Luffield. Careful not to touch the curbs and unsettle the car coming out of the second half. I am trying to push this sled faster, find a microsecond here, wait a little longer before I get on the brakes, and it is not enough, not nearly enough. The car is so slow I could be writing letters home. Or someplace.

Damn.

The car reels out with the outside wheels on the rough grip of the concrete rumble strip at the outside of the track at Woodcote, getting a clean exit, no wheel spin and foot to the floor up through the gears from second and down the main straight, flat out, foot to the floor, come on, come on, crossing the finish line knowing that I am down at least three, maybe even four, whole seconds behind Hill and Senna. A lifetime in Formula One.

Maybe Senna could make this car go faster, but I can not.

A second and a half later, coming into Copse at the end of the main straight, it happens again—the engine cuts out just before I get on the brakes. It has happened so often today, you would think I would be used to it. But I am not used to it. It never happens the same way twice, and it scares the hell out of me every time. My heart has my teeth marks all over it. They have been rebuilding the course, and Copse is a different corner now. Now it's much easier than it used to be. Or should be easier. You enter Copse very early. From close to two hundred miles an hour in sixth, just dab on the brakes down to fifth, and with a much sharper turn in than the old corner, just shave the inside where they've chopped off the old curb. Now it's more like a kink than a corner, so you are right on the power very early, going wide on the exit, and you are hard on the power going uphill, getting into sixth before Maggots. Unless, of course, your engine is choking and coughing.

Letting up on the throttle on a Formula One car is like standing on the brakes in your favorite Ferrari. Complicated by a loss of grip. As the car loses power, I entered the turn more slowly, down to say 175 instead of 190. The difference in speed isn't apparent to the spectators, but without the power of the engine to pull me through, the car loses downforce, the glue that keeps me on the track, and the front end starts to slide wide, getting out of the groove, where the rubber is, out onto the slippery edge of the track coated with dust and covered with little rubber pellets scrubbed off the tires of twenty-four Formula One cars pounding around and around. Then the car twitches sideways as the power comes back on again in a rush, sending me charging for the infield before the power cuts off again, and I get the car straightened out and the power comes on again and I am on my way, up the hill toward Maggots, having gained the attention of the small crowd on the outside of Copse, who have come to watch tire testing. They have had a wonderful day, watching me. Here comes the clown. Looks like he's coming into the corner too fast again, panicking, almost losing it, and then stomping on the accelerator again, driving with the delicacy of a Brahma bull. And with about as much speed.

The problem comes and goes and it will not go away.

The day is almost over. And I let up. To hell with it. Almost every time I try a hot lap the car starts to stall at the end of the main straight. Once it came back on just before I turned into the corner. Seven hundred and fifty horsepower coming on in a rush, pushing the car straight ahead out of control when I want it poised and easing the weight onto the left front corner of the car, turning in, like having a chainsaw suddenly swing around on you.

We have changed the black box, the spark plugs, the leads, and checked every conceivable electrical part, from the battery to the alternator. The telemetry readouts tell us the problem is electrical, but we cannot see anything that pinpoints the problem.

Russell passes me going into Stowe, with Alesi hot on his heels, lining up to pass my teammate at the end of Vale. Let them go. I have had it for today.

I cruised around through Vale, taking my time. Coming into Abbey again, off the line to let Hill through, the Williams screamed by me like a shock wave. A flash of blue and gold, sparks flying, and it was gone. I went through the double left of Priory and Brookfield and the double right of Luffield. Not my favorite turns. The cars slide this way and that way in a meaningless little dance for the Paddock Club grandstand, to make the five-hundred-pound-a-day punters think they are seeing something. I peeled off the track and through the pit-lane chicane and into the pits, pulled into my slot and turned it off. I never think of it before, so it is always a surprise when I switch off a Formula One car. The incredible silence as the world returns to normal sounds and normal speed. No more two-ton Cuisinart on the eardrums. No more all-body vibro. No more slamming back and forth and side to side. The peace and quiet's a shock.

Pat Hutchins, the crew chief, bent over me and I said, ''Roll it back in. It's still doing it.''

''We'll find it,'' he said. ''The Hozuki guys say they think they've got the answer. One of the airflow sensors is picking up some strange stuff. Don't worry, we'll track it down.''

I hoped so. It was like driving a loaded gun. You never knew when it might go off.

Jeremy Buckingham, Naughton's man from Emron, crowded in, his short, stocky body covered in a yellow slicker in case it rained, his earphones wrapped around his neck, his eyes squinting. ''You're not hitting the kill switch by any chance, are you, Forrest?'' he said. ''I mean I know it's unlikely.''

''Could be, Jeremy. You know I always like to give the crowd a wave there as I'm turning into the corner. I'll have to try a couple of laps with both hands on the wheel.''

''Come on, Evers, this is serious.''

''OK, why don't you check and see how many Hozuki technicians it takes to trace an electrical fault?''

''Fuck you.''

I had it coming. Of course it is serious. Formula One racing, if it is about anything, is about being the best in the world, no excuses and no glory for second place. Which may explain why I do not suffer amateurs gladly. Even well-intentioned ones. Buckingham had busied himself with inventories and statistics; setting up flowcharts for the components and putting items on a replacement schedule. All good business school stuff. And what I probably should have done. But none of it made the car go faster. Getting organized cuts down on the fuck-up ratio, and you have to be meticulous about every change you make to the car, because every change affects the behavior of every other component. So you keep computer records of every single change and the effect of that change so you don't start from scratch every time you raise the rear wing a millimeter. That's good management and you can't go faster without it. But good management is not what going faster is about.

Going faster is all about power—getting it, using it and getting more of it. Power from the engine company, power from the fuel company, money from everybody. Because money and power are inseparable, especially when the power is measured in horses. Still, I thought, I should lighten up.

Tire testing is way more relaxed than a race weekend. Tire testing has nothing to do with testing tires. The only tires out there were Goodyear and they were fine, thank you. What we were doing was getting the car set up for the French Grand Prix the next weekend and for Silverstone the week after that. So you are racing yourself, trying to get the best setup. There just happen to be other cars out there. The fact that every lap is timed and we spend half our time staring into monitors to get the latest readouts from the other teams is just coincidence. Still, there is time to cruise the pits and say hello to old friends, and see if maybe they have the front nacelle off the car, see what their new monoshock suspension looks like.

I stretched my legs by walking down past Ligier and Benetton and Correlli to the Tyrell pit, where Ken Tyrell was leaning his tall frame over the pit wall. "How are you, Ken?"

"I'm worried," he said, his great hawk face turning toward me, teeth pointing in different directions, eyes squinting at me through horn-rim tinted glasses. "They better get these damn guardrails fitted before the Grand Prix or we're going to have all the rail birds falling bum first into the pit lane." Next to him black steel rails were stacked up along the walkway.

"You mean Jackie wasn't the only one who was concerned about safety."

"I'm concerned when the safety is mine. I've seen you getting all crossed up in Copse. What's your problem?"

"If I were a better test driver, I'd know."

"Don't worry about it."

"Ken, the car is cutting out and coming back on again. Maybe you are relaxed about seven hundred and fifty horsepower turning on and off at a hundred ninety miles an hour, but I am not."

"That's what you get for using pump fuel." A little jibe there, about our lack of a fuel contract, and with it the strange and evil-smelling concoctions that gave the fortunate teams 50 extra horsepower. Our fuel came from the petrol pump in the pits.

"Well, what is it I shouldn't worry about?"

His face swiveled as his driver, DeCesaris, screamed by.

"Being a test driver," he said. "The great drivers are not the ones who go out there, burn up the track and come back in and tell the technicians to dial up a quarter of an ohm on the left front wing end plate sensor. The great drivers," he turned his back to the track and folded his arms, grinning, warming to his story, "the great drivers don't give a damn for the technology. And they do not have political opinions worth listening to or *Vogue* leading taste in decor, and they are not necessarily fun to be around. But the great drivers do share one great and overwhelming talent. The great drivers sit in their driving seat, and when you nod, they put their foot down and blow the doors off the test drivers."

"Berger says the only real difference between him and Senna is that Senna knows how to set up his car better. All those years Senna had in Go-Karts and Formula Three."

"That's his story. You let the techies sort it out. All you have to do is get in the car and put your foot down."

"Sounds easy to me. Let me give you Evers Universal Law number 12: 'Everybody's job is easier than mine.'"

"Well," he said, "I'll give you that. Your job is a hell of a lot easier than mine."

Evers UL #13: A racetrack is the worst place in the world to look for sympathy. In fact, if you are looking for sympathy, don't even think about being a racing driver.

I wandered back down to our pit. Ferrari had shut their doors, hiding something. At least they had doors to shut. Silverstone, with all the other construction in the pits, hadn't got around to putting the doors back on all the garages yet. It didn't matter much; the weather was cool and clear, and we didn't have any new technical developments to hide. But with luck we would at the British Grand Prix in two weeks' time.

In the distance, the CSN broadcast truck at the end to the grandstand was retracting its antenna, packing up. My teammate Russell Simpson pulled in to change tires, the pit crew practiced a race change, and he accelerated out again, kicking up a cloud of cement dust from the construction. I went into the garage, grabbed a pair of earphones off a counter, went back outside, across the pit lane, and stood up on the pit wall, next to Alistair.

"How's he doing?" I said, putting on the earphones.

"We've taken a little off his rear wing to give him a bit more on the straights. He's doing around 1m 27.095s, about a second quicker than you."

"I never got a clear lap."

"Well, go get one."

"Fix the damn car."

"Talk to your electrician."

Russell came by, on it, trying hard. On the radio he said, "Tires are hot. I got two hundred more on the straight." Meaning he was getting more speed and going for a good lap.

Alistair gave me a thumbs-up, happy that his aerodynamic tweak seemed to be working, and I was thinking I should be glad it was working for somebody when, without warning, a dog attacked me.

Out of nowhere.

Coming fast.

There was a low growl in front of me, I could hear the jump after the run, there was a huge scream of rage from the beast in midair, and instinctively I half fell back, half turned to defend myself. Into the path of Milese in the Minardi. And as I fell, I reached out for Alistair, grabbing the back of his jacket, pulling him back with me, and Alistair started to fall. Milese was flat-out accelerating and lifted in the fraction of a second before impact.

Like a dream the way the mind picks up speed and the details shine. My back is falling toward the tarmac, and I have a strong grip on Alistair, turning him, trying to pull myself up but pulling him down too, and he reaches out and grabs Buckingham's yellow slicker, pulling Buckingham back with us, and it is enough, just, to slow us down, in our slow-motion fall onto pit lane, so that Milese blasts past us as my head hits the tarmac where, a hundredth of a second ago, the car had been, and a half a second later, Alistair and Buckingham come tumbling down, Humpty-Dumpties off the wall.

Chapter 15

Falling back, thinking, What dog?

I could swear I saw, must have seen, the long, thin lips pulled back, the pink-and-black gums and the wet teeth in the wide-open mouth. The dog was raging. Coming in throat-high.

Thinking, Plenty of time. Reaching out for Alistair's shoulder, missing, and then, in the slow fall backward, just catching his shirt with my fingers. The scream of Milese's Minardi approaching, as Alistair begins to fall back and turns his head slowly toward me, his legs buckling with my weight, his shirt starting to tear in my hand. Like Phil. In a sense peaceful, still floating in the air but no way relaxed. How could they be so stupid? To do it again. To me, the same way. Alistair's arms are stretched straight out, moving up and down like a marching toy. His head is turning away from me. Toward Jeremy. Who is not looking and tries to brush Alistair's hand away. Jeremy is wholly unprepared for the shock of Alistair's weight and then mine, which pulls him sharply back a step and then another step, where there is nothing to step on, just air. Jeremy's mouth is opened wide in surprise, his round, gold wire-rim glasses coming off. And his billowing yellow jacket in the blue sky coming down, growing larger as I feel the hot rush of the car passing underneath me, the push and then the vacuum, and the noise and the smell of oil, of chemical exhaust, of hot rubber passing underneath, and the crack of the back of my skull on the pavement as Alistair's shoulder descends into my shoulder and Jeremy falls gently down. Forrest.

A long way away, "Forrest?" My name.

"*Forrest*!" I want to stay asleep, here in the warm dream. Falling. I opened an eye, and a large, fuzzy head loomed over me.

"I think he heard me. *Forrrrest*!!"

"Please," another voice said. "He should be resting."

"It's OK," I said, opening my eyes to the face over me, her short brown hair hanging down, the nice mouth with lipstick. "Hello, Susan."

Her face pulled back, into focus, revealing a pale green ceiling. And a thundering headache. I closed my eyes again.

"Come back here, Forrest."

"Perhaps we should come back later," the voice behind her said.

"This is later. *Forrrest*!!"

I opened my eyes. "I'm resting now."

"Alistair has a dislocated shoulder, Jeremy has a broken nose, and I want to know what happened."

"I'm fine. Thank you for asking."

"I know you are. I've seen the X rays."

"What happened?"

"You crashed, Forrest. Without a car. Hard to believe, but both Alistair and Jeremy tell me you stumbled backward, fell off the pit wall and pulled them with you. Everyone else seems to agree. But I thought I would ask you."

"Because you suspect."

"It's in my mind, yes."

"You didn't see it."

"Of course I didn't see it. I was home. Playing Mum. Thinking all the children were with me."

"You heard I fell off," I said, feeling unbearably heavy and tired. My eyelids had weight.

"I heard my driver took out half my team falling off the pit wall."

"What time is it?"

"Just after six. Do you want anything?"

"In the evening?"

She nodded. "Same day."

"I need to talk to Alistair. What do the doctors say?"

"They say I should find a driver who can make his way down pit lane without falling off the wall."

"What do you think happened, Susan?"

"I don't think. I mean, I wasn't there when it happened. I mean, I have no idea what it was, but I have a feeling it could have been the same thing that happened to Phil. Whatever the hell it was. I don't want to think about it. The doctor says you can leave in the morning. They think it's just a mild concussion, but they want to keep you here overnight for observation. What did happen, Forrest?" Her brown eyes were open wide, afraid.

"I'm not sure. I need to talk to Alistair."

"He's gone home. Hours ago. You should get some rest, and I should get home and feed the monsters."

"Give them a hug for me."

"Here's one for you." She bent down low, smelling of perfume and lavender soap, held my head gently in her hands and kissed me. Lightly. Not long. On the mouth. "I'm glad you're OK," she whispered in my ear. "Tell me in the morning." She rose up again, Mum tucking a child into bed. Towering over me. My eyes were closing to the taste of lipstick.

"Drive carefully," I said.

"Walk safely," she said.

Chapter 16

Nurse Caroline cranked up my bed so I could keep an eye on my rubber eggs. I dropped a fork on the lumpy yellow mound, and the fork bounced. Interesting.

The yellow liquid in the plastic cup tasted like tin, while the coffee in the foam cup was flavored with newspaper. Fascinating.

Nurse Caroline was just tall enough to peer over the top of the bed. She had a pretty round face, long hair and shoulders that cranked up two hundred beds a day. She was still standing there, an expectant look on her face. Then she held out a telegram for me. "Somebody loves you," she said. I took it, and she gave me a sad, too-bad-you-have-to-die smile. And a wave good-bye.

A get well message, I thought, from a fan. Oh, look, all the way from Tokyo Telegraph and Radio. It said,

Forrest: Naturally I am disappointed in your performance, specifically your lap times. You wanted direct control of the team and you have it. If the car is not functioning properly, the responsibility is yours. Your times are not competitive, Russell's are not appreciably better and those responsibilities, for the cars and for him, are also within your assignment. There can be no excuses and I am not interested in comedy. EFORT must be a first-rate operation. Must be. EFORT is the designated standard-bearer of the Emron Group into the twenty-first century. Call me. Need to discuss ways to be more competitive not less. Get well soon. Sam.

Naughton's note gave me an insight into why international management is so universally loathed—the expectation that the distant voice from on high knows better and will be obeyed, along with helpful hints from twelve thousand miles away. The chances of my calling him were below zero. He was right about the responsibility. The responsibility for running the team was mine. I had asked for it. But whatever was interfering with my car and pushing me in front of a race car was outside my control. Although not necessarily outside his.

"Good news, I hope." A teenager with a stethoscope around his neck stood at the foot of the bed. "Dr. Manning, Mr. Evers. How are you feeling this morning?"

"No aches, no pains, I feel fine. I didn't know doctors still wore stethoscopes."

"Don't get me started on this hospital's equipment. Think of it as the new Micro-Disk Walkman. Glad to hear you're feeling good. You should go easy for a bit. I wouldn't be surprised if you had just a trace of a headache."

"We racing drivers are famous for the speed of our recovery," I said. And famous for our brave wit in hospitals.

"And for thick skulls, if yours is indicative." He wrapped a black rag around my arm, pumped it up and stuck his cool stethoscope here and there. "Well, you did have a good thump, but I don't think it has done you any great harm. You may experience occasional nausea. And just a bit of a headache. If either persists after a couple of days, give us a ring." He wrapped up his black rag and looked down into a manila folder and back up at me, blinking his eyes with fatigue. "Your clothes should be in the locker. Take your time, no rush. But do bear in mind we will require the bed by nine this morning. A *serious* injury, I'm afraid."

He moved through the curtains to interview my roommate, a man whom I never saw and who screamed regularly, although I never found out why.

The clock on the wall said 6:38. I swung my feet over the side of the bed, and my head ballooned with glowing volcanic sludge. With great care, I lifted one foot and then the other back up onto the bed and lay back on the pillow and closed my eyes for a moment.

"Mr. Evers? Mr. Evers?"

I opened my eyes quarter-mast. Hoping whoever he was wouldn't notice. Some scruffy kid.

"Mr. Evers, they say they need your bed? It's nine-thirty?"

Half-mast. He wasn't going away; he was coming around to the side of the bed. And he wasn't a kid. He was a grown man dressed like an art student.

"Good morning, Mr. Evers? I'm Mike Cooper from the *Northampton Eagle*?" He had a Northerner's habit of making statements sound like questions? His hand stuck out, waiting for a shake.

"And you want to know about my accident?" I said, unintentionally mimicking him. He was pale and thin, about thirty-six, with short black curly hair, blue eyes and silver bracelets on his arm which was not sticking out for a handshake like I'd thought. It was sticking out holding a tape recorder.

"What's to say about your accident?" he said. "Geezer falls over backward. 'Snot what you would call front page, know what I'm saying? What it was, thing I wanted to know was, what's Virgin really like?"

"She's short."

"Come on, you gotta have some little tidbit for the fans?"

"She's your average billionairess. Short, just like the Queen. Hand me my shirt."

"She's a greedy little bleach-blonde bimbo who's into masturbating in public. How are you this morning, Forrest?" Susan said cheerily. "And why are you putting your shirt on inside out?"

Susan shooed the reporter away with promises of lunch and an in-depth look at local Formula One team premises. "Next week. Call me," she called out to him as he was leaving. Susan was wearing one of Phil's white shirts with a cocoa suede vest, a short pleated green skirt and loafers with no socks. Her long brown hair was pulled back with a gold hoop. "Come on, get dressed," she said.

"Why is everybody in a hurry this morning?"

"You are the one who said he wanted to see Alistair. I rang him and he said he will only be home until noon. He has to go in for an MRI on his shoulder. The one you dislocated. I've brought your car."

"Do you have a ride back to Pury End?"

"You're coming with me."

We went cross-country toward Cambridge, through little villages like Bletsoe, Thurleigh and Staploe. Although I didn't see much of them, apart from a blur of red brick and half-timbered houses, with window boxes and here and there a thatch roof

"Much prettier than the A-45," Susan said, "and just as quick." She drove with the easy and nerve-wracking confidence of a woman who has grown up zooming up and down the molelike tunnels they call country lanes in England, charging into six-foot-wide blind comers at sixty, hedgerows on both sides blocking out the sun, darting into the tiny little laybys for no apparent reason, until another car, driven by another Nigella Mansell, charges by in the other direction going sixty, waving thanks. Whatever the women of rural Britain are up to during the day, they are in hell of a hurry to do it.

"You didn't have to come," I said as she pulled back out, the Vauxhall accelerating as hard as it could. There is something sexy about a woman's legs moving up and down on the accelerator clutch and brake, and Susan had very good legs, suntanned and smooth, with good muscles, and I was going to have to do something about my love life before I started grabbing women in the street. Or while they were driving.

"I don't *have* to do anything. You, on the other hand,

can't do much of anything. The doctor said you are not to drive, read, watch TV or go to a movie for two days. Besides, I want to know what you and Alistair are up to.''

"Nothing, if we don't get there."

"You can be such a wimp, Forrest. We missed it by a mile. I could drive this road blindfolded. Go back to staring at my legs if the road bothers you."

"You are in a feisty mood this morning."

"Compared to most of my mornings for the past few weeks, I am an absolute sweetie."

"That's a one-lane bridge coming up."

"Hold on."

Alistair's house was the latest in eighteenth-century aero-dynamic development—a low, thatched roof just below the crest of a green field and, inside, wide plank floors, stone fireplaces big enough to roast an ox and exposed beams. I impressed the ancient grain of one beam on my forehead going through the kitchen, understanding in another volcanic flash of pain why Alistair walked with a permanent stoop. The alternative was brain damage.

Alistair held out his left hand to shake, saying, "Mind the beams." With his arm in a sling, he looked more stooped than usual.

"I'm sorry," I said. "Is it painful?"

"More," he said, "than I can possibly explain. Hello, Susan."

Susan gave him a delicate hug and a long kiss on the cheek, going up on tiptoe. "Don't they give you painkillers, darling? Darvon, something like that?" she said.

"He doesn't believe in things that dull the mind." An electric wheelchair with a small figure in it hummed into the room. Her eyes were wide, black, intense. When she rolled into the light from the kitchen window, she looked very young—nineteen or twenty—and she was smiling happily. "The booby asked them for mescaline, but they pretended they'd never heard of the stuff. Hello, you," she said to

Susan. She took her long, delicate fingers off the joystick that controlled the machine and held out her hand to me. "Hiya, I'm Merrie. Her indoors, if you don't mind a cruel joke. I've heard bags about you, Evers, and I must say I don't think he's done you justice."

We shook hands, and Alistair said, "Merrie, my wife and co-owner of Soft Air. Do you want to tell them about the accident, darling?"

"Heavens no. He's so crass sometimes," Merrie said to us, as if Alistair weren't there. "We were in a motorcycle accident just before we were married, and he thinks everybody we meet wants to know all about us flying side by side through the air. It was all quite sweet. Look, I know why you're here, and I don't want to intrude because I'd be bored stiff. So why don't you let me get on with doing a few housewifely things which I rarely get to do, like make the tea and sort out some biscuits for you. Nice to meet you. Oh, Alistair, before you go, would you reach down the digestives?" Merrie did a pirouette with her chair, neatly wheeled over to the cupboard and came to a smooth stop. Her movements with the wheelchair were precise and elegant, probably a reflection of the grace she'd had before her accident. Reaching behind, she pulled out a long, polished aluminium pole with pincers on the end, like grocery clerks use to get tins and boxes off high shelves. Something Alistair must have made for her. She poked it in the air, running the pincers along the top of the dresser, demonstrating where she couldn't reach.

"I put them up on top so you wouldn't gobble them all up, and now I can't get the damn things," she said.

Alistair winced as he reached up with his good arm and found the biscuits on top of the cupboard. He helped himself to one before giving the package to Merrie, and, munching, he led us out of the kitchen.

"She usually likes to tell people all of the gory details," he said. "It gives her some weird kind of pleasure. But she's all right."

"Is there anything I can do for you?" I said, nodding toward his sling.

"Sure. Stop looking so glum, old chum. Like looking in the looking glass. Course, I'd have done exactly the same to you if I thought I was descending in an accelerating arc into the path of a Minardi. A Ferrari wouldn't be so bad. Almost a kind of heraldic honor to be run down by a Ferrari. But a Minardi! That's about as fast as Merrie's wheelchair. Which," he said, stopping in the hall for a moment, "is not all that slow. I've had it up to fifty on the downhill. It's got six 12-volt car batteries and an aircraft starter motor for power. It's probably the only wheelchair in Britain with a seat belt, although Merrie won't buckle up. Wish she would—it's two miles down to the village."

"You built it yourself?" I asked.

"All my own work. I'm working on another with a suspension, proper steering and some bodywork to keep the rain off so she can get into town when the weather is bad." He led us through the house to the back, where a glass conservatory housed his workroom. "Welcome," he said with a sweep of his hand, "to the playroom."

It was a large, airy conservatory. High overhead, glass panels let in the summer air. Birds and jet fighters and butterflies and commercial airliners, biplanes, dragonflies and flying wings suspended from the ceiling were moving gently in the breeze along with Formula One cars, ocean racers and flowing abstract shapes that might have been part of something else. Each one was finely detailed and brightly colored. There was a bank of computer screens and keyboards along one glass wall and a large drawing table in the middle. At the far end, against the transparent glass wall, with the sky as background, a large scale model of the Wright brothers' plane hung at eye level. My art, if you can call it that, is in the passing moments. Finding an extra thousandth or, if I am lucky, hundredth of a second where nobody else can. And then it is gone. So I have always admired someone who can make something so permanent it can hang on a string, or a wall. If you have ever looked at an intake manifold, you know that mechanical engineers are the real artists.

"I made that old thing when I was twelve," Alistair said to me, leading Susan by the hand to inspect the fragile construction close up. "I'd built a couple of the Leonardo da Vinci models, and I wanted to start at the beginning of stuff that actually works, that you could step into and fly. But my problem was the engine. The original was an old lump I couldn't duplicate. I could have stuck a Volkswagen in it, but that wouldn't have been right, and where can you get a good VW engine for fifteen pounds, which is what I had. So I settled for a model. Most of these are projects I've worked on at one time or another. Except for birds and bugs, of course."

" 'Only God and Angels Fly,' " Susan read off a plaque on the model. "Where did you say that came from?"

"That was Bishop Milton Wright, 1903. What he said just before his sons left home for Kitty Hawk." He put his good arm around Susan's shoulders and turned to me. "How are you feeling, Forrest? Not as bad as you look, I hope. Any lasting effects, like a sense of humor?"

"None so far. I'm not supposed to watch TV or drive for a couple of days. I think I can stand it. The only real pain has been sitting in the suicide seat with Susan driving. I don't want to die young."

"Oh, stop it, Forrest. We hardly got out of third gear."

"Susan shifts out of third at eighty-five," I said. Susan smiled sweetly at Alistair.

"I know," he said, giving Susan a hug, "I know."

He went over to his computer, switched it on and sat down, the screen glowing blue, red and green. "In the future, you won't have to go by road, Forrest, and all of this stuff," he waved an arm at his models, "will be obsolete. It sounds weird, but we are not far from the day when most of the traveling we do will be by computer. It's a bit more energy efficient and somewhat safer."

"Might even do sex by computer," Susan said to me, looking over his shoulder. "That would be a lot safer."

"I'll take my chances," Alistair said.

"What about the rabid dogs?" I said. "Are they safer too?"

Alistair looked back at me. "Rabid dogs?"

"Remember what happened when Phil was killed?"

"I saw it happen, Forrest. But I'm far from sure what happened. Does it bother you if we talk about it, Susan?"

"Don't worry about my feelings, they ran out weeks ago. And I'm tired of people pussyfooting around me. I don't know that there's much that I can contribute. Apart from the fact that Phil could not have stepped in front of race car. Not under his own steam."

"He was wearing Alistair's earphones," I said. "Just like I was, yesterday."

"You didn't just stumble back." Alistair switched off his computer, got up and went over to one of his biplanes. He gave the propeller a spin.

"I can't be certain," I said. "I've tried to sort it out and it sounds dumb. I thought I saw a dog, but I don't think I did because I can't remember what it looked like. What's a dog doing there, on the track? I've tried to remember what it looked like and I just can't get a picture of it. I had the feeling that it was big and fast, and I do know that it came from lower left and was charging for my throat. I heard it and I thought I saw it but I couldn't have seen it. It scared the hell out of me. Does that make any sense at all?"

Susan said, "Not if you are talking about Phil. There wasn't any dog anywhere near Phil. I saw the tape. Besides, they don't let them in the pits, do they?"

"No. But what you are saying, Forrest," Alistair said, "makes sense. You heard of virtual reality?"

"Only when you mention it six times a day."

"Well, to understand it, you have to go back to Heilig's convergence stuff in Mexico in the fifties and NASA's Ames

Research Center in Mountain View, California, in the 1980s
for the first prototypes."

"I don't have to understand it," I said. "I just want to
know what happened."

"What we're talking here is 'auditory visualization.' "

"*Alistair,*" Susan said.

"Would you prefer 'auditory intuition-amplifier'?"

"I'd prefer something simple. Without jargon."

"Well, you know stereo sound. Where you hear different
sounds and different sound values in each ear. Like you
would in a concert hall. Except, if you are wearing earphones, which are normally much better than speakers, it's
not so convincing when you move your head, because the
sound values stay the same any way you turn. Well, recently
they have been doing some virtual-reality stuff where they
give you the sounds that you would hear if you moved your
head. Like if you hear a dog coming up at you from left to
right, and when you turn your head, the dog sounds like he's
coming for your face."

"It didn't last very long."

"You wouldn't believe it if it did. For a second or two—
just long enough for you to turn your head—that's all you
need to think you better get the hell out of there. There's
another part to this. The human eye sees about one hundred
and eighty degrees side to side. If you hear something that
is outside your peripheral vision, it throws more importance
on the sound. You turn toward the sound, and now it's coming right at you—the reality is very persuasive."

"Somebody was watching me."

"Must have been. They would have to time it. You know,
have it ready to broadcast when a car starts coming up pit
lane."

"But I don't think they were watching me. I think they
were watching you."

Alistair said, "Sounds like they are really stupid. I don't
look anything like you."

"Maybe they are stupid. Or maybe they just didn't know I had your earphones on. How much do you know about Sam Naughton?"

"You leave Sam out of this," Susan said. "Sam's all right."

"Listen, shall I see if Merrie has tea ready?" Alistair said. "This could take some time."

Chapter 17

"Another bite?" This was Tom Castleman, asking in his hushed, Sovereign-of-the-British-Empire voice. Pure gold lying under the velvet plush. His financier's voice, the one he used to snow the bankers in New York. The proffered bite was sea bass, silky, smooth, white and so lightly smoked you hardly noticed it.

"No, really, I couldn't," Susan said, bending forward, helping herself. She had on a short, silky aqua summer dress with a low neckline and plenty of Susan moving freely beneath.

"Then you'll help out too, won't you, Forrest? Shame to waste it. It was flown in on AeroMexico this morning. Probably swimming off the coast of Vera Cruz yesterday." He spread his hands apologetically. "They'd lumber me with the stuff every day if I'd let them. I set up a fisheries program with a wonderful little man, Renaldo Ramirez, Mexican Minister of Agriculture, and he sends these treats over from time to time as a little gesture of gratitude. Project is still in the pilot stage, but when it gets off the ground . . . " Tom lifted his hands high and wide, palms up to indicate a sky's bounty of profits.

"What about another shrimp, Susan? They are good, aren't they. Although personally I prefer the smaller ones. Smaller ones," he said, jaws working, "are sweeter. Come, come, Evers, a few bites won't hurt. Otherwise Margaret will toss them to the pussycat.

"Do you know Mexico?" he said, turning his full attention to Susan. "Don't believe anything you've heard. Once you are outside the cities, it really is the most exquisite country in the spring. An ecological Eden where we are. You must come for a visit. Possibly, as a team owner, Susan, you could tell me why, in this day and age, people still want to watch racing cars run round burning fossil fuel. Or why men like Forrest here go out and risk their hides in them. Makes no sense at all to me."

"I'd love to come visit sometime," Susan said. "But my children wouldn't like being left behind."

"Children? Really? I wouldn't have guessed. There can't be many. I wouldn't have thought you were more than twenty-five."

"Twenty-eight," Susan said. "And two. Children."

"Ah well, bring them. There are always children running about in my house." Tom Castleman smiled his slow, satisfied smile. The one that used to mean he was about to strike. I was astonished at how much he'd aged. He still had the long, athletic frame, and those slightly bulging brown eyes that looked as deep as optical instruments under the long lashes. But his stomach had gone round and his shoulders were beginning to stoop. There were age spots on the backs of his hands, and his sleek head was balding now and silver. Almost as if he were withdrawing into semi-retirement.

I should have known when he suggested lunch. In the old days he never had time for lunch. Once, years ago, when he had contacted me about the ins and outs of corporate sponsorship and I suggested we talk over lunch, he said, "If you have to have lunch, take one of my accountants. She can tell you what I want."

Beyond and below the formal garden, with its geometric hedges spaced evenly across the lawn, the Thames strolled through the English countryside. It was another warm and sunny day, and we were outside on the terrace, at the front of Burnham, Castleman's English country house. As opposed to his Bel-Air or Maui or New York or Kyoto house, or the grandiose palace he had been building for the past five years on the Pacific coast of Mexico.

Castleman leaned back, sweeping his wineglass across the view. "It is marvelous, isn't it? You are privileged to be here, you know. If I wasn't here, you'd have a hell of a time. The National Trust opens Burnham to visitors on alternate Thursday afternoons from one to two-forty-five, by prior appointment only, every February." He laughed at his joke. "For the tax break."

"The stately homes of England," Susan sang, waving her wineglass, "how beautifully they stand, to show the upper classes, still have the ruling hand."

Castleman laughed. "Yes, I always liked that. One of the reasons I still come back here. In the summer at any rate. It's so clear in Britain, so well defined, isn't it? The upper classes have all of the money and pay none of the taxes. The middle classes do all of the work and pay all the taxes. And the lower classes scare the shit out of the middle classes. Excellent," he said, draining his glass of Montrachet.

"Actually you were quite lucky to catch me here. It's all rather out of date, don't you think? A leftover from the days when I thought I was building an empire. I ought to turn this pile into a hotel for all the use I get out of it, although the pool is nice if you can bear the bills for keeping the thing warm enough to swim in. I really think I will turn it into a hotel. Let the American tourists play duke and duchess for the weekend." He leaned forward, imparting his secrets. "The government can be quite generous if you want to play Basil Fawlty. They'll even get some other bugger to play Basil for you and guarantee you a return plus forgiving the taxes." He gestured toward the shrimp on their mound of melting ice. "You sure?"

"No thank you." I wanted to get this over with. Castleman might have gone into semi-retirement, but I always had the feeling I should check my wallet when I spent any time with him. He never did favors. He only repaid debts. With as little interest as possible. To his little paradigm of Britain's class structure he could have added his own, the vulture class, hovering just above and scaring the shit out of the ruling class, waiting to pick up the carcass the instant they let the profits drop.

"You remember Texon," I said.

"Of course. It's the first thing you mention every time we meet. How you put me onto them. And how they gave me eighty-five million to go away." He smiled easily at Susan. A man with wives, mistresses, corporations, houses and fortunes scattered around the world. As if Susan would be a pleasant addition. He turned back to me, the smile giving way to a trace of pain. "That damn near killed me, Evers, and I'm still waiting for a decent return. I don't have to tell you what a pit petroleum has been for the past five years, but you seem to think I ought to be forever grateful. What is it you want this time?"

"It wasn't just Texon, which I read you now hold a thirty-percent stake in."

"Which I paid for."

"And Courtland. Which I gave you on a silver platter."

"Come, come, dear boy," he said, doing his impression of the landed gentry, "to the point. You said on the phone you wanted to know about Emron. What is it you want to know about Emron? I certainly wouldn't put any money in." He swiveled slightly in his chair, half-turning to what looked like a laptop computer on its own little round table next to him. His long, slender fingers played the keys like a piano player. He looked back up. "In fact if you've got any money in, I'd try to get it out if I were you."

Susan put down her fork carefully, staring at him. "What makes you say that?"

"Frankly I think the large international corporation is a doomed species. Just like a dinosaur. You've got one tiny little head in some dying city like London or New York or Rome trying to take all the decisions for a body spread all over the world. And the natives are eating them alive. Just my opinion, of course, but you can bet this one will be extinct before the end of the year.'' He looked down at the vivid green-and-black screen alongside him. The numbers, as far as I could tell, were constantly changing, as if it were receiving information. Which was surprising because there was no electrical cord.

"This clown Naughton,'' he said, looking up for a moment and then going back to his screen. "One day I'm going to open my collection of chief executive officers to the public. The ones I've stuffed and mounted on the wall. He's had a negative earnings curve accelerating down for the past five years, and what does he do? He does what CEOs with no brains all over the world do. He cuts middle management in half every year and cuts ten percent of his total work force and extends the lease on his corporate jet and pays himself a 2.5-million-dollar bonus. He tells *The Wall Street Journal* Emron's problems are 'exogenous variables.' He means external problems he can't control: the world economy, falling consumer confidence, the Gulf War. My God, it is his *job* to anticipate what the problems are going to be. If he isn't keeping his ships off the rocks, what the hell is he doing besides banking his bonus? Even if he didn't anticipate the Gulf War—I mean it looked obvious enough to me—even if he didn't see it coming, with his companies he should have made a *bundle* on it. And look at this,'' he said, peering into the screen we couldn't see. "He cites write-offs, failed acquisitions. But he never blames the CEO. Well, they never do, do they? They should be falling on their swords, and they give themselves golden parachutes, greedy little buggers. What else?'' He punched some more buttons. "Reading between the lines, I'd guess Naughton made heavy payoffs in Washington for military contracts that got cut after Irangate.'' He looked up, a look of triumph on his face, "And then he was caught napping by the Gulf War, double squeeze just as his consumer sales are falling. His broadcast companies don't look too bad. Some of them are almost breaking even. Oh, right,'' he said, "look at this. He's got that Phelps thing, so I don't think I would want him for an enemy. They make the CIA look like my little pussycat.'' He bent over the table, making little sucking sounds.

''Phelps,'' Susan said primly, ''is the world's largest security company. Surely that is a growth area.''

Castleman's head rose up above the table again, giving up on finding his cat. ''The only growth area, my dear Susan,'' he said, putting his hand on hers as if to reassure her, ''is in governmental work. Very few governments these days want to commit themselves to doing their own assassinations. So they quietly farm it out. Of course the secret of the modern assassination is to engineer it so nobody ever suspects it was an assassination. But even that work, I'm told, is tapering off. It's not my field, so I don't really know. They might just be getting better at their bookkeeping. This broadcast network he's got, CSN . . . What is that, Cable Sports News?''

Susan nodded.

''Looks like he could spin that off to raise some cash. Although, if I were him, I'd hate to lose my network. Like having your soapbox taken away. Some cash but not nearly enough to keep him from sinking.''

He turned again to his screen. ''Ah yes, here it is coming up now. That's what I thought. I knew it—he *is* broke. Absolutely flat, running on empty. He has, let's see . . . His next loan obligation is due, good God, in three weeks. That should make interesting reading. If you want to invest in Emron, wait three weeks until the banks come crashing down on him. If you were quick, you might pick up Phelps for five pence in the pound.''

''Yes, you might,'' I said.

''Well, if I do, don't go claiming it was your idea, Evers. Carl,'' he called out over his shoulder, ''bring us a pot of your excellent coffee if you would be so kind.''

Later, as he and Susan swirled 150-year-old brandy in their snifters and a young woman wearing glasses and a swimsuit cleared the table, Castleman leaned toward me, his voice a half whisper. ''Forrest, that stuff you wear . . .''

I looked blank, thinking he meant my linen slacks, my dark green polo shirt.

"That Formula One concoction," he said, impatient. "That scent you are touting in those photos of you rolling around with half-naked women and that Virgin character. Does it really work?"

"Oh, absolutely," Susan said over the rim of her glass.

Driving out Burnham's long, winding drive, through the grove of beeches and out into the lush green fields that surrounded the estate, Susan rolled her window down and put her head back on the headrest, the afternoon sun making a gold halo around her hair. "I have a confession to make," she said, rolling her head toward me, her eyes a little dreamy with brandy.

She looked lovely, seductive, but I had to ask her. "About why you told him Formula One works when you know I don't wear the stuff?"

"I have no idea what you wear. I was just pulling the old lecher's chain. For all I know you bathe in it."

We drove out of the gates and I turned left, toward Maidenhead.

After a while she said, "I mean about Phelps."

"What about Phelps?"

"I hired them. Two of them. Phelps approached us at the beginning of the season, right after Phil signed the deal with Emron. They said that for very little money more than I'd pay for two computer analysts I could have the analysts plus 'the added benefit' of Phelps Security."

"Phil signed with Emron? I thought you shepherded the sponsors, and signed the contracts."

"I did. I do. But Emron made a point of dealing with Phil. Sam Naughton personally called him, said he admired what Phil had done. Said he was a fan of Phil's, said sponsoring us dovetailed with his plans for redirecting Emron into high-tech."

"And they are still on the team?"

"Laurel and Hardy."

"That explains the stupidity. What did Phelps mean by 'security'?"

"We'd had a couple of break-ins—computer terminals stolen, some racing tires. Nothing serious, but it made us think that next time, unless we did something, we could lose a car, plans, software. Several teams last year had break-ins. Where was it? Phoenix—you were there. You remember, March had their brake lines clipped. Can you imagine? And we do have several million pounds' worth of portable machinery. Not just the cars, but the computers and the transports. And on top of that, or underneath it if you like, we have our secrets. You know, all our little tricks that we like to think nobody else knows. So I guess we were all a little jumpy. Anyway Phelps said their technicians were trained in electronic systems and surveillance and they could provide security for all of that. They had all this snazzy equipment of their own. And they connected to a central control board, and Phil thought it would be good for the team, reassure our sponsors, make us seem up-to-date. You know how the little bugger liked gadgets."

Susan put her hand on my knee. "Do you think you can get around this camper, Forrest? Or would you like me to drive?"

I passed the lumbering, silt-stained camper, and we drove in silence for a while. Susan said, "Do you?"

"Do I what?"

"Nothing."

Dear Susan. Dear sweet Susan. Susan's breasts were full, free, pendulant, swaying over me. With wide strawberry-pink aureoles coming to a soft point. Brushing from time to time, against my chest. "Forrest," she said. Her mouth was full and sweet, and her kiss was wide open.

"It has been so long. Years," she said into my ear, whispering her secret.

I thought, Months, but I wasn't about to contradict her.

What did I know? What I knew was that she was warm and soft and easing up and down. The long and slow, loving slide up and then pausing for a moment. Teasing me. Giving me time to think it felt as if we had been together forever. And then slowly sliding down again, holding her tummy in, sliding down so the tips of her nipples were just touching me. Kissing my forehead, saying, "Forrest." The way my other Susan, Susan Evers, still calls herself Evers, the way Susan first wife used to make love. Her kinky streak, she called it. Wearing nothing, only high heels, squatting over me, rising up and down and squirming. The proper prim and trim British executive in her tailored suits and sexy underwear. Her secret life.

The silky girl.

"Susan, Susan," I said, rising up to meet her. "This is not right."

"Well then," Susan said, "you tell me what is." She was moving down again, twisting her hips slightly. "Because this feels right to me," she said, moving up again, toward the ceiling, "just right." She put her hand on my shoulder, bending down over me. "Just this once, darling. We'll only do this once. Only once. We're not hurting anybody. You're going to France tomorrow."

She sat back and was still for a moment, then hands on my stomach, she pushed off, rising up again and pausing. "Is this right," she asked, "the right way to do it? The way you like, like this? I've never done it with anyone else before. Do you really think once is enough?"

I sat up enough to put my hands on the small of her back. And felt her breasts spread against me.

"Once," I thought, "is never enough. Once," I moved my hands down, feeling her contract around me, "is too much. Or not nearly enough."

Susan smelled of sleep and a vague musky perfume and the oyster smell of sex. Moving up and down. She had spirit and courage, and she was delicious, voluptuous, especially from this angle, looking up. How easy this is to do and how impossible to undo it. Never undo it. She wasn't even beginning to be over Phil. Josh and Sue Two were Phil's children. Another man's family. I should have a family of my own, get started. Affection and desire weren't enough. "Never enough," I thought.

"Oh, wake up, Forrest," Susan said, "we're friends. Very good friends. We can be lovers if we want. We don't need permission. This isn't the Middle Ages." Her hand reached behind her to cup my balls and squeeze. Long, slender fingers. Sharp manicured nails. "Just this once won't hurt anybody. Really. No one has to know." She squeezed me hard for emphasis. "Wake up."

She let go, and her hands were on my chest, pushing me. Shaking me.

"*Wake up.*"

I opened my eyes, and Susan was standing beside the bed in her old slate-blue silk robe, leaning over me. She was shaking me. "Wake up, goddamnit, Forrest," she said.

"*Wake up!*" Tears were streaming down her face. "Merrie is on the phone." Her voice was shaking, starting to lose control now that I was awake. "Alistair's crashed."

And I knew what had happened to Alistair. Knew it. And realized that I had known it would happen. That it was bound to happen.

And I thought, I have been acting as if I am in a game. In a dream. And this is not a game. Not a dream.

Not at all.

Chapter 18

"Where *is* the sugar, Forrest? Why can't I find the sugar?"
Merrie waved her aluminum pole in the air, its rubber-tip
pincers threatening pots, plates and glasses on the shelves
over her stove.

"I don't take sugar in my tea, Merrie," I said. "It's three
in the morning. I don't want any tea."

"Where did that son of a bitch hide it? He is always hiding
things. Was."

Merrie whirled her wheelchair around and rolled up to me
in the middle of the kitchen. She had a small and classic oval
English face, smooth and pale, large black eyes under heavy
eyebrows, straight dark hair, a small delicate nose and mouth.
She couldn't have been more than twenty-two or -three. And
she was small, sitting like a child in her wheelchair, her legs
dangling helplessly out of her nightgown. She squeezed her
eyes shut, trying not to, but she couldn't help it, and her
face, getting red, squeezed and wrinkled. She dropped her
aluminum pole, put her hands to her face and cried.

I knelt in front of her and took her hot, wet face in my
hands. "I'm sorry, Merrie. I'm so very sorry."

I felt sorry, stupid and responsible. I had known this would
happen to Alistair. And I hadn't done anything about it. He
was a friend; he was only twenty-six. I knew him and I
trusted him with my life every time I went out on the track
and he had been in danger and I hadn't taken it seriously. I
don't know how I could have stopped it, but I could have

tried. I could have done something. Anything instead of nothing.

Merrie looked up at me as if there might be some hope in my face. She looked away. I stood up, and after a long moment she said, "Everybody is sorry, Evers. Everybody is always so sorry. It's their way of saying they are glad it's me that's crippled instead of them. I don't blame them, but what good is sorry? Sorry doesn't help anything."

She looked away, trying to control her tears, then she came back to me as if I might have some answers. "Like who is going to help me get into bed now? And who is going to help me get up? The bastard. I *need* him. First he makes me a cripple, then he does everything for me so I can't even get out of bed without him, I can hardly even pee without him, and now he's gone. No good-bye, no nothing. I could kill him." She started to laugh through her tears. "Oh Jesus, what a son of a bitch. I'm sorry too, Forrest. I'm sorry I'm making a scene. Sorry I don't know where the sugar is. Sorry for Alistair. And I wish I had never met the selfish son of a bitch. But if I catch you feeling sorry for me, Forrest, I will bash you with my pole. Can you hand it to me? Thanks. What did he look like?"

"I didn't see him, Merrie. He was gone . . . "

"Dead," she interrupted, "Alistair is dead."

"Alistair was dead by the time I got to the hospital."

He was dead long before and he had never had a chance. They had said it was better if I didn't see him. "Are you a relative?" the nurse behind the Emergency desk asked. "Well we couldn't allow you to view the body in any case. But it is much better if you remember him alive, believe me." I believed her.

"Do you need help getting into bed?"

"No no no. Of course I can *do* it. I was just whining, feeling sorry for myself. I'm allowed but nobody else is. Stop looking so grim, Forrest. Getting in and out of bed is just one of the hundred acrobatic exercises we 'challenged' people perform all by ourselves without benefit of a net. Try getting out of bed sometime with no leg or stomach muscles. It isn't pretty to watch, but I can do it myself.'' She stretched her arms and yawned.

"I am exhausted. I would love a cup of tea if you want to do something useful. I mean, I could do it. But if you would make me a pot and find the sugar and tell me about what happened . . . if you can bear it.'' She wiped her cheeks dry with her sleeve, like a child.

"You sure you wouldn't rather wait until the morning.''

"It is morning.''

"I don't know what happened.''

"You went out to the accident. You must have seen something.''

"They'd all gone by the time I got there.''

Except for a last police car, a white Rover with the red and yellow stripes along the side. Jam Butty cars they call them in the North. Its headlights on the tire tracks through the wet grass and shining on the tree. And the oak with bald, glistening, splintered yellow patches where the bark had been torn off. Wet with sap and spattered. I asked the policeman behind the wheel if they had found anything in Alistair's car, any records or computer discs.

"You don't think it was an accident, do you?'' Merrie said. "Look in the cupboard over the sink. Sometimes he hides it up there.''

"Why would he hide the sugar?''

"Dr. Quack says it isn't good for me. Look behind the soup bowls. Did they find anything?''

"They said they went through the car and there wasn't anything.'' Which was not quite true. The two policemen were in their car alongside the little winding two-lane country road, finishing up their report, drinking coffee out of paper cups and listening to the radio. Nothing else going on in rural Cambridgeshire. They said that they found him halfway through the windscreen, with blood all over the BMW, soaking the upholstery. That he had exploded against the tree trunk, bounced back into the car and there were bits of him under the seat, skull fragments. That they would have another look in the morning when the light was better and the car was dry. Another idiot, they said, going a hundred and ten miles an hour who didn't wear a seat belt. Probably drinking to boot. "Stay outside the yellow cordon, sir," they said. "We don't want you stepping on anything." Inside the yellow plastic tape there were the footprints of the mechanics, the police, ambulance workers and who knows, spectators. It looked like the side of a pitch at a village football match, the grass and leaves wet and trampled. The earth still fresh from the wrecked car plowing up the grass as it was towed backward. Small black shining ponds of blood or oil, shining black and gold in the headlights from the police car. Something caught my eye. A small white section of bloodless flesh. A piece of Alistair's lip or hand—there was no way of knowing from this distance. The ants were just finding it.

"You didn't see anything?"

"I'll go back in the morning and look when there is some light."

"Oh, good, you found the sugar. Three teaspoons, please. How fast do you think he was going?"

"I didn't see the car. The police said over a hundred."

"Rubbish. Alistair always drove quickly; that's why he bought that whacking great thing. He is a scientist. Was a scientist. He never once drove recklessly. Besides you can't go that fast on that road, even in his car. He's driven that road, thousands of times, so it isn't as if some corner would surprise him. Even on his motorcycles he always drove well within his limits. And no, he doesn't drink and drive. Never." She handed her white mug back to me. "You didn't put enough sugar in. Another teaspoon, please."

"No wonder they hide it from you. The question I was thinking, Merrie. Why would he be coming back from his office in the middle of the night? I mean, he must have been coming from his office; it's the road between here and Team Joyce. Did he say anything to you?"

"Say anything to me? Don't be an idiot." Her voice was getting light, almost careless.

"I thought he might have been working. Or making copies of his programs. Backing up his systems. Working on a new idea. Logging onto the Cray in California. Something like that."

"My God, Evers, you really don't know, do you? I thought everybody knew."

She just left it there and there was a long silence. Finally I had to ask, "Knew what?"

"Knew he was having an affair with Susan. For years, Evers. For two bloody years. Living in the same house and you really didn't know?"

I thought of ways to disappear, through the slate stones of the kitchen floor, to go to sleep and wake up from this dream. Walk out the door. Anything to get away, fall off the world.

"Well, don't just stand there with your mouth open. He told me. He told me all about it before it happened. Before we were married. For God's sake, Forrest, sit down before you fall down, and I'll tell you. We were at Bristol together. You would have loved him then. Alistair was outrageous, funny, the way some very bright men are when they are so much quicker than everybody else around. I was reading physics with courses in aeronautics and I thought there cannot be another man half as bright and half as charming who is also reading aeronautics. God, he had a motorcycle. Brilliant." She laughed, and I caught a glimpse of the bright and beautiful student. "He never had a chance once I made up my mind. I was very pretty, wasn't I? And I adored him, just adored him. I would have done anything for him. Well, maybe Alistair didn't look like God's gift to you, but spend three years as an undergraduate at Bristol with a bunch of pencil necks, and I promise you Alistair will look like Matt Dillon and a young Sean Connery rolled into one. And when we had the accident, he wasn't touched, Forrest. OK, a couple of bruises and scratches, but he didn't even need a sticking plaster. My back was broken; four of my vertebrae were smashed.'' She took a tentative sip of her tea. ''Still not enough sugar. Sit still, it'll do.

''So I had seven months in the hospital and I knew I would never walk and he asked me to marry him. He said he was having an affair with Susan and he wouldn't give it up and would I marry him, and I said yes.''

She bent forward in her wheelchair, her eyes streaming. ''I was pretty,'' she said.

Alistair had built a ramp up to their bedroom at the end of the house, and I walked behind Merrie's humming wheelchair into the high and wide room with the beamed cathedral ceiling and the big bay window. In the west, the first light was a rose pink rim on the edge of the dark valley. Here and there in the distance there were the white winking headlights of the early risers and the red taillights going home. I pulled back the blue-and-green comforter on their four-poster bed and lifted Merrie out of her wheelchair and into the soft bed. She seemed to float she was so light. She looked up at me, her large black eyes red-rimmed, blinking. I bent down and kissed her forehead.

''Maybe it is a mistake,'' she said as I pulled her comforter up. ''Maybe it wasn't him.''

I went out to my car and drove back to Pury End. Five miles from Susan's house, the police had gone and there was enough light to get out, step over the yellow plastic ribbon and look. I didn't slow down.

I let myself in the front door, went quietly up the back stairs to my room, packed my suitcase in ten minutes, threw it in the back of my car and drove to London.

At five-thirty in the morning, getting into London on the first day of July, the air was clear, and the traffic, as they say on GLR, was light. And, as the gray light gave the buildings and the trees color, the world seemed light in another way. As if part of the substance were missing. As if overnight, every other molecule had dissolved and the houses along the Notting

Hill were only partly there, lightweight, ghostly. Not transparent yet, but not quite solid either.

Some survey, somewhere, estimated that Britain's children will see over a hundred thousand acts of violence and over ten thousand murders on television by the time they reach eighteen. I don't know that I have seen that many on television, because I rarely watch it. But I can tell you that when you see real violence, up close, it seems almost familiar, as if it were a scene from a movie or a news program you can't remember. It also seems different, unfamiliar. As if it were shot in the wrong lens, too close and too bright. Spots of blood on a splintered tree trunk, soaking into the fiber of the wood, stay wet and scarlet in your mind. Just when you think you have been numbed in the horror department by the endless limbs of actors, soldiers, dummies and grandmothers being blown skyhigh on the late night movie and the evening news, the ants feeding on a piece of your friend on the ground come crawling single file inside your brain to remind you that the groove of horror you thought was dead is alive and squirming. Shock dulls the mind, but you know you will carry the image vibrating with horror. From now on you will never look at any friend the same way again. There will always be that chance for them. And for you.

Violence, close up, blows away the certainty of your life and it will not come back.

I pulled up in front of my flat in Holland Park, realized I would have to get up again at nine to feed the parking meter with a fistful of twenty p. pieces, thought to hell with it, let them clamp and tow the Alamobile away, Susan can afford it, walked up the four flights to my flat, opened the double locks and walked past the stack of mail, mostly brown envelopes, and the winking telephone answering machine, went into the bedroom, pulled back the comforter, kicked off my shoes and the phone rang.

I let it ring and I was asleep before the answering machine picked up.

Chapter 19

The sun was warming the foot of my bed, waking me, announcing noon. I rolled over, picked up the phone and rang Susan.

"Where the hell are you?" she said. "I've been worried sick. This is a hell of a time for you to do a runner on me. Are you trying to make me say how much I need you? What the hell are you doing?"

"How are you, Susan?"

"Oh God, how do you think? Forrest, where are you? Why aren't you here? The police have been in and out all morning."

"Did they ask about you and Alistair, your relationship, being lovers?"

"That's none of their business. Or yours. What does it matter, anyway?"

"You never told me about it."

"Of course I didn't tell you. I didn't tell anyone. I was trying to keep my marriage together . . . Look, I don't want to talk about this. I feel rotten now and I need you here. Why aren't you here?"

Push the button and, presto, Forrest appears. "Susan, you are not alone there. You've got Jeremy Buckingham, Jim Barton; you have a team of forty people there packing up for France. You've got kids, the au pair."

"The team left hours ago."

"I'm leaving in half an hour for Paris. I've got a meeting with Panaguian at Chantal at six, then I'm driving down to Magny Cours."

"Can't you put it off? Take the FOCA plane in the morning from Luton? You don't have to be in Magny Cours tonight. Nobody will be there."

There are times when I think I have spent my life running from obligations. "You'll be fine, Susan. You don't need anybody there now. Are you coming to France, to the Grand Prix?"

"I'm staying here. With Josh and Sue Two. I couldn't face anybody now." There was a long pause. "Good luck, Forrest," she said. "Will you ring me?"

"Of course I'll ring you. Susan, do you know if our friends from Phelps, Laurel and Hardy, were in the shop last night?"

"I don't know. They could have been. Ask them. You'll see them Thursday." There was another pause and I could hear her crying. "I'm sorry," she said and hung up.

It had been easier than I'd thought. And much harder. I was running out on her when she needed a good friend. She was manipulating me like a puppet. She was in terrible pain. She had lied to me. The truth was in there somewhere between the lies and the pain.

The truth was I did have to be in Paris at six and it was as good excuse as any to get out of the mire, look around and see if Don Quixote in his rusting armor wanted to dive back in again. And sink. All I really wanted to do was to hold the wheel in my hands and drive. Maybe, in the days before sponsors, television and global marketing plans, it had been as simple as showing up at the track, risking your neck and, if you were lucky, winning the chance to risk your neck again. Now there were two lives to be accounted for. Neither of them my responsibility really. Neither one of them could I ignore. I showered, dressed for a marketing meeting with the world's leading *parfumerie*—dusty blue silk jacket, white T-shirt and baggy jeans—packed and called Merrie.

"Forrest," she said, "I'm glad you rang."

"How are you?"

"Infinitely better. Much, much. I'm supposed to be taking

lithium, and I'm not sure, I might have missed a pill, but it doesn't matter, the next one comes up in what two hours.''

I knew about lithium. It's what they give manic-depressives to keep them steady, off the terrible highs and lows. I once put a friend of mine in the hospital because he stopped taking the stuff. His wife called and I came over to his house and it looked like they had had a hurricane inside. He had pulled every book off the shelves, he was tearing down the wall between the dining room and the kitchen and every thought he had ever had was right at the front of his brain, all at once, trying to get out at the same time. Merrie was sounding like he had—urgent, fizzing with energy, but more lucid, at an earlier stage. ''Anyway,'' she was saying, ''I want to get at that garden while I've got the chance. This must be the limbo stage, when you know what you're supposed to feel but you don't? You know, Forrest, like an acrobat, one toe on the wire, whirling your arms, trying to stay upright, thinking you're a half a second away from flying and there's no net.''

There was a sharp intake of breath. ''Maybe tomorrow it'll hit me and I'll feel sorry for myself and weep for Alistair, but I haven't had a second today. I've been talking to the police. God, they are the worst bureaucrats, and what can I tell them? He was here now he's not. One day, they say, at a time. Every neighbor for five miles has been round offering cake and sympathy, and I finally got rid of them, all of them looking concerned and smiling bravely. They mean well, and heaven knows I am going to need every one of them, but a relief I can tell you to have them gone. I've been going through Alistair's stuff he's been doing on your car. Do you mind?''

''Of course I don't mind. What stuff?''

''Well, two things. He probably didn't tell you I had been working with him. He never tells anybody about me. Saves him going into the long explanations. Told anybody. But I was getting back up to speed on that transfuser. I mean if I don't do something, I am just going to sit and weep, so let me do this because I think he missed a tick.''

"Missed a trick," I said to give Merrie a chance to draw a breath.

"Just one. You probably know that one of the things that makes our virtual wind tunnel work is knowledge-based design, so we can take into account not only the topical data but also punch in the techniques for design and analysis, so we can see the multiple consequences of hypothetical material and production changes. I mean, the thing, that transfuser, is a nightmare to draw in 3D. I mean, just plotting the transverse centroid of the tunnel leading into the three ducts at the end with all those wandering shapes, and conforming to the intrusions from the power unit, suspension, gearbox and exhaust—it is an immensely complicated thing to draw and even more difficult to reproduce with an acceptable degree of accuracy in carbon fiber once you get the shape right, so I thought if I could dial in a faster production technique, maybe there's a way we could speed up the production of your bloody transfuser. Have it for Silverstone. You with me?''

"I'm hoping to catch up in the end."

"You will, it's simple. I think there's a way, using very high-temp liquid in place of water, we could form the carbon fiber almost overnight instead of building those complicated forms. But I need to get back on the Cray in California, and they'll need another pile of money before they'll let me do that.''

"Merrie, I have no idea what it is you want to do, but go ahead and do it," I said, giving her an authority I doubted that I had to give. "What was the other thing?"

"I've been thinking about the person or the persons that killed Alistair. I've thought about it and I want to kill them. Do you think you could find them? I mean, you must know something, and I'd really like to know because what I want to do next is to figure out a way for them to die.''

"Take your lithium now, Merrie."

"Sure, right away, but what did you say to the police?"

"I haven't talked to them."

"Well, what are you going to say? I know you don't think it's an accident, so what are you going to say? Or are you just going to run off to France and act like it never happened?"

"I don't know anything."

"Who knows anything? I want to know what you think, Forrest, because I know and you know it didn't just happen."

She was almost screaming on the phone. In an hour or three or tomorrow something or someone would cut the string and she would nosedive straight down. In the meantime she was flying, but she was also right. It couldn't have just happened. What I thought was that Alistair's BMW, the 850i, was like the McLaren, fly-by-wire. When you stepped on the brake or the accelerator, you didn't pump hydraulic cylinders that pushed the callipers onto the brake rotors and you didn't push the cables that opened the throttle, you sent an electrical input into a computer. And anybody who knew enough to program a computer chip could program it so that the throttle stuck open, the engine would not switch off and re-programmed the ABS system to hold the calipers off the brake discs. It was mildly sophisticated work, but Phelps had the resources. It could be linked to a timer, say, ten minutes after the car started. It would take less than two minutes to replace the main chip in the car's computer. Anybody with a screwdriver could do it. About the only thing a driver could do—once he realized the car was accelerating full throttle and the brakes didn't work, and neither did turning off the ignition—about all he could do, while he tried to keep the car on that dark, narrow and twisting road, would be to slam the car into low, which would account for the skid marks. Thinking about it, I realized that there was no reason they couldn't have programmed the headlights to turn off. If Laurel and Hardy were able to rig earphones and transmit electrical interference to my race car, they could have done it. If one of them was still at the race shop. But I had to find that out first. I should have talked to the police. It was too late now, I'd miss my plane. Tomorrow.

"Forrest?"

"I think somebody might have rigged the car's computer. It's an idea. I have to look into it."

"Shouldn't they pull the unit then? I mean at least protect it until you know what to look for?"

"For somebody who is flying off the walls, you are pretty quick, Merrie."

"OK, I'll take the lithium. And I will call the police, get them to do that. But you have to tell me more than that and you have to stop treating a doctor of aerodynamic physics like a child."

"You know Machtel?"

"Everybody in the field knows them. They were calling Alistair twice a week. They wanted to buy him out. He said he thought he had them by the short hairs, because once he got his program running and debugged, it would be worth a thousand times what they were offering him. You think that is a connection?"

"How much do they know about you, about your work?"

"I don't know, probably zilch. I don't think Alistair mentioned me, and I don't think he ever talked to them in any detail, but I wasn't there, you know, every time he talked to them. I mean, for example, did he ever mention me to you?"

"I don't think so."

"So don't worry. I'm OK. Look, if you like, I can set up a kind of code when I log in on the Cray, so nobody knows who I am. Get Laurel or Hardy to give me a ring and they can set it up."

"They are the last people you should talk to."

"Are they really?" she said with what sounded like a smile.

Chapter 20

It was the year of fawn, honey and champagne at Parfums Chantal. Fawn velvet carpet, honey silk walls, champagne suede topping the oval conference table in a room with a movie screen at one end and no windows. Panaguian took off his pale cream, butter-soft, natural hanging brushed silk jacket, hung it over the back of his chair and loosened his grape tie as a sign of the seriousness of the occasion. Down to work.

His personal assistant, Catherine, in a crisp tailored chardonnay silk suit with natural shoulders and a pink silk blouse hiding small happy breasts pointing this way and that way with her every breath, poured espresso into tiny cups. Catherine's face, in contrast to the lively action under her blouse, was on permanent hold. She drew an audio cassette recorder from her pocket and pointed it like a weapon at Panaguian. Every word would be recorded for all time and, if necessary, used as evidence against him. The average life expectancy of a marketing manager at Chantal was fourteen months.

"This has not been an easy year for us," Panaguian said. "Women are using less perfume in the recession, there is a strong movement toward more natural scents like," he curled his lip in distaste at their competitor's perfume marketing coup, " 'Soap.' And men are returning from their business trips with the eighth of an ounce bottles in place of the more generous quarter and half ounce. Historically luxury goods are the first to go in an economic downturn and we are no exception to history. So our total volume is down four hundred and fifty thousand liters last quarter and our revenue is down thirty-six-percent across the board, globally. In light of our reduced revenues we are conducting a major review of all of our marketing strategies and, I regret to say, revising our budgets downward an average of forty-two percent across the board.

"The one exception to this unfortunate scenario," Panaguian said, his face brightening into a display of white teeth in his dark face, "is Formula One. In every market to date in our rollout introduction, sales have exceeded our forecasts by an average of thirty-eight percent and in one case, in Brazil, by one hundred and twenty-nine percent. I am happy to report we have a serious supply problem in Brazil. The one little cloud in Formula One's otherwise sunny sky is repeat sales. Repeat sales are very low. But test markets in Helsinki and Milwaukee indicate that we will have the answer to low user satisfaction next year when we introduce Formula One Extract.

"We are monitoring the reaction, from some sectors outside our market, that Formula One is a sexist exercise of masculine power, an accusation we are doing everything we can to encourage, since, as you know, our primary target group is sexually insecure males under thirty-five. And product use studies along with consumer groups in South Africa and North America report that Formula One is, uh, somewhat less than a hundred percent effective, which backs up those low repeat sales figures. But since our buyers do not read consumer reports and are not feminists, I only mention these as interesting sidelights. Forgive me for going through this stage setting, Forrest, but I want to be sure that our friends from the creative team at Jonathan Reynolds, our British agency, are fully briefed. They have not always fully understood our problems in the past."

Panaguian nodded toward a dark, nervous man with a pockmarked face and a pencil in his mouth and a thin woman in layers of gauze, leather, vests and scarves. They flicked their eyes toward me and back to Panaguian, hostages, I guessed, to some former crime of judgment that had nearly lost them the account.

"Forgive me rambling on." Panaguian was rolling his shoulders, just warming up. "You know a Frenchman talks until he hears what he wants to say. We, of course, have had to do some fine tuning of our campaign. A little icing on the cake, you might say. Yes, of course, Virgin is very expensive. And we are aware of the danger of her, what is the word, overbearing? Overshadowing? Overshadowing, the importance of Formula One. But, as we have seen, that risk is more than overbalanced by the anticipated massive increase in media exposure. To date, I am happy to say she has been enthusiastically received by all of our agencies around the world except for Britain. A stroke of genius, our German agency called our signing Virgin to partner Forrest." The two British advertising people smiled weakly. "What was your phrase?" Panaguian said, looking at them for the first time, hands on the table, leaning toward them. "That Virgin is 'past it.' As if she were overripe fruit. *Of course* she is overripe fruit. We are not stupid. That is why we get her for so little money. Comparatively little money. For Virgin. Not much more out of our budget than Forrest here."

This was news to me. Did that mean they were paying Virgin over six million? The agency woman shifted uneasily in her chair, toying with one of her scarves.

"It is your *job* to make her fresh. England is the most important market in Europe for us. Potentially the biggest. Even bigger than Italy. And besides, the Englishmen have the most need of this." He was holding up a bottle of Formula One, a long, narrow bottle that looked a little like a test tube, with a narrow neck and a tiny rubber stopper. The 'sexual attractor' I was meant to be the spokesman for. Or of, or whatever it is that spokesmen do besides hold up the bottle and smile. "We have all the advertising and publicity in place," Panaguian said, his dark smile showing white teeth. "But I want something more to introduce this. A scandal, yes?"

The advertising agency nodded yes.

"*Ta dahhh!!*" Virgin was in the door, a glass of champagne in her hand. She was wearing tight magenta pants, a kind of bullfighter's silver jacket, a magenta halter that squeezed her breasts up to overflowing, bright white hair and too much makeup. She looked tired under her makeup, but the buzz of her energy had us all up on our feet. "Hi, Panny, you old poove," she said, giving Panaguian a light kiss on the cheek, nodding to the British creative team and slipping her hand in mine. "Hi, honey," she whispered in my ear.

"Sit down, sit down," Panaguian said, spreading his arms wide. "We were just talking about you."

We sat down, Virgin squeezing my hand, as the woman from the agency was saying, "We were thinking along the same lines, Panny . . ."

"Mr. Panaguian," he corrected her.

"Mr. Panaguian."

"I thought the whole point of Virgin was to avoid a scandal," I said. "That photograph of me holding a married woman's three-year-old had a quote, 'Negative reaction among single male adults under twenty-five.' You said it reminded them of the 'negative' consequences of sex."

"Yes, quite," the English adwoman said, leaning protectively over a pack of cigarettes. She tapped a Gitane on the table, lit it and exhaled the aroma of French bars and cafés. "After the excesses of the eighties coupled with an ongoing recession, we've seen a moral reaction across Europe. There's a new emphasis on family, and you were in danger there, Forrest, of being seen as the invader of those values. Which is very different from being seen as the sexy, available, rich sportsman. It's OK to be a fantasy figure as long as the fantasy doesn't threaten the hearth at home."

"We were talking about a scandal," Panaguian said, an edge in his voice. He had heard all this before. "A *new* scandal."

"Yes, well, the advertising and PR that most engages," the dark woman picked a flake of tobacco from her lip, "our imagination is the most effective. We've all seen explicit sex and we are bored by it.''

"Speak for yourself, sweetie,'' Virgin said, smiling happily.

"I'm just reporting what showed up on our latest tracking studies. Seventy-four percent—''

"I have another meeting at seven and a date at eight,'' Panaguian interrupted.

"Right. OK,'' she said, "so what we have organized and you have approved,'' she nodded to Panaguian, who did not return the nod, "is that Forrest and Virgin have the most amazing night out in Paris—all hand-held video, the stuff in the street, getting in and out of the limo in black and white, and the interiors we'll shoot in color; we go with them to the absolute epitome of the classiest café, restaurant and most outrageous club in Paris from the British point of view, and then, when they return to the most fabulous suite in the most fabulous hotel in Paris, we stay outside the hotel, I mean we see them go through the doors, across the lobby and into the elevator, and I've checked and the elevator has one of those old-fashioned bronze arrow dials so we can see them riding up and up, and the last shot we are down in the street looking up at the only window that has the light on, like the room of the princess in the castle, and the last frame we see the light in their room go out.''

"That sounds more like a fairy tale than a scandal to me,'' I said.

"Sure, right. What you have to realize is that Britain is the most conservative country in Europe. And we have the richest imagination. Except for France, of course,'' she added quickly, hearing Panaguian stir in his chair. "So we can't show too much if we really want to engage their imagination. Besides,'' she said, smiling for the first time, "we don't want our audience seeing you as mere human beings. I mean I saw those shots you did of the two of you in Canada. Talk about feet of clay.''

"Those foot shots were very effective here in France,''

Panaguian said into Catherine's cassette recorder.

"It's run out," Catherine said, brushing back her long tawny hair with an expression that made you wonder if it would take a car bomb to engage her interest.

"It's time you get going," Panaguian said. "You'll have all the videotapes in my office in the morning?"

"We'd like to edit them first," the woman from the agency said.

"Edit them first, second, I don't care. As long as you have *all* of the footage on my desk at eight in the morning. I am paying for all those shots and I want to see every one. And I expect to see a rough cut, two-thirty at the latest. That will give you tomorrow afternoon and tomorrow night to finish with a track. I will look at it Friday, here at nine A.M., and if you haven't fucked it up, we can ship to the British, what do you call those censors, the ITA, so they have it Monday morning and we can be on the air, on schedule for our, what is your word, blitz, Wednesday, Thursday, Friday, Saturday for our run-up to Silverstone."

"I'd like to help you out," I said, "but I've got a hotel reserved in Nevers tonight," I said.

Panaguian looked at me for a moment then turned. "Catherine. Cancel his hotel." Then he turned back to me. "Tomorrow, Mr. Evers, you can be a racing driver. Tonight you will be a god."

"I appreciate you've all made plans," I said, "but so have I."

"Mr. Evers, whatever your plans may be, we have our agreement and our budget. And if you wish to be included in our budget, may I suggest that you enjoy your stay in Paris tonight. Otherwise there will be no point in going to Magny Cours tomorrow."

Virgin, still holding my hand, gave it a little squeeze and looked up at me like a child who has had an accident with her milk. "Forrest, I'm sorry. But I have to fly back to LA tomorrow. Please? For me? It'll be OK. You'll see."

Chapter 21

Parisians stepped around the vans—spewing lights, cables, reflectors, assistant directors with clipboards, grips and sparks in their dirty T-shirts—as if the clutter of moviemaking were always there, always turning rue del Ancienne Comedie into an obstacle course. The Parisians hardly glanced at the bright white light blazing into the early evening out of Les Deux Maggots, one of the last of the tin-topped corner bars in Paris.

Les Deux Maggots could have been the bar where Jean Gabin picked up the suitcase with Jean-Paul Belmondo's pig inside. It looked like a bar where Jeanne Moreau might be sitting at a corner table with Natalie Blye and Gerard Depardieu would be wiping the counter, wearing an apron. Might have been, but wasn't. Madame de La Fromage was behind the bar, her face sagging like ripe Brie. She was looking back and forth between the clock on the wall and the camera lens that refused to swing her way. (Laurence, the film director, had hired the bar for an hour and a half, Madame had been paid up front, and like the old hooker she probably was, she couldn't wait for us to be out of there.) The video lens was focused on Virgin and the six-foot-one-inch racing driver in the red, yellow and green leather jacket that was all the rage in LA, the one with the Indian head on the back.

Laurence, with the pencil in his mouth, his face drooping like a burlap bag, poked his video camera in our faces. It was all b&w hand-held stuff, MOS (Mit Out Sound), and he was next to us, in front of or behind us, and rising up from behind the bar, and sneaking up behind us with his zoom lens, pulling us through the storefront glass. After a couple of minutes of small talk, we ignored him.

Virgin said, holding up a glass of bright green liquid, "The first person who says, 'We can't go on meeting like this' has to pay ten thousand dollars."

"Meeting like this was your idea," I said, peering into a short, untouched glass of French beer. Another video camera circled behind Virgin, focusing close up, no doubt, on my nostrils.

"Don't say I didn't tell you."

"I won't say a word," I said. "Just before you came in, in Panaguian's office, they were all claiming this 'night in Paris' was their idea."

"Yeah, well," she said, waving her hand, "if you have a good idea and you want to get it done right, give it to somebody else. I gave it to Sheila, my business manager, and I said 'Run, sweetie. Don't come back till it's done.' Are you OK?"

"I'm all right, Janice. I didn't get much sleep. You look a little tired yourself."

"I just flew in on an overnight from LA. So I don't feel like a daisy, OK? What's your excuse?"

"A friend of mine died last night."

"Oh Jesus, Forrest. I'm sorry." She looked up at me, just herself for once. A delicate porcelain face under Slovak brows. "I know it's dumb, but if there is anything I can do . . . I mean, if you want to talk about it or something." She gave my hand a squeeze.

"That's sweet of you, Janice, but that's all I've done about it, is talk."

"Well, what else can you do about it? Sometimes it helps to talk, you know."

"Suppose, Janice, he was your friend and you knew, not because of what you saw but because you knew him, suppose you knew it wasn't an accident. And more than that, suppose you knew who killed him and how they did it. And you knew that they had done it before. And you think that they will probably do something similar to you unless you find a way to stop them.''

''You don't do drugs or anything, do you?''

Laurence moved us to the corner of bar, with our backs to the door. And that's where he took the famous shot, the one that ran in all the newspapers, shot from the street. Our backs were to the camera and we were framed by the open door, standing at the zinc bar, the rows of aperitifs and digestifs behind us, our faces reflected among the bottles, the shelves and the soiled light. You can see just enough of Virgin to know it is her. She is turned just slightly to the right, one famous boob profiled, showing, miraculously, a tilt against the force of gravity, her platinum blond head tilted up at the same angle to show her hair cut short, cupping the back of her head, and her left arm draped casually down across my back, her left hand squeezing my butt, her fingertips disappearing for that casual, obscene and meaningless touch that has always been Virgin's trademark. Just two lovers, starting out on a night on the town in Paris. Followed by film crew.

We did some shots of the two of us getting into a Citroen DS decapotable, the Marilyn Monroe of French convertibles, an upside-down bathtub car, with fifties ultra-swank. Virgin snuggled up alongside me, legs curled up on the red leather upholstery like a teenager. Laurence crawled over the side into the backseat. With his video camera on his shoulder, shooting us as I drove, he gave me directions for Tour d'Argent. Virgin let her hand rest lightly on my knee and said, ''I like your hair, you know. Kinda boyish, like one of those Roman senators. What do you think, Laurence, should I put my hand in his lap or you want to save that for the restaurant?''

''Shoot it both ways,'' Laurence said.

''Wait for the drive to the hotel,'' I said.

La Tour was just a few blocks away, on the banks of the Seine, and after the indifference of the French on rue Ancienne Comedie, it was another world. I suppose the crowd came from where most pop scene crowds come from these days—the PR budget paid them with Virgin T-shirts, Virgin baseball caps and a promise of a glimpse of the icon along with discount coupons for her new CD. When we arrived and the doorman stepped forward to open the car door for Virgin, searchlights crisscrossed the sky, and behind the crowd, Notre Dame Cathedral rose out of the Seine. I thought they were all there for Virgin. Until, in between their calling out, "*Veergin, Veeeergin,*" I heard women calling, "Forray, Forray."

For some wacky reason the way they pronounced Forrest reminded me of years ago when I was towing my Formula Three car around Europe. I was looking for a campground in a pine forest I'd heard about in the South of France near The Camargue. And I couldn't understand why every time I asked directions for the *forray des pins,* the locals all rolled around on the ground and kicked their feet in the air. Until one of them stopped laughing long enough to explain that the way I pronounced *pins* (peen) was French for penis. So I had that image of the *forray des* peen in my head when I heard them calling, "Forray, Forray," "Look at me, Forray."

I hadn't seen the French newspapers, so I didn't know that one of the pictures of Virgin and me that they had taken in Canada—the naked feet, with mine on the inside pointing down, Virgin's on the outside pointing up—had run in full-page ads in most of the papers that morning. In a moment they were all over the car, women saying in French, "Give me a sniff, Forray, just a whiff." There were more of them after Virgin than me, but she was used to being mobbed. She put her head down and bolted for the restaurant. Hands reached out to touch me, and I dove into them, through them, and, getting one painful grab of the balls, I made it into the sanctity of the restaurant that has had the reputation of being the finest restaurant in Paris since Michelin began awarding stars. A maître d' dabbed my face with a cool towel and led me to the lift where Virgin was waiting, grinning.

• • •

"How's your duck, Virge?"

Virgin held a sliver of impaled purple flesh on the end of her silver fork. "I guess it'd be rude not to eat it, huh?"

"It's what Tour D'Argent is famous for—Caneton Presse."

Virgin took the piece of duck between her white teeth, her lips smiling wide for the camera pointed at her. She had a way of turning everything into camp. Even chewing a piece of dead duck. "You know why they call this La Tour D'Argent?" she said between her teeth. "'Cause that's what it costs to eat here." Behind her the Seine glittered darkly in front of the square stone bell towers and the flying buttresses of Notre Dame. Over her shoulder a giant silver duck press, screwed down tight, oozed squashed duck.

"You don't look so good, Forrest. Maybe you should try pretending you are enjoying yourself, act it out. You can always be paranoic later. Think of a garage full of Ferraris or whatever you guys think of. Hey, really," she leaned forward across the table, her breasts grazing the white cloth on either side of her plate, "if you are going to be anyplace, sweetie, then you might as well be here." She sat back in her chair, flinging her arms out, "with me. In this restaurant. OK? It's not so bad, is it? I mean, it's not like we're paying. Which is funny 'cause I'm probably the richest person in this room. Maybe in Paris. I could buy this place if I wanted."

"I doubt it's for sale," I said, turning a dark ruby glass of Château Margaux '64 in my hand. I'd had a sniff, even ventured a sip—a small pond of voluptuous, priceless wine on my tongue, complex purple blooms trickling down my throat. One sip was it. Over my limit. I was driving on Sunday.

"You wanna bet? How much you want to bet this place is owned by a Japanese consortium strapped for cash? You trying to get that wine up your nose?"

"You win." I laughed. "How's it feel to be able to buy anything you want?"

"Like Caligula. Except you can't buy everything you want. I mean it's nice to have nice houses and know you've got lots of money for the rest of your life. And it's nice to do something goofy, you know, like take the dancers in my act into Jean Paul Gaultier and tell them to buy anything they like. And they're all over 'wheeeee.' I mean they make a couple of hundred a week, so that's a real treat for them. But the more stuff costs the more complicated it gets, with accountants, lawyers, insurance. A lot of people get involved and the fun just kind of evaporates. It's hard to enjoy a big diamond when you are surrounded by a bunch of fat guys in bulletproof vests cocking their Uzis. The other trick is you don't want to drive yourself crazy thinking what you want because it's always going to turn out to be something you can't have. So what do you want?"

"I want to be the world champion. I want to simplify my life, without complications."

"So what's the problem? If you want something, go get it. You want to know what I want? I want to be rich and famous."

"That's what everybody says they want, Lousky."

"Sure, but they don't want it bad enough. I mean maybe if the kids in my class hadn't called me Lousky, I'd still be in the burbs, shopping at Price Club and banging some guy watches Monday night football. But you have to have something to give, you know. You want to be rich and famous, you have to make them want you."

"You liked that mob down there?"

"I loved that mob down there. If they weren't down there, I wouldn't be here. And I love their money. Hey, it's fun to be rich, Forrest. Come on, it's not a hard question, what do you want? Seriously."

I thought of Susan, her affair with Alistair, and I hoped she had nothing to do with his murder or Phil's. Susan, Sue Two and Josh—my substitute family. I thought of my empty flat in Holland Park, a shell of a real life. I thought of how long it had been since I had felt a woman's arms around me, and how I could stop Naughton from rolling over me. Stop him, sink him. Without a trace. I would see him in a day. I wanted a simple life, and I didn't have enough what, something, to call a life, let alone simple. I thought of this pretty, tough aggressive thirty-eight-year-old woman across the table, still playing at being a girl, tough as a rubber doll on the outside, a needy little girl screaming inside. Virgin, Janice Corlowski, framed by the lights they had set up on stands, shining on her with the blessing of the electronic media. Her large blue eyes red-veined and blinking. She had arranged this, set it up, almost on a whim, and flown twelve hours to be here. For what? For the promotion? For me? And I thought how tired I was of being somebody else's pawn, a player who did what he was told in a larger game.

"What I want to do," I said, "is win Formula One races."

"That's one of the things I like about you," Virgin said, reaching across the table to touch my face. "You are such a child, happy with so little."

Maybe, from her perspective, it was a small thing. But I have a hard time thinking of anything that takes everything you have, as small. Maybe that was my mistake, thinking that it would be enough. That if I just played my cards right, the rest of the world would go away.

"And you are such a grown-up," I said. "Unhappy with so much."

"Bullshit," Virgin said, loud enough to turn heads beyond the mini-spots they had scattered around us like footlights and spotlights on a stage.

"Then why are you here?"

"Forrest," she said, taking my hand. "What do you want me to say?"

"Say, 'good night.' "

"Good night? What the hell do you mean?" The color in her pale face was starting to rise. I'd heard she had a ferocious temper. I wondered, idly, what she was like when she didn't get her way.

"Hey, I read about this place in *Gourmet* magazine," she

was saying. "This is supposed to be the greatest restaurant in the world. They have a pear for dessert you wouldn't believe. We got a scene to make at Catafalque. There's that new girl, the French one, what's she call herself, Coquille, does all those sex things on the stage, I've got to see her, everybody's talking about her. They're all set up over there for us. I came all this way to see you and that's what you want me to say is 'good night' ?"

I pushed my chair back and stood up.

"Virgin," I said, "my friend died last night. I'm going to the hotel now, and you can come with me if you want. Or go check out Coquille. I am going to bed."

"The *fuck* you are," she said, standing up.

I nodded to the maître d', who was standing next to Virgin in case she wanted anything, and to Laurence, who was kneeling on the carpet, shooting up at her, and walked out through the silent, staring, well-dressed men and women with their knives and forks held still in the air.

I took the lift downstairs, walked out the front door, slipped the doorman a fifty-franc note and stood looking into the faces of the few determined souls who were standing behind yellow police barriers. They looked back without interest. The real stars, they knew, were still inside. The doorman held open the door of the taxi, and there was a small cry of surprise from the crowd, then several cries of "*Veeeeeeergeeeeen.*"

They ducked under the barriers, and she had to push her way through them, Laurence and the photographers holding their cameras high, lights popping. And it was one of those shots, the one of her pushing through the crowd to get to me, that the PR folks sold to the British papers. That was the shot that Panaguian said was pure genius. She caught my arm and whispered in my ear. "You are a real prick," she said.

I told the driver the Crillon. Virgin rolled down the window. "Don't get the wrong idea," she said, leaning out the window and waving to the crowd, the camera lights flashing like fireworks. "I am not running after you like some little puppy." She rolled the window up and sat back. "I flashed on going to Catafalque. Some stinko little snapshooter is going to catch me and this Coquille in the same shot and I am going to look like a dead parrot next to her."

"You look fine," I said. In the semidarkness of the back of the taxi, she looked fresh, beautiful, all eyes and mouth.

"I look like a dead parrot without her. So how do you think I am going to look next to a nineteen-year-old kid? Sometimes these days I get so tired," she said, rubbing her eyes.

Virgin sat back in the taxi seat, sulking as we crossed the river. "You ever use any of that stuff?" she said, looking out the window at a tourist boat lit with candles, gliding under the bridge.

"What stuff?"

"That Formula One stuff, dummy. The stuff we're supposed to be pushing."

"It's a trick," I said. "I think they make it out of floor wax."

"I got a bottle," she said, turning her head at the last minute. "You want to see if it works?"

Chapter 22

We were running.

Our taxi pulled up as close as it could. It was early for a night in Paris, way early, before ten, and our press schedule didn't have us checking into the hotel before one. But it was not too early for a small mob of photographers and fans to be waiting outside the hotel. I thought we might be able to slip through them, get out of the taxi and walk into the crowd as if we were two of them, hanging out, waiting for the action to arrive. In the dark of the taxi I'd forgotten that Virgin is a visual foghorn, visible for five miles. Her platinum hair and grape octagonal shades, and the frothy pink-and-purple cut-below-the-navel silk outfit with the black basketball sneakers could only be camouflage in Hollywood. As soon as the first flash exploded in a balloon of light, the cry went up: "*Veeeeerrgeeeeen. Veeeeeeergeeeen.*" I dove in first, Virgin following close behind, keeping low, knees pumping, pushing our way through the flailing octopus of arms, legs, video cameras and bleached-white screaming faces.

"Forrraaay, Forrrraaaay," some women cried out from the sea of "*Veeeeeerrrrgggggggeeeeeeeeeennnn*"'s. Churning through the crowd, I was groped, hard, from several directions. No more little sad-eyed passive groupies offering to lie down under you. These were the new breed—active, aggressive. Taking what they could get with both hands. Gropies.

The lobby of the Crillon Hotel is like an old viola, encased

in wood paneling the color of old champagne and honey.
Built in the decade before World War I by the Tattinger
Champagne family, out of two eighteenth-century Louis XV
town houses, and facing one of the great, grand and beautiful
urban spaces in Europe, the Crillon is a museum to serious
money. Money flows in and out of the lobby with the quiet
ebb and flow of an ocean tide. Money grand enough to float
empires of steel and wine in a sinking economy. Money of
sufficient depth to support fourth, fifth and sixtieth generations of Hapsburgs, Romanoffs, and Rothschilds. This is the
High Sierra of money country, where the merely rich are out
of place. Currency traders, film stars and overnight computer
millionaires are directed to the Ritz or Plaza Athenee, if you
don't mind. We are so sorry, we are fully booked. Come
back in a couple of generations. The desk clerks, sharing the
weight of the immense financial burdens of their guests, normally wear frowns of concerned subservience. They looked
up with mild interest when Virgin and I hit the front doors
like commandos.

Virgin screamed, ''*Keys*,'' and without pausing, a pale
young man in a gray suit, behind the front desk, turned,
pulled a heavy bronze key with a tassel out of the rows of
boxes behind him, completed his turn and looped the key up
in the air. Virgin caught it on the fly as we ran across the
lobby. The normal guests, dressed for some ancient postwar
ceremony like Cocktails, froze like statues, and we dove into
a walnut-paneled lift.

Heavy breathing in the lift. Virgin said hi to the blond
man standing in front of the buttons. He nodded, pressed the
button, the doors slid shut, and we rose above the tide of
tourists, fans and photographers crashing on the shores of the
lobby below.

The lift stopped, the doors opened and a bellboy in green
uniform led us down the hall to front of the hotel. ''I will
be here, Mademoiselle Vairgeen *et* uh, Monsieur, outside
your door, *tout la nuit*,'' he said, taking the key and opening

the door to our suite, "to be sure absolute you are never disturbed."

Virgin didn't give him a second glance; she was used to this. She went to the front windows and pulled back the curtains. Down below, the show was over and the crowd was already breaking up, heading in different directions across the square like fans leaving the stadium after a concert. From time to time a flashbulb went off, the last bubbles in the champagne.

"Stupid shits," Virgin said, staring down. "Why don't they get a life of their own?"

"I thought you liked them."

"I liked them when I thought you and I were starting off on the greatest evening of all time. Before I knew you were such a prick. Before you fucked it up."

"OK, I fucked it up, Janice. Your perfect evening. It sure wasn't mine. You keep telling me, live in the present. Here and now," I said, putting my hand on her shoulder. "Look out there on the square, Janice. Look how beautiful it is now. And how simple, as if a child could have done this square, the geometry of the streets, the simplicity of the French logic. Then, for fun, look up to the Arc de Triomphe in the distance there, and then across to the Seine, the lights along the river and the dome of Les Invalides rising up on the other side. Stop. For a moment, and think how far you've come to be here, looking out at one of the most beautiful views in one of the most beautiful cities in the world."

"With one of the worst pricks," she said, starting to smile. She ran over to the huge bed and bounced on it, lying flat on her back, kicking her feet with the black basketball sneakers up in the air. "OOOOOOOeeeeee."

She bounced back up and ran into the bathroom. An echo to her voice, touch of the cave, she said, "Ohhhh, it's all marble and it's lovely, Forrest. Think of all the rich asses that sat in here."

"You think of them," I said, as she was closing the door, "I'm going to bed."

The shower went on, almost covering the sound of the toilet flushing a little later. The shower sprayed on, and I took off my clothes, pulled on the too short hotel robe with the gaudy crest and sat on the bed to wait. I heard Virgin singing in the shower, some show tune I hadn't heard before. Some Virgin song she must have been working on or just made up. She had a powerful bluesy voice, raspy when she got into the chorus:

> *This is our only night,*
> *the only night we have alone.*
> *This is our only night,*
> *and tomorrow I'll be alone.*

Really belting out the chorus:

> *Love me tonight if you can*
> *Take me tonight if you dare*
> *Love me tonight 'cause tomorrow,*
> *you bastard, I'll leave you alone.*

Virgin came out of the shower barefoot, in a long cream-silk robe tied with a sash, her hair wet, toweling her face, looking fresh and scrubbed. She sat down on the bed next to me and said, "I'm sorry your friend died."

"Me too," I said. "I'm sorry I ruined your evening."

"It's not over yet. You gonna take a shower?"

I nodded yes, and she leaned forward, kissed me lightly on the cheek and said, "I'll wait for you."

The marble shower room was Victorian, with a variety of bronze nozzles and a huge old-fashioned bronze shower head that poured down water like warm rain, washing away the grit and heat of the day. I toweled off, left my robe hanging on the door hook, went back into the room and got into bed next to Virgin, who was watching me from her pillow. I switched off the lights, and the moon shone a clear blue light through the floor-to-ceiling windows.

Virgin bounded out of bed and across the room to switch on a floor lamp. "Is that OK, a little light?" she said, standing with her face in half darkness next to the lamp shade, the yellow light falling down across her body. "You can turn it out later if you like." Her arms and legs looked like a long-distance runner's, the hours of daily workouts showing in her sharp muscles and long tendons, standing out in the warmth and shadow of the lamp. Her tummy was going soft, though, and time had added extra padding to her hips.

She walked back across the room, her breasts pink and pretty, bouncing against each other. World's most famous mammaries, seen by hundreds of millions, in magazines, on TV and billboards around the world. "How come I feel so relaxed with you?" she said, snuggling under the sheet.

"We've been in bed together in every page in Paris today. You're just bored."

We lay on our sides, facing each other. Little lines ran back in small fans away from her eyes. Without makeup her eyes looked smaller and so did her mouth, less aggressive. A touch of reality. Her hand found mine under the covers and held it. Thinking of the need to say something, I said, "When was the first time you made love?"

She closed her eyes for a moment, remembering. "Oh, Daddy, Daddy," she said. Then she opened her eyes, not smiling. "Just joking. Is this a magazine interview or what?"

"This is an 'or what.' "

"OK, 'cause I already answered that question in *Vogue, Rolling Stone, Time, The Face* and *Vanity Fair*."

"What'd you tell them?"

"Different stuff. I forget. When was the first time you made love, Forrest? I mean really."

I rolled back on my back, thinking of an afternoon in Norfolk. Janice's hand grazed across my stomach, and waited.

"I was about fifteen, or sixteen. And I was in Norfolk for the summer. My parents were separated, and the way they divided me up was I spent my school terms in a freezing

British public school in Bristol and then summers to alternate one with my father and one with my mother. And that summer, when I was supposed to go to Arizona to spend my holiday with my mother on her ranch, my mother took up with some guy—''

''What guy? Be specific.''

''I don't know. She said he was a Hollywood director. I think specifically he did beer commercials. She went to live with him in Beverly Hills, and it was decided that what would be best for fifteen-year-old Forrest, who was not exactly the best behaved boy in the school, was a dose of my father's stern Norfolk Puritan care for the summer.''

''He was really strict?''

''He believed in punishment. Something was always my fault. So the first thing he did that summer was have me shovel out the barn, which took about a week. What you have to understand about the barn is that it is a Grade II medieval daub-and-wattle pile with a thatch roof and five hundred years and thirty yards of mold and rising damp. And when I finished shoveling medieval cowshit, he had me patching the thatch roof. And one day, it was hot, and I thought to hell with it, to hell with being his peasant. And I climbed down the roof and walked out across one of his fields.''

''Where I grew up we didn't have fields. We had a back-yard with a patch of grass, a sandbox and a swing. He was rich?''

''He wasn't rich, but he had a lot of land. He was the vicar, and he acted like he lived out of the poor box. He had two thousand acres that had been in his family since the twelfth century. Originally a gift of Henry II to my father's ancestor, Bishop Everard of Norfolk, 1156 to 1178. Anyway, I thought it was about time I took a day off. So I went across the fields, took my shirt off, and when I got to one of the canals that run across Norfolk, I lay down on the bank and I fell asleep.

''I woke up with rain in my face. But it wasn't really

raining, there were three girls ... OK, not girls, young women, in shorts, standing over me, dripping water on me. Their hands cupped and letting it seep out. And I was looking up at their bare legs.

"They had hired the boat for the day—Sarah and Michelle and Fay—and they had been out cruising, sunning themselves, drinking wine, and they were a little drunk. Sarah, I remember, was round and short and didn't wear a brassiere. Which I thought was fantastic. Fay was the pretty one with the long legs. And Michelle had blue eyes and a little smile for me every time she looked my way. They decided I was their mascot. A kind of pet. Which I was happy to go along with. It made a nice change from shoveling shit and thatching a barn roof. And I knew the local canals, so I went with them, thinking this was really wicked and sophisticated, floating down toward the sea with women who were old enough to be in Cambridge. And we drank some cold wine— I'd never had cold wine before—and Michelle, who had these wonderful perfect breasts and blond silky hair, said she wanted to show me something below deck, and I stumbled down the stairs. I knew what was going on, although I wasn't sure what I was supposed to do."

"What did you do?"

"She put my hand on her breast and she asked me if that felt nice."

Janice moved my hand under the covers onto her breast.

"And I said yes, that felt very nice. And she asked me if I was too warm, and I said yes, I was. And we both took our clothes off. And I was shy because I had never had a hard-on in front of anybody before. And when she saw me, she said that was a very good sign."

Janice lifted up the sheet and looked down. "When I was a kid," she said, "we used to call them 'boners.' That's a very good sign," she said, letting the sheet fall back down.

"Then what?"

"Then she lay back on the bunk and her breasts sprawled out and her legs were apart, and she reached up and took my hand and pulled me toward her.''

Janice pulled me toward her, her legs apart, her breasts sprawling. "And?''

"And then she kissed my chest.''

Janice buried her face against my chest and gave me a soft kiss with her tongue and her lips. "And?'' she said, not looking up.

"And then she touched the tip of my cock with her finger.''

Janice reached down and tentatively touched my cock with the tip of her finger. "And?''

"And then she started to tell me about the first time she made love, when she was in her first year at Cambridge.''

"What?''

"There was this famous rock singer who came in for a concert—''

Virgin sat up, her world-famous breasts hanging over me. "You're making this up.''

"Only the part about the women.''

Virgin got up out of bed, pulled on her silk robe and went over to the window, staring out over the square and the river. After a minute she sighed, her shoulders dropped and she came back to the bed and sat down, looking down at me. "Why are you doing this to me?'' she said.

"I am not doing this to you.''

"OK, why are you not doing this to me?''

I sat up, face-to-face. "You are beautiful and desirable and you give me a hard-on like a telephone pole . . . ''

"Mr. Romance. Five years ago you never would have had a chance. You should have seen me, Forrest.''

"Last night I wouldn't have had a chance. But not tonight. I feel bad and it's a bad time to make love with you.''

"You never know,'' she said, eyebrows rising.

"Janice, I am tired of doing things that can't be undone.''

"Oh horseshit. If you want something, take it.''

"That's what you do, you just take it?''

"Well, yeah, that's what I do. Why not? You pay for it

one way or another. You pay for it whether you take it or not. Nothing's free. What's your problem, Forrest?''

"That story about my father. It reminded me that Phil—''

"What Phil? I thought we were talking about me.''

"The Joyce team owner. You might have read about it in the papers. They killed him in May, at Monaco.''

"'*They* killed'? What are we talking here, some goofy paranoia? The guys that shot Kennedy?''

"It's not paranoia, Janice. When I was telling the story, I realized I had thought of Phil, well, as a lot of things, but part of it was as a substitute for my father. He was happy, funny, generous . . . all the things my father wasn't.''

"Listen, you want a family, Forrest, start one. That way you get to be the daddy. Damn, you lead me on, you give 'cockteaser' a whole new meaning—are you trying to blame that on somebody else too? You want something, you go get it. A season in Hollywood would do you good. Take or get taken.''

"You don't understand. The man who killed Phil and killed Alistair will try and kill me.''

"So do something for Christ's sake. Call the police. Go get a gun. Or a bodyguard, Forrest. I got these guys from Phelps, and they are good, you never even see them, but they are there. Jesus, you are weird. Who are we talking about here?''

"You don't understand.''

"What? What don't I understand?''

"I killed a man once. I can't do it again.''

She looked at me. Waiting.

"Two years ago at Monza. It was at the Formula One race. I made him crash headfirst into the wall. His car exploded in a fireball and he died.''

"I thought that's what racing drivers are supposed to do—crash and burn.''

"It wasn't funny. I still see his car hitting the barrier. I can still smell him burning.''

"Yeah, OK,'' she said quietly. "I can see you wouldn't

want to do that twice. Look, I don't know the story, but it sounds to me like maybe it wasn't that simple. Or maybe you just like remembering it because it excuses you. As long as you got that, you don't have to do anything now, right? 'Cause if you did, you might kill somebody again. That's the only reason it matters now, it lets you off the hook. If you want to be a spectator, go stand with those assholes outside the hotel. Who are we talking about here?''

"Your old friend, Naughton."

"Naughton? Naughton is just a money guy. His favorite weapon is a checkbook. He wouldn't kick a dog out of the way, he'd move the road, you know what I mean?

"Who else you want to blame? You want to blame your daddy because you don't have the guts to be one. You think somebody killed your friends and is after you, right? And you are not going to do anything about it because once you did something and you didn't like it. You have to know, Forrest, Naughton's in Tokyo. He's been there for days. Move over," she said, shrugging off her robe. "If you don't want to make love with one of the world's greatest fantasies of all time, she is going to sleep."

"That's the great thing about fantasies, you don't have to act them out."

"That's a hell of a thing for you to say," she said, rolling over on her side, away from me. "You find a better fantasy than me, give me a call. I'd like to meet her."

In our sleep we had fallen together like two spoons, with my arm over Janice as if we had been lovers. I was half-waking, half-asleep. Eyes closed. I smelled her warm and musky female scent and felt the old warm urge building. I had risen between her thighs, and Janice was moving her legs back and forth slowly. Just an inch or two. A soft scissors. The sweet girl. The old hooker. The brassy broad with a heart of brass. The rich and famous bad girl. I put my hand on her, cupping the weight of the world's most famous breast, warm in my hand, feeling her nipple rise under my fingertips. She rolled over to face me and kissed my cheek. "Of all the guys in the world," she said. "What did you say your name was?"

"Of all the crummy joints," I said.

"I think you must be wearing that stuff," she said.

"Scouts honor," I said, kissing her on the neck.

"I could do a lot for you, you know," she said. "Like you could forget about Naughton and all that. Forget about the rest of the season, come back with me to Hollywood. Help me count my money and throw it up in the air. I could get you a good part in something. No problem. You'd be good in movies."

"I'd stick out like a wart in Hollywood. Don't make me any promises, Janice. You're fine. You don't need any extra spin."

"You gonna do it?"

"As soon as I work out how," I said.

"Let me know when you work it out," she said. "I'd like to know about it."

Janice rolled away from me, on her side, into the spoons we had been before, ribs showing in the cool light of the moon coming in the window. And after a few moments she moved back into me, opening. The oldest offering, before language. The most vulnerable. After all the exposure and the hype, the old deep need for comfort, warmth and the connection. I moved up against her, and Janice reached down to guide my cock and move it back and forth against her in a warm, slippery and teasing slide.

Ah, well, I thought, catching the power and the rhythm of the tide, feeling her open and close, open and close against the tip of me. I'll do this. Just this once. Before I put my armor on.

When I woke again, the light was on the horizon, outlining the dome of Les Invalides through the floor-to-ceiling windows. I got up, got dressed in my running shoes, T-shirt and jeans, went out the door, past the sleeping bellboy propped against the wall, down the stairs and through the silent lobby to run along the Seine. Two-and-a-half miles out, two-and-a-half miles back. To clear my mind and keep the sinews and muscles taut as piano wires. I would be driving tomorrow and I needed a workout. Feet going slap, slap, slap on the uneven stones, a kind of water rhythm, with the sky growing lighter and the traffic building up to its daily stall. And on the river, on the barges with their flowerpots and laundry hanging on clotheslines, the men and women were boiling coffee and staring out at the river slipping beneath their feet. Riverpeople, living completely separate lives, moving to a different flow.

When I got back to the room, the bed was empty and she was gone, checked out.

There was a note on the night table:

> *F,*
> *Sorry, but I gotta run too. No hard feelings, OK?*
> *Love, V.*

Except the V was crossed out and underneath it she had written, J.

Chapter 23

My wheel is nose high, alongside my knee, and it is lifting up, off the track, cocked to the left. The weight of the car is leaning outside to the right front on this downhill goddamn corkscrew that screws you up before you get a good shot at what passes for the main straight in front of the pits. The car is heavy, clumsy, loose. As the back end is starting to come around, I still have my left foot lightly on the brake and my right flat to the floor, mashing the goddamn thing, looking for a little extra power in third, punishing the son of a bitch like a Go-Kart, steering on the throttle, throwing it to the inside of the track so I can carom off the curbs and get back to the outside so I can bounce off that curb to kick this slug up the straight. And I have given it too much boot, the inside rear wheel is spinning, the engine coughs and sputters as it hits the rev limiter and loses power just when I want it and the back end starts to come around, making me look like a cowboy, sliding the car way over, getting off line. I try to compensate by twitching the wheel, lifting for a microsecond to get back on the power, goddamn all computers, seeing the wall of faces in the distant grandstand rising up like a jury. They are well over a hundred yards away, but I see their faces while I am sitting there, a passenger waiting to get back on the power again. The power kicks back in, the little drama is over, I steer though the hairpin and pound down the straight of this goddamn track, thinking of Mo Nunn's old dictum that a competitive driver will try to overcome the limitations of an uncompetitive car and you cannot do that.

Fuck.

I am out here up against the limits, and when I go over them the slightest fraction, the world tilts and comes swinging back in my face. Sending the car bounding off the curbs in a messy dance that will end up ripping the wheels off and wrapping the front wings around my neck if I don't back off and wait for the car to collect itself, scrub off some speed, lose some more time. Whole tenths of a second slide by. Meanwhile the money cars with a hundred and twenty-five more horsepower, a hundred and fifty pounds less weight, better aerodynamics and a suspension system that looks ahead a quarter of an inch and irons the track flat—while I stand around on tiptoes, waiting, waiting, waiting to get the power down—the money cars are fast fading down the straight, disappearing into the vanishing point. Magny Cours is a brand new track, and you may quote me when I say it stinks.

Magny Cours is one of the new generation of Formula One race facilities. Which is to say it is not a racetrack. Or circuit as they used to say in the old country. Magny Cours is a computer-generated marketing exercise designed for maximizing profit, land use, driver safety, sponsor sign sites, TV angles and crowd control. Racing never enters into the equation. Even so, Magny Cours is not all bad. It could even be a decent track if they would take it out of the box. As it is, crammed into that French field, it is a few bent straights held together with hairpins. Not one great curve that commands your attention like Eau Rouge at Spa or Lesmo One and Lesmo Two at Monza. My bloody Lesmo Two.

Not that it is easier to drive than a real circuit. It is harder, much harder, because even with computer-run traction control, computer-activated active suspension, computer-controlled automatic transmission and computer-controlled two tons of downforce at speed, your modern, totally-up-to-date, hundred-million-dollars-in-the-making Formula One car is a mess on slow corners. On slow corners, the supertrick cars, the Williams and McLarens, have no downforce, lose their balance, and you can't put the power down except a little at a time as dictated by your traction-control chip, lest you sit around smoking your wheels. Except, of course, compared to the cars that pound around without the benefit of a hundred million dollars of computer hardware and software. Compared to me, the computercars are slot cars on a slot track. And I am a pig on ice.

Down through the corkscrew again, and damn, the back end kicks around again in the downhill hairpin corner (called 'Lycee' and which I seem to have trouble learning) leading into the straight. I have screwed it up because the track is warming up and losing grip. Which is no excuse. I have screwed up because I am pissed off, and I get on the power too soon, punishing the car, losing more time in another useless, ugly slide. This driver's dance I do, with my hands and feet in a thousand intricate simultaneous and related high-speed movements and manipulations among the pedals, the steering wheel and the gearshift, this flailing useless dance, will soon be on public display along with morris dancing at village fetes. See the racing drivers in their funny antique outfits covered with patches doing their dance with their asses two inches off the ground.

In the future the real drivers will sit in corporate suites and push the Go button, and the computers will take care of the rest, while the driver/analyst gets back to the serious business of marketing: target-user psychographics, competitive distribution patterns and ten-day brand-share analysis. Now appearing in corporate headquarters everywhere. Coming soon to your home computer screens. Push a button. Let us know what you think.

Jeremy Buckingham is leaning his pudgy body over the pit wall, holding a sign with my time. Jeremy, our new crew chief, a.k.a. the "I'm a financial guy" marketing manager from Emron, who never understood why Emron should back a team that "wasn't even sixth," is telling me I have lost another whole second. Which would put us around twentieth, barely in the race. I was pushing the car too hard. Overheating the tires. Losing my concentration. Letting my emotions get in the way. An unprofessional, stupid and dangerous thing to do. A racing driver needs emotions like a bull needs roller blades.

And my mind was wandering. Knocked off center by the sound of my own whining. Ask any racing driver how it feels to be at the back of the pack after you've run up front. No, don't. You have better things to do. I let up, radioed Buckingham the tires had gone off and cruised around off line to come into the pits. It was only Friday morning. Plenty of time. Time to chat with Naughton, fresh back from Japan. Time to see what Laurel and Hardy had on their computer screens, the murdering, sneaking bastards.

I hardly knew Naughton. He had enough power to kill Phil and Alistair from a distance. Controlling a group of companies with a worldwide revenue of 2.4 billion, all he had to do was snap his fingers and Phelps Security would come running. Naughton was under heavy financial pressure, cornered, Castleman said. He was in Japan when Alistair died, and in New York when Phil was killed. No one could possibly connect him. I needed to draw him out in the open, expose him. And I had no idea how to do it. But I did have the beginning of a plan. A nasty, dirty, underhanded con of a plan. I would be his enemy. It was lonely at the top; he could use a enemy. Every man needs an enemy in these days of falling skies. I would take his dirty hand and lead him out into the light, where he could shoot at me.

On the cool, air-conditioned top deck of the motor home, banks of computer screens glowed with truth in numbers. Hardy sat at one keyboard, looking at the off-loaded monitored data, with Laurel standing just behind him.

"Hi, Forrest," Hardy said. A friendly man to everyone. "How's it going?" He had the numbers in front of him. He knew exactly how it was going. I ignored him.

Jim Barton, my race engineer, sat at another keyboard, looking at the analytical data. He turned in his chair and looked up at me with the depressed, furrowed look of a tax accountant, running his hand over his bald scalp. Jim had an endless capacity for detail, and patience. Sorting through the numbers, he needed both. Naughton, the audience of this computer show, stood just a little behind them so they would have to turn to speak to him. A slight nod toward the accusing screens acknowledged my arrival.

Naughton was out of his leathers and back in his race team supremo outfit of purple EFORT polo shirt, collar turned up in back, "EMRON" stitched discreetly on the breast pocket, "C-i-C" stitched above that, standing for Commander in Chief. His little joke. And naturally he was sporting stone washed, faded and sharply creased designer jeans to signify "one of the lads," ending perfectly without a break on black leather air-pump Mephistos. He had a habit of looking better informed than anybody else in the room, like he was holding the missing pieces of the puzzle of life in his left hand. He was a handsome, tall man with long silver hair, accustomed to being the man in command. His long face wore heavy corporate responsibilities in the furrows on his forehead. His jaw sticking out said he was a man who played hard and was big enough and strong enough to bend the rules if he had to, for the greater corporate good. The kind of clear-eyed, focused-on-the-big-picture, wide-horizon gaze that made the cover of a business magazine look good.

Thursday afternoon he had shown up at the track on a big black BMW bike, wearing a tight black leather motorcycle outfit, complete with white silk scarf and heavy black motorcycle boots up to the knee. With his silver hair slicked back in a ponytail, sunglasses staring up from the top of his head and Caribbean tan, he looked like a fine new hip fascist—Storm Trooper Naughton, Supreme Commander of the Corporate SS.

The only glitch in Sam's new Eagle of Industry image, planned for an upcoming cover story in *Forbes*, was that the French truckers had gone on strike that weekend and blocked the main roads. So when Sam's parade—limousine with Sam, followed by Imaggi, the fashion photographer, with five assistants, including a blowsy middle-aged woman with a picnic basket full of makeup for the great man, his public relations team, a personal secretary and an executive assistant, for a grand total of one limo, two vans and five cars—took the back roads, hoping to get set up for his PR shots quietly without attracting any attention, everybody in France was on the back roads. Among them a French student photographer who happened to be stuck on the same back route, just behind the Public Relations Officer's car, and who stopped when Sam's limo stopped a few hundred yards short of the N-7. The student photographed Sam stepping out of his limo in his leathers. She also snapped the bike being wheeled up to the Captain of Industry, and she shot the long-haired Imaggi, *Vogue*'s fashion photographer of the year, popping away as Sam stood there with the crotch rocket between his legs, gloved hands on the handlebars, head thrown back. The local papers who knew what was good for them carried the official version, but the French, German and Italian left-wing press and the British tabloids had a field day with Sam's long leather legs getting out of the limo, and Sam grimacing as the makeup "girl" dabbed his cheek with powder as he sat on his machine between takes. My personal favorite, the shot of the PR woman holding Sam's hand for balance as he threw his leg over the bike, with the limo waiting in the background, made international TV. The *Daily Mail* called him "Bikey," and the name stuck in the paddock that weekend.

Although I never heard anyone call Sam Bikey to his face. Even in his pristine jeans and fresh-out-of-the-plastic-wrap shirt, Sam had presence. He held his head still when he talked and people turned and listened. The mover and shaker talking about moving and shaking. Big-money people have that golden attraction. You think you might learn something about how to hold on to the stuff if you get close. And the closer you get, the more uneasy they get.

We were staring into the computer screen in the motor home, and Naughton said, "Looks like you've got your hands full with the car. You're a second-and-a-half behind Russell, Evers.''

"Russell's driving better. If you want a reason, I'm going slower because I'm driving harder. Finding the limits of the car, Sam,'' I said, "by going over its limits. The tires are overheating and it's sliding around. The setup is OK; we're not going to find much lap time by changing the setup. We're just short of horsepower and downforce. I'll take another second-and-a-half off this afternoon in qualifying. Unless the sun comes out and slows up the track for everybody. Either way, we will be in the top half.''

"Let's start looking at some of the places where you lost time,'' Sam said, ignoring me. Two weeks on the team and he was the information junkie. "You can always find your answer,'' he said, "in the numbers.''

There are two hundred and fifty-eight on-board data gathering measurements you may look at, at any given instant and/or at any given point on any lap of the modern Grand Prix car. Revs, gear ratio, slip angle, coefficient of friction, throttle position, brake-pedal deflection, force of acceleration or deceleration are some of the most obvious. Bump-stop deflection, tub torsion, tire-wall deflection, and their effect as noted by the laser ride-height sensors, are among the lesser measurements we consider. Plus, if you wish, we could calculate the deflection of the bump stops inside the dampers. And I swear to God we do. Along, of course, with the track conditions, radius of the turn, track surface condition, road camber. And you may relate all those measurements to the settings on the car; that is low and high piston-velocity bump in the dampers, spring rate, inertia and movement, ride height at each corner, roll bar and wing adjustment, to name a few.

Alistair once calculated that if you printed out all the measurements of all of the moments of all of the laps of racing and practice for just one car over any Formula One weekend, you could fill every shelf of every library in Britain with absolutely meaningless information.

With so much to look at, we don't look at most of it. The

eyes go blind staring at the rows upon rows of numbers. We look for the weird moments, what the driver remembers. A good driver spends a fair amount of his time committing little moments to memory, like the car feeling light coming into the left-hand sweeper at the end of the pits straight, leading into the long right-hander on lap 17, just coming into the right-hand part. He then spends a good deal more of his time seeing if he and the techies can find what "feels a little light" in the numbers. I didn't care a Hockenhiem about the numbers. On the other hand I wasn't blowing the doors off anybody. I was just spinning my wheels.

"Is Russell running more wing?"

"Two degrees more in front," Hardy said, "three degrees less in back."

"Check and see if his turn in is sharper. If it is, let's try that."

Hardy looked at me with the blank stare of a security guard, suspicion and resentment just under the surface. His real name, sorry, I don't know his real name. The name he gave us was Luchs. William Howard Luchs. He was about six two and weighed over 250 pounds. He had a beefy round face, little beady eyes, and he combed his sparse black hair across his scalp for camouflage. His arms bulged out of his sleeves, and around one thick hairy wrist he wore a thin gold watch with a thin gold band. He chewed gum.

Hardy's partner, Laurel, hung back, behind him. Laurel's specialty was electronics, on board and off. He looked more like a retired halfback than Stan Laurel, but the name was too good to pass up. The name he gave us was Richard Sykes. Whatever his real one was, we called him Laurel, because he did have the watery blue eyes and a flat kind of face. I never saw him smile.

Hardy punched the numbers on his keyboard, the screen flickered, and a grid of numbers came up. "It's not sharper," he said in his mild high voice, "it's more gradual."

"But his entry speed is lower," I said, looking at the screen. "Let me look at his exit speed."

Hardy punched in a command, the numbers all changed, and he raised his eyebrows. "Guess what, Forrest. He's coming out four miles an hour faster than you. And using less of the track." Hardy gave me a little self-satisfied smile.

"How fast was Alistair going when he hit the tree?" I said, unable to resist the temptation to wipe the smile off his face.

"Forrest," Naughton said, putting his hand on my shoulder, "can I have a word with you? In private."

"Fine," I said.

We went downstairs and into the bar at the back of the motor home. There was a half moon of a gray leather couch against the back wall, and the walls were paneled with black wood mirrors and chrome, with hidden lighting and a deep burgundy carpet. It had been Phil's idea of elegance, a hushed leather-and-wood cave. Phil had loved putting his feet up on the glass coffee table and holding court with his favorite journalists.

I eased myself into Phil's easy chair. Naughton lowered himself down on the dark gray leather built-in sofa and stretched out his long legs. "I appreciate that you are upset by Alistair's death," he said. "But I can't have you talking like that to my crew."

His crew. The new captain. He hadn't even bought the team yet, but because he had the money, or at least because Susan thought he had the money, it was "his."

"Alistair," I said carefully, "went through the windscreen and hit a tree head-on. There were pieces of his face in the grass, alongside the car." I wanted him to see it, bring it home to him in his safe place. "Alistair was a friend of mine, Sam. I also tend to get a little touchy when I'm pushing the car as fast as it will go and it's not fast enough. But you are right. Why should I take it out on old Hardy. I'll go down and tell Hardy he's a pussycat."

"I'm glad to hear it. I feel uncomfortable," he said easily, "when there is any discord on my team. I had no idea you were this upset. We are all very sad about Alistair's death, but I have to tell you this is the time for Team EFORT to pull together. Irresponsible statements like that don't do anybody any good. Least of all you. Besides," he said, permitting himself a small smile, "I have some extremely good news."

He was right. This was sticks and stones. I hadn't meant to say any of it, but it came out, out of control like my driving. I missed Alistair with an ache. And felt the ants crawling in and crawling out, single file. Poor bastard. "We could all use some good news," I said.

"I met with George Hozuki, as you suggested. Very impressive CEO, very impressive. And I'm grateful to you for steering me in his direction because I think we might be able to do some business. We can help them on our side of the Pacific Rim, and he can give us entry into some of those closed circles of distribution for some of our financial products in Japan."

I smiled my good-for-you smile.

"Well, of course, you know, you've met him. But he was very impressive, Evers. His grasp of statistics is just phenomenal. Although I have to tell you I like the way the Japanese do business. They have twelve guys all bowing, agreeing with everything you say, and seventeen corporate ceremonies they want you to go through before they get to the meat and potatoes, and at the end of it I usually say, 'Bullshit, here's the figures and here's what we are going to do.' And nine times out of ten they say yes. Russell, my man . . . ''

I looked up. My teammate was in the doorway, diagonal grin. Sweating, in his driving suit, his face streaked.

"Come in, sit down. Get Sally to bring you some ice water.

"See this boy," Sam turned to me, lowering his voice for stage effect, "I have great plans for this boy. Russell is going to be world champion, aren't you, Russell?

"My boy," he said, his voice coming back up to normal, "I was just telling Forrest how George Hozuki is part of the new breed in Japan. Come on, sit down, I've got some good news.''

Then, back to me, forgetting Russell, ''Very direct, very fast. Nothing wasted. We started in the afternoon at his office and went on into the evening. Covered a hell of a lot of ground. Ended up in his private club. A scene you would have liked, Evers. The two of us lying naked on our stomachs on tables in the steam room, massaged by naked women, a little pocket tape recorder running so we don't lose anything. Doesn't exactly sharpen the mind, being rubbed by naked ladies, but he has a habit of thinking out loud, so we understood each other. As I said, I like the way he does business. Anyway, about the good news, the new engine.''

''I didn't know they were working on a new one.''

''Well, he told me they have been more than a little embarrassed, especially in their home market, by their performance and by our performance in Formula One. As a result they have been working flat out, twenty-four hours a day, in secret.''

''The Japanese always work flat out. They run to work.''

''Well maybe he was just humoring me. His first idea was that they should wait until they have at least a hundred more horsepower to make a real impact on the competition. Trouble is, as you well know, we can't wait. We are after a moving target here. If you are not constantly improving, you are falling behind. I told him we had to work together. I said we would put one hundred percent behind promoting Hozuki.''

''Meaning me. You think promoting Hozuki will sit alongside my promoting Chantal.''

''Jesus, Evers, if you can push that stuff, and the figures I've seen say they can't ship enough of it, you can push anything. You were my ace in the hole with him. By the way he sends you his warm regards.''

Naughton leaned back against the sofa, tilted his head back and closed his eyes. The corporate seer. ''You see, I think— and that is what is so interesting about George—I think we are on the verge of the concentration of tremendous power

in the hands of a very few people. That is what we are doing
with these global electronic networks. It's going to be painful
getting there. Our current political process just isn't equipped
to deal with global problems. This is what I was talking
about with George. The Japanese understand the need for
these global networks. They know there is going to be an
upheaval that will make the depression of the 1930s look
like a country fair.''

Russell was twirling a piece of ice in his glass. He picked
it up and swallowed it. Naughton heard the sound, opened
his eyes and watched Russell for a moment, collecting his
thoughts. ''I run a number of companies, and I have no doubt
that some of them may disappear. But at the end of it, whatever happens, information is concentrating. Information at-
tracts information. And the use of information is power.
Which, of course, is what the EFORT Team is all about. We
had a great conversation.''

''What'd he tell you about the new engine?''

''My understanding, Forrest, is that what he calls a new
engine is essentially the same as the one we have now. But
they have found another seventy to eighty horsepower. So
the good news is more power. And the good news is we
don't have to change a thing to slot them in. They've redone
the heads and pistons, gone to airsprings for the valves, and
lost some fifteen kilos. Hozuki are airfreighting them to us
now, and we should have them for Silverstone.''

I thought how delighted Alistair would have been. Like a
kid with a new bike. The more power you have, the better
the diffuser works. With more power you can run more wing.
With more wing you can stop quicker, turn in sharper, go
around the corners faster. Or, on a fast course like Silverstone, leave the wings alone and fly down the straights.

Russell, an empty glass of ice water in his hand, said,
''How soon? We need to get some track time before
Silverstone.''

''Sooner than you think. If we can get them through
French customs, we should have two of them here Saturday

morning. I doubt we'll have them in the cars in time for qualifying, but unless we have a problem fitting them in the cars, you should have them for the race. Which should surprise some people. When is the funeral, Forrest?''

His question brought me up sharply. If he had killed Alistair, if he really wanted the team to fail, why come back with new engines? The thought occurred to me, not for the first time, that I was entering into the dark places where I couldn't see the surface. Maybe, I thought, I should just shut up and drive. ''They hadn't arranged it when I left London,'' I said. ''I'll ring Merrie this afternoon, after qualifying.''

''Oh yes, his wife, right? The poor girl in the wheelchair. How's she taking it?''

''Better than you might think,'' I said.

He stood up, looking down at me. ''Let me know if there's anything I can do,'' he said, putting his hand on my shoulder. ''Anything she needs. I suppose you know I'd been in touch with Alistair over acquiring his little outfit. If the right moment comes up, when it's appropriate, Forrest, you might mention to her that I am still interested. Although, without Alistair, I'd have to take another look at the figures. How'd you like the Crillon?''

Chapter 24

"What?"

Her voice was thick, sleepy. "Hello, Merrie."

"Who is this?"

"Forrest. How are you?"

"Just great, Forrest. What do you think? I'm in a wheelchair and Alistair is smashed to pieces. What the hell do you think?"

"I thought you were doing well the last time I talked to you."

"Well I'm doing shitty now. What do you want?"

"Talk to you, hold your hand over the phone. See if there is anything I can do."

"Have you seen the British papers?"

"What's in the British press?"

"Not a lot. Just a couple of them yesterday, *The Mail* and *The Guardian*, ran an obituary on Alistair. Just a couple of lines. And the *Daily Express* had a piece about his accident that had a nifty little innuendo. They said he was not known to have been drinking before."

"Is that what the police say, that he'd been drinking?"

"Not officially, but it's what they've been telling the press. I can't stand this. I can't stand this mess. I want it finished."

"When is the funeral?"

"I'm burying him in a couple of hours. Six o'clock."

"You didn't tell me. I wanted to be there."

"He's not yours. Or mine. He's dead and I want him in

the ground. I want people to stop talking about him. I want it over with. His mother's coming to take me."

"I'm sorry."

"Don't start that. We're all sorry."

"The last time I talked to you, you wanted to make that diffuser work."

She sighed. There was a long pause. "Yes. I know. The underwing."

"You mean the bottom of the car, the undertray."

"Call it what you like, it is an upside-down wing. I mean it's a venturi but the point is that it acts like a wing. If you had active suspension on the car it would be one thing. The whole point of an active suspension is to keep the aero platform absolutely level, do you understand? That the car is an aero platform? Sure, the ride is nicer, and if you clout the curbs, the other wheels will stay flat on the ground, but the whole point of active suspension is to keep the aero platform stable. But your car doesn't have that stability. So if I mess around with the strakes of the diffuser and enlarge the diffuser chamber so there's more air pulled through the venturi, it sounds good, but I don't know what effect it will have on the pitch of the car, moving the center of pressure. Without active suspension it could take weeks to sort out the wings and the dampers and springs."

"You thought you could put together something quickly. For Silverstone."

"Forrest, I was high then. In shock. I can't possibly. Even if I wanted to, Forrest. After I talked to you, I spent ten hours straight at the computer. Alistair was bluffing."

"I never knew him to lie."

"Yeah, he was good, wasn't he? I mean the trick is that there are lots of programs around where you can do the algorithms for any part of the car, like the wheel. Or maybe the rear wing. But they are all separate parts, and if you run them separately, you might learn something about the aerodynamics of it, but you won't know how it affects the whole car. What he was trying to do was run all of the separate bits in tandem. The program he had was an interface that he had between Fake Space's virtual reality wind tunnel and the team's CAD/CAM. But it was immensely complicated, it's full of bugs, and there is a lot of it I just don't understand.''

"He told me he was using a program from Fake Space Labs. That if you had the whole car in the computer with CAD/CAM, you could test the whole car in a wind tunnel.''

"Right. As I said. What he didn't tell you is that it doesn't work. He had twenty graduate students working on it, and from what I could tell, they were at least a year and maybe five away from getting it running. Some of the big companies like Ford, General Motors have these crash programs where they run crash tests in a computer. But we just don't have the software. I thought he did. I thought at least the linkages were there. Maybe it's here, someplace, I don't know. It's a mess. My life is a mess. I can't tell you anything.''

"Merrie, it doesn't matter if you can't do the diffuser. You'd said you wanted to. If you don't, don't worry about it. You also said you'd ask the police to pull the black box from Alistair's car. I don't suppose you did that?''

"I didn't do anything. Can't do anything. I want Alistair buried in the ground, and then I want to sleep for twenty days, and when I wake up, I never want to think of him again.''

"So Naughton didn't have anything to be afraid of.''

"Well, I don't know what his problem is, but I think if Alistair really had anything he would have sold it to Naughton. I mean, I think what he was doing was making his program sound more advanced than it really was. Scientists shouldn't exaggerate their own work, but they do. They're optimists. It's what gets us through the drudgery.''

"Naughton still wants to buy your company.''

"Do we have to talk about this?''

"Would you like me to call you tomorrow?''

"Isn't tomorrow the race, the French Grand Prix?''

"I could call you after the race.''

"You're coming back to England, aren't you?"

"Sure. I'll hitchhike with one of the drivers. There's usually an empty seat on one of their jets."

"Stay here."

"I don't know—"

She cut me off. "You asked if you could do anything and I'm telling you. Come spend the night here. Please. For me. For Alistair. Just for the one night."

"You think you'd sleep better?"

"Oh, I'll sleep all right. Don't you worry about my sleep. I think I know how to get the sons of bitches that smashed Alistair and I'd like your opinion."

"I thought you were going to sleep for twenty days."

"Don't think, just come."

From the terrace of the Château Ballade, where we were staying, you could see the Loire winding through the bottom of the valley and, on the little one- and two-lane roads running through the grassy fields and patches of woods, lines of traffic flowing slowly, trying to get around the roadblocks, backed up for as far as the eye could see. On the white wrought-iron table in front of me there was an empty white demitasse coffee cup, a sugar bowl, a small spoon, a torn ticket from the waiter and the machine that plugged into the rest of the world, wrapping it in its net, shrinking it visibly, daily, the vehicle of choice for mainframes, banks, defense departments, designers in separate continents and racing drivers trying to keep up with the acceleration of their lives. It had started as a local party line and continued to grow ever since. The hackers and the phone companies didn't even call it a telephone. It was now an "endset." And the perfect vehicle for conveying Merrie's pain into my ear. Like a line of ants.

Outside the entrance to the Château, at a discreet distance enforced by the Nevers gendarmerie, a small group of teenage girls and older women waited near their cars hoping to catch a glimpse of the sexy racing driver. The one who was in all the sexy ads. The man who was absolutely irresistible.

Sexxay Forray. Who, if they saw him up close for a day, would bring their vague sexy dreams crashing down. I began to understand Virgin's contempt for them. Didn't they have anything better to do?

I looked at the telephone sitting there on the white table like a black toad, the rural French countryside dozing green and hazy in the late afternoon sun. Looked at it a while longer and decided it was not going to get any easier, picked it up and punched in Susan's number.

"Hello, Susan."

"Forrest, I'm glad you called. I was trying to think of the good things, and one of them was you might call."

"I said I would."

"Yes. You did."

There was a pause. I said, "How are you?"

"I'm all right, Forrest. Kinda numb. I feel like I've been through this before. Like I ought to know what to do next. But there isn't anything for me to do. Sue Two was asking about you."

"Is she OK?"

"She and Josh are fine. Josh has decided it's time he had a bicycle. I'm not sure. I picture him going out on the road and getting hit by a car."

"Get him one of those cross-country things and tell him he has to stay on your property. By the time he breaks the rules, he'll know how to ride. I just talked to Merrie."

"Oh, I feel so rotten for her. About her. How is she?"

"She's up and down. On lithium. She's burying Alistair this afternoon."

"Do you know where?"

"She didn't say. I think it'll just be her and Alistair's mother."

"I always felt so bad about Merrie."

"But you loved him."

"Good heavens no. What gave you that idea?"

"You were married with children and you were having an affair with him. That's the usual excuse. Love."

"Oh, Forrest. You are such a romantic sometimes. I loved Phil. Really loved him. He had physical problems you don't know about. He said, fine, go ahead. It seemed like such a nice neat simple solution. Merrie couldn't, and Phil couldn't. And Alistair and I would meet once a week. We weren't secretive about it, and now I wish we had been. It would have been kinder all round if we'd kept our secrets. Anyway it was coming to an end. We both felt bad about it, and all of that show of honesty we did to make us feel better just made everyone feel rotten. In the end it was a habit. I can't bear thinking about it now. Wasn't qualifying today?"

"You sure you are OK? Normally you'd be glued to the monitor, watching the Marlboro race reports."

"To tell you the truth I've been out in the garden, sitting on that bench under that old plum tree that ought to come down and crying and getting sick of myself. For crying. For being so stupid. I'm glad you called. How'd you do? Where are you on the grid?"

"Twelfth. Russell's fourteenth."

"No wonder you're not bragging about it. Is something wrong with the setup? Is that the best you can do?"

"Naughton came back from Japan with new engines under his arms. The team is fitting them now. He says there's another seventy to eighty horsepower. If they don't break, we should be in the points."

"What about after the race, Forrest? Are you coming back here? I mean, you will need to start right in for Silverstone next weekend, and you know the old 'going up and down the Motorway doesn't make any sense' story. I've put clean sheets in your room."

"Merrie asked me to stay the night."

"Oh."

"She's confused and she's in pain."

"Sure. Of course. Forrest," she said, hesitating, "it may not be possible. But if you could find a way, could you do something for me? A favor? Could you tell Merrie I'm sorry?"

"If you really want to say something to Merrie, wait a few days and call her or write her a note. She doesn't want anybody's pity, but she is going to need help."

"Forrest . . ."

I waited.

"Forrest, please don't you turn away from me too. I didn't do anything. And I need you. I need your friendship."

"I'll work on it, Susan."

Chapter 25

At ten P.M. the air was hot and still and the sky was purple and gold with the last of the sunset.

Rather than drive past the small group of women waiting for me outside the Château Ballade (Should I wave to them, try to sneak past without being seen, sign their bottoms?) and then circle around the French Truckers roadblock to La Renaissance in Magny Cours, to join the big-money players of Formula One at feeding time, instead of all that hassle, we walked under a striped canopy down to the river, where it was cool. An old, blue nineteenth-century boathouse, mounted on stone piers like a blocky Chenonceau stuck out over the river.

Much smiling, shaking of hands. Yes, Monsieur Evers, we have your table. Maybe tomorrow you catch Monsieur Senna.

Inside waiters and busboys and girls in uniform were moving as silently and gracefully as fish through Restaurant Glorie Loire, Château Ballade's newly opened shot at a star in the Guide Michelin. The carpet was new and pale blue, the tablecloths pink, and through the arched windows, opened to let the cool air flow through, the sea-green Loire rolled by underneath and on three sides. On the fourth side, across an expanse of lawn and topiary, the château—originally built in the thirteenth century as the summer home of the Duc de Orleans and occupied several times by the British—rose up from the countryside to bathe in the golden light from the setting sun. The Loire River sparkled green and gold through the open window next to our table.

Naughton's face was in the sun, and his pocked cheeks took on a golden sheen, making him look carved out of metal. His face slowly creased into a smile. "This is a rare pleasure, Forrest. What a good idea," he said, looking down at the wine list.

"Normally I'd be dining out with one of our major sponsors the night before a race," I said. "Why should tonight be different?"

"Why indeed," he said, looking up and enjoying the golden evening light playing on the river. "Owner, sponsor . . . it sounds impressive, but all it means is I get to watch you have all the fun."

Leaning back in his light green shirt and immaculate light blue jacket, the long silver hair on his round boyish head fringed with gold by the sun, he looked as at home as if this were his dining room and always had been. As if he were a descendent of the Original Duke, the world his personally engraved oyster. A con man's confidence. If Castleman were right, Naughton would be broke and probably under investigation by the serious fraud squad in two weeks. "I have to admit, Forrest, this is the first time I've had a chance to unwind in weeks."

"Apart from the massage in Tokyo."

"Oh, Jesus, Forrest," he said, sitting up sharply. "That was a high-speed engagement, full battle stations. I held my own, may have even come away with a trophy or two. But that was work. That is my work, what I do: negotiation; give and take, mostly take. Your George Hozuki is a world-class player. So it was also a learning process."

He put the wine list down and leaned forward, confiding. "The things I learned in that one afternoon. The Japanese are into an electronic world corporate America is only beginning to see. Give you one little example: the way they get around taxes. You know caller identification? Somebody calls you and your phone displays the caller's phone number? We use it to build up a file on the people who call Emron.

Well, that is sandbox stuff for the Japanese. They are into fifth-generation CID now. For example, there are one or two Japanese banks that can identify transfers by sender in a nanosecond. And if you are one of their favored customers, with your own special little tag in the computer, they can take your little parcel of, say, twenty million yen, dollars or whatever, split the money into twenty-five thousand parcels among, say, two hundred and fifty banks halfway round the world, bounce it off the appropriate satellites and have it safe and sound and underground in a vault in Budapest or the Cayman Islands before you can say 'laundry.' And in that little twinkling, your money will be in some underground account for some opaque tax-free corporation without a trail, because the program alters all the numbers before they go on the log. I'll tell you, these guys are the Ninja of international finance and they've got more money bouncing around the satellites than God. Course the hot tip banks these days is Eastern Europe. Smart money is in Hungary right now.''

Sam ordered a bottle of '61 Château Petrus to go with his frogs. I ordered a bottle of fine vintage Evian water (a very good week) to accompany a seafood salad (*salade jardin du mar, compose Chef Marceau Martin*), which I would chew on while I meditated on the cudlike diets of six-foot-one-inch-tall racing drivers with wide shoulders who could barely squeeze into their shrinking cockpits. On every table around me, men and women were complacently wolfing down some delectable morsel that I dared not taste lest I gain an extra ounce to drag around the racetrack. No point spending nine thousand pounds on a titanium suspension assembly to save three pounds in weight if your driver gains four pounds at the dinner table. I was already the heaviest driver in Formula One and paid the penalty of a second a lap over the lightest. Yes, just the de-caff lo-cal salad, Waiter, no oil and no freshly baked bread with crispy crusts and light steaming memories of childhood when there was butter. I'll just chew on the pink tablecloth, if you don't mind, keep my teeth in shape.

"One of the secrets of business," Sam said, as the wine waiter gestured for a pretty teenager in operetta costume to run down to the cellars under the château and fetch one of the last bottles of '61 Petrus in the world, "is to sign your own expense account."

In some ways Sam seemed quaint. One of the old school of business who thought it was hip to brag about fraud. Formula One used to be about simple aggressive men battling it out on the racetrack. Now it is about complicated men battling it out in the boardroom. Simple, as I'm sure you appreciate, is the positive in that equation.

"How is your business doing, Sam?" I said. "From what I read, I hear you have your hands full." From what Castleman had told me, he was in free-fall with no parachute.

"You may as well know, I think Emron is on the verge of a hell of a breakthrough. I've got to go to LA on Monday, tape a part of a presentation we're making to the D.O.D. And on the way back I'm picking up Senator Dickerson and Representatives Walker and Giordini, on the Armed Services Appropriations Committee. They've agreed to be my guests at Silverstone, and I think once they catch a whiff of the excitement, not to mention the technology of Formula One . . . Course that means I'll need to depend on you and to some degree Susan to look after the team . . . "

"The press doesn't seem to share your confidence."

"Well, the shots I've been taking in the press make me wonder if the hassle is worth it."

"They don't give the money away, do they, Sam?" You have to steal it, I almost added.

"Money is not the point," he said mildly as a wide, shallow porcelain bowl was placed in front of him, a buttery pond of *créme de cuisses de grenouilles en champignonnade*. His soup spoon slid in carefully, holding the lumpy liquid as he blew on it to cool. "The point," he said, "is jobs." The spoon disappeared in his mouth for a moment then darted back quickly down to the bowl. "Show me a country that doesn't need jobs right now, and I'll show you a damn fairy tale. Every country in the world is desperate for jobs.'' His voice and the spoon picked up speed. "The world economy is slowing down so fast it's going to take us a hell of a time to get it going again." Spoon. "What I am doing, Evers," blowing, slurping, "is swimming against the tide." Spoon. "Financing the reconstruction of people's lives by giving them a steady income." Blowing and slurping. "And in those," spoon, "countries where they need it," blowing and slurping, "teaching the skills for our workers to be wage earners" spoon "and taxpayers," blowing and slurping, "a plus in their community." Spoon. "If nobody is making any money," blowing, slurping and spilling an unseen drop on his immaculate light-blue jacket lapel, "nobody pays any taxes." Spoon. "Nobody pays any taxes, governments go broke." Blowing and slurping. "Governments go broke, people go berserk." He chased a little lump, tipping his bowl to catch it.

"Making money to save the world." I could have argued with him. He was paying slave wages in third-world countries and acting like he was bringing water to the desert. But I didn't want to argue with him. I wanted to hook him by the scrotum.

"Yeah," he said, swirling the wine in his glass, sniffing it. "It's nasty work, but somebody has to do it. You always this prickly before a race?"

"Always."

He swooshed the wine around in his mouth, pursed his lips, swallowed and smacked his lips. "You sure you won't try a drop of this wine? Might improve your disposition."

"But not my lap times," I said. One day I will make some lucky somebody a lovely maiden aunty. No alcohol, no *créme de cuisses de grenouilles en champignonnade* for the greedy driver. Sam's spoon gathered in the last little bit of frog, and his mouth snapped shut on his spoon. Hero driver's spoon gathered dust.

"Enzo Ferrari used to claim a couple of glasses of wine improved his drivers' lap times."

"That was because they were driving Ferraris. It helps to have your brain fuzzed to drive one of those things. I didn't know you were a fan, Sam."

"Fan? What the hell do you think I'm doing here? Christ, I've heard people this weekend bitch about paying three hundred dollars for a seat in the grandstands. I've paid millions to be here. Because I love it."

Sam hadn't paid anything, and I suspected he was planning to milk the team for whatever money Susan had in it. I thought he'd bought Team Joyce to stop Alistair from developing his virtual reality wind tunnel. But far be it from me to be undiplomatic. I said, "Horseshit."

Sam looked just over my shoulder, beginning to smile.

I felt soft hands on my neck and smelt a light, musky perfume. Felt as much as heard sniffing sounds. I turned and looked into a yellow scoop-neck dress where small perfect breasts were swinging like pink-and-white birds on a swing. Where the perfume was coming from. "My name," she said, "is Glorianna. And I am in room fourteen. Alone until ten. Then I go to sleep."

I looked up and she had that sleek-as-a-seal, dipped-in-oil look that some expensive French women have. "Talk to him," I said, looking up into the face of a woman in her late twenties and nodding toward Sam. With her smooth face, hair slicked back, she looked as if she had just come out of the swimming pool. She also had a wide, full mouth, the kind that looked as if it could engulf either half of you. Just now her mouth was displaying very white teeth. She wore little gold earrings and just enough makeup to look rich. "He has all the money," I said.

She stood up and considered Sam Naughton, who was grinning widely at her. "Oh, money," she said. "Money is so disgusting."

She bent down over me again so I could smell her perfume, feel her warm breath. She said, "It's very easy, Forrest. Glorianna. Fourteen. You won't forget. I will go change now." And she walked away, across the restaurant and out the door, back up to the château.

"My God," Sam said, watching her yellow behind sashay across the dark lawn. "If I hadn't seen it with my own eyes, I wouldn't believe it. That Formula One stuff works."

"If it works on me, it's a miracle," I said. "I never wear the stuff. What works is all the hype around it."

"You going to take her up on her offer, you old dog? Go up to her room? Find her lying on her bed in maybe a satin nightie, sprawled on the bed, moaning with desire? Christ, I wouldn't mind pumping that broad." He was having fun, imagining it.

"Hard to know what she has in mind, Sam. I doubt it's me she's after, because she has never met me. Maybe she wants to see how her husband reacts to finding her riding a foreign gentleman. Maybe she's just found out she's HIV positive and wants to share her problem. You never know, she could be a publicity stunt. Maybe somebody has hired her for God knows what public scandal, and maybe she's just silly enough to get all sexed up over a photograph in a magazine. It doesn't sound likely, but why don't you splash on a bottle of the stuff and knock on her door, find out for yourself? I should warn you, though, Sam. I've had a lot of women who look like fantasies chasing after me in the past few weeks. And it never works out the way you expect."

"Depends on what you expect. If I didn't try out my fantasies, I'd probably still be working in an insurance claims office. You were saying 'horseshit.' "

"I was saying the reason you bought the team, Sam, was to stop Alistair from proving that a virtual reality wind tunnel was alive and working before your government contracts were signed."

Sam took a deep mouthful of wine, looking at me while he held it in his mouth. As he swallowed, a small trickle of red wine came out of the corner of his mouth. He wiped it away. "Evers, this dinner was your idea. I was looking forward to it. I thought we might mend our fences, maybe even be friends. I thought it was going to be pleasant. A pleasant exchange in a pleasant place between two men. I think I should remind you that I have responsibility for several thousand employees. For their jobs and to some real degree for their families. And I cannot tolerate and I will not tolerate crap like that. Say that in public and I shall have to protect their jobs and sue you for more than you ever dreamed existed. Now, are you sure you wouldn't like a drop of this divine beverage?'' he said, picking up the bottle from its little wicker casket and pouring himself another glass.

"Sam, I wouldn't be surprised if you'd poisoned it."

"Evers, if I could, I certainly would," he said, smiling easily. "Just a drop?"

"Just a drop," I said, smiling back, thinking I was sinking the hook. "Just a drop."

Chapter 26

Big Sunday grin. Wall-to-wall. Inside the white Nomex sock with holes for my eyes and my mouth, encased in a helmet the size of a watermelon and behind a lexan visor, I am grinning like a lost dog in a new home with a full supper dish.

On Saturday morning Russell had followed me around the track at Magny Cours while I went looking for time. Time was lying loose all over the track, waiting to be scooped up by cars with more horsepower. Picking up time with will-power was more difficult. Imola, for example. Imola is a fast right-and-left uphill S-turn that crests on the apex of the left-hand section, the second part of the S. There, the car goes light as the track drops down slightly, leading into Château d'Eau, an open hairpin. Coming into Imola, accelerating hard in sixth, you drop down into fifth and ease back on the throttle as you come out of the turn, before getting hard on the brakes. By tightening my line on the exit, leaning the weight of the car hard on the outside front wheel, I found I could get on the throttle a fraction quicker and harder, gaining a whole tenth of a second. The car still was light, and the nose went wide onto the curb, giving my hands a hell of a knock, making the back end threaten to come around just when you had to be sure you were lined up straight for Château d'Eau, but there it was, a whole tenth of a second, with only part of it lost to the front tires scrubbing off a little speed.

In the afternoon qualifying session, riding up on the curbs, spinning our wheels, keeping the car out on the far edge, flinging ourselves headfirst into corners, hurling around that cramped little track, we managed to qualify twelfth and fifteenth on the grid, Russell never getting a clear lap and three-tenths of a second down on my time. I had never driven harder or better. I drove the car faster than it was willing to go, grazing the edge of the track and coming within a whisker of turning myself to pulp. It is not easier in the middle of the field, it is harder. Much harder.

Hozuki's new engines arrived at ten o'clock Saturday night. After a banzai dive into the innards of Russell's car and mine, digging out our old engines tube by wire by bolt by bolt, the mechanics had the new ones in, with considerable help from the Hozuki technicians, by two-thirty in the morning. Then the damn things would not start.

Would not start.

They tried everything for three hours and nothing worked. They had given up and were about to take out the new engines and put the old ones back in when one of the Hozuki technicians looked in the empty engine crates and found an envelope with the new software. Then, whoop BLLAAAAAAT screeeeaaamMM. *They ran.*

For Sunday morning's warm-up we had gone out cautiously, on full tanks, not wanting to break anything before the race, and gone seventh and eighth fastest, both of us feeling we could have been quicker but wanting to save our engines for the race. Hozuki engines, from time to time and for no consistent reason, thus far in the season had the life expectancy of a hand grenade. So we would be gentle with our new babies.

Big grin. First one in a race all season. The power band has shrunk to the width of a watch band. From 12,000 rpm to 14,500 there is power; below that the engine stumbles and falls. There is also a harsh vibration that frags my vision above 10,750. Martini in front of me is sending up a micro-dot fog of oil, filming my visor as soon as I strip off the cover. The car is still a mess in the turns and it doesn't matter. I am grinning because when we get through the corkscrew they call Chicane and through the diabolical Lycee hairpin leading onto the pit straight, I will pass Martini because I have the power. I will put my foot down and whoom, no waiting, it happens. What a difference seventy extra horses can make. Even if they are mean, unpredictable and ill-tempered. Even if I could use another seventy to run up front. A racing driver never has enough power, but this is a real start. *Baaaannzzzzaaaiii Hozzzzuuuukkkkiiii!!*

Pedal to the metal, like the old days, the car is actually moving. Up behind Martini, grit from his tires spitting at my helmet like buckshot, coming right up underneath his tail, the air thick and boiling from his exhaust, getting a tow from him on the main straight, the grandstands on the left, the pits on my right, so I miss my lap board, doesn't matter, up through the gears, third, fourth, fifth, going under the bridge, I pull out of his noise grit and the heavy stink of his exhaust and out into the clean air and past him into sixth gear and into the long, sweeping left-hand turn, still hard on the throttle, clear of him now, in sixth position, hot damn, the Ferrari of Jean Alesi in sight and I can catch him. Russell is right there in my mirrors, ten feet behind me, in seventh. I snick down to fifth for the long, sweeping 180-degree right-hand turn, slightly uphill, constant radius. Set the speed and stay there until you can get hard on the throttle, back into sixth and ride up the gentle hill with the engine on full scream.

The narrow power band forces me to drive like in the old turbo cars, where you kept the engine revs up to keep the turbos spinning. A little left-foot braking, keeping my foot on the throttle while braking with my left foot, keeping up the engine speed, meant that I didn't have to wait around while the engine climbed back up to where the power was. It was tricky in the Adelaide hairpin ahead of me. Coming down from over 190 miles an hour to a crawling 55 in forty yards, braking so hard my eyeballs force my eyelids open wide and my whole head turns to a lead ball straining forward trying to squeeze out of the front of my helmet. My body gains five times its weight while I try to get the balance just right between braking, keeping the power up and steering on the throttle because the front end doesn't want to turn at fifty. The trick is turning in early very fast, letting the car scrub off speed while it drifts out, fingertip control, all four wheels breaking traction. You do not do this unless you are going very fast and you are just a little crazy. I would be slapping myself on the back for this trick if Russell weren't on my tail, giving every indication he would go even quicker if I would get out of his way.

I am not getting out of his way. Alesi slows early for the Adelaide hairpin, and I am, for the moment, catching him at magnum speed, his car the red pinpoint of focus as I crest the rise on the back straight, growing larger as I am right on the redline at 14,200 rpm. To hell with saving the engine now. It is fine, strong, and I am catching him. We are catching him. Alesi disappears around the hairpin and I look for my braking point, a pole on the spectator fencing with a broad yellow stripe on it and I start to ease on the brakes with my left foot, keeping my foot to the floor then letting up on the throttle, turning in early, letting my speed carry me out and there is, through the noise of the tires and the wind and high-pitched whine of the gears, a crunch, a lurch left, the back end starts to spin out of control, and I see the purple nose of Russell's car coming into spear the side of my car, and his left front wing skates inches over my head, sailing free through the dark sky like a scythe.

His front wheels are locked, turned to the right, and they are sliding, not turning at all with smoke billowing out from where they are melting against the black track. The nose of Russell's car moves in with the deliberate speed of a ship coming into dock and crunches the side of my car. I am just hanging on, bounding across the road, across the dirt and strip of green grass into the walnut-size gravel at the outside of the turn as my foot comes off the brake and hard on the throttle, anxious to keep going, not get bogged down in the stones, and my back wheels spin, crunch over his shattered purple nose cone, sending up a rooster tail of dirt and rocks behind me, all over him, to hell with Russell, as I scrabble back onto the track, spinning the wheels to clear them of the dirt and rocks stuck to their hot and sticky surface, and almost run into Martini, who has just slipped past us.

Doesn't matter, I will catch him again if I haven't flat spotted my tires, they feel OK, no vibration yet, and I am back on the track, back into the race, foot down, I have only lost a second-and-a-half at the most, not sure if anything is broken and thinking there are probably bits of broken racing car and dirt blocking the radiators. I should probably come in, but I will give it a lap if everything feels OK; shifting into third under the bridge and my engine dies.

Zero.

Nothing. Dead. Goddamn Russell. Goddamn me for not seeing him in my mirrors. I roll silently down the track for a few yards, trying to get some response out of the engine, and there is absolutely nothing, just the amazing silence you hear after the blast of war stops. I switch the car off and roll over onto the infield grass on my right, out of the way and out of the race as the rain starts to fall.

Chapter 27

"How could you, Forrest?"

One of those questions that makes you look out the window. It had been raining in France, so naturally it was also raining on the hills of Cambridgeshire. Proving Evers law of English weather: If, at any one time, there shall be rain falling elsewhere upon our planet, there shall also be rain falling upon England. On the other hand the sky would still be light gray at ten P.M. No small compensation for Blighty's cold climate.

"The yellowjackets think there is a glitch in the software," I said. "Yellow jackets" was our shorthand for the Hozuki technicians, who wore immaculately pressed yellow sport jackets with their names stitched in Japanese characters on the breast pockets. Whatever their names might have been, they couldn't recognize our earnest attempts to pronounce Hirioshi, Nobuhiko, etc.

I put down my cup and leaned against the counter. This could take a while. "When they rolled my car in the pits garage, it started right up, and died. They couldn't restart it, so they're downloading all the telemetry and rerunning the race on their computer in Nagoya. The yellowjackets will have revised software tomorrow by modem."

"That's just great, Forrest. I don't care about glitches and software. Listen to me. How could you run into Russell?"

"It's great to talk to you too, Susan," I said, waving Merrie away. She was threatening more tea. "Russell got too close behind me. He was catching a tow down the straight. Catching a little extra to pass me on the inside going into that hairpin. And when he put on the brakes, he didn't have any downforce and his wheels locked up. He couldn't turn, he couldn't slow down and he plowed into me."

"Rubbish. I saw it on TV, so don't blame it on Russell. They replayed it five times. James Hunt was furious. He said you turned in too soon on purpose to knock Russell out of the race. You destroyed my team just to keep Russell from passing you."

"Oh well, if James Hunt said so on television, it must be true. Ask Russell if you have your doubts. And why are you blaming this on me? I thought you wanted friendship."

"Well, yes, isn't that a hoot? Silly old me wants to be friends with a geezer whose main claim to fame is pushing 'Formula One, the Sexual Attractor.' Splash on a dose of magic and watch the ladies spread their legs. I mean, really, Forrest. Doesn't that sound just the least bit primitive to you? Not to mention sexist and ridiculous? You men are such babies. You'll do anything for the promise of a fuck."

"Susan, you sound pissed."

"What?"

"Drunk. You sound drunk."

"I am not drunk. Just drink-ing. There's a difference."

"Look, if I didn't take Chantal's money, I couldn't drive." I was about to add that she didn't have any problems accepting their money, but she was off in another direction.

"That might not be such a bad thing. At least I wouldn't have to see you swanning around with Sam's bimbo."

"I didn't know Sam had a bimbo. What bimbo?"

"Virgin, dummy. Virgin met him at the Paris airport. Very touching. The two lovers flying in from opposite sides of the world to meet in Paris. Sam the 'embattled financier.' Virgin, 'the aging but still active megastar. The Financial Legend Battling for a Comeback.' It was in the *Daily Mirror*. I could look it up, if you like."

"It doesn't matter," I said. "We're just good friends." A weak joke to hide the knife sliding between the ribs. Keep it light, smile and keep dancing and playing the fool. Nobody minds, nobody cares. I didn't love Virgin. She wasn't what you would call lovable. But she had spirit, I thought, and for a while there we had been lovers. At home in each other's arms. And legs, come to that. What was Susan doing reading the *Daily Mirror*?

"Forrest, I'm sorry," she said. "I didn't mean to be so rude. I am a bit jealous if you want the truth."

"Jealous of who?" I wondered out loud.

"Virgin, naturally. Forrest, of course I want your friendship. I just don't want you smashing up my team."

I did the old male thing, what we do when we are presented with a peace offering. I hit back. "It's not your team, Susan. You sold it."

"Not sold, sell-ing. I've only signed a statement of intent. I'm signing the contract tomorrow morning. The lawyers are driving up from London."

"Tell them to stay in London. Don't sign it."

"Of course I'll sign it. I'd be a fool not to. Besides, I said I would."

"You still want to stay home and look after Josh and Sue Two?"

"Well, yes, of course. Sure. Except Josh is in school all day, and Sue Two gets cranky if I hang around her all the time. And she's got this playschool she goes to in the afternoon. So while you were all off to France, I was sitting here in this empty house staring out the window. I had this nice homey picture—Susan Joyce, Super Mum, arms full of happy children and a kettle on the stove. But if you want to know the truth it hasn't even been a week and I'm bored out of my skull. I miss you. I even miss Laurel and Hardy. I miss having too much to do."

"Can you hang on for another week before you sign?"

"What's the point, Forrest? We're getting further behind in our technology, we are losing money, half our sponsors are threatening to bail. I'm afraid if I start playing hard to get Sam will cancel the whole deal."

"You asked me to fix your contract if I didn't think it was right."

"I remember."

"I need one more week."

"I have to sign it. It's all agreed."

"You don't have to sign anything. Naughton hasn't put up any money, has he?" There was a pause. "His deal is wrapped around his putting up no money because he doesn't have any. You heard Castleman. Naughton's going belly-up in a week. You'll lose your team for nothing. You don't owe him anything, Susan. Make up an excuse. Say you need another week to research Emron, project their profits. Which is not a bad idea. Say your cat is sick. Say anything you like, it doesn't matter. If nothing else I think he's so desperate to get his hands on your cash, he'll double his offer."

"There isn't that much cash."

"One week. You said you wanted my friendship, Susan, and I'm working on it."

"I must be mad but all right. Work on it for one week, for me. If you'll promise not to run over Russell again. Give Merrie my love if she can stand it, poor thing. Take a little for yourself."

"How is the old bag?" Merrie said.

"She said to send you her love."

"Fuck her."

"For a racing driver," Merrie said, putting the last dish into the dishwasher, "you cook a lovely chicken. You'll make some woman a lovely wife."

"So people keep saying. I hate to see a woman eat out of a tin."

"It's not so bad. And it's not tins. I've got a fridge full of stuff I haven't even looked at, from the neighbors, the church, the women's committee. The local Conservative party sent a duck pie." She rolled down the ramp that Alistair had built for her, along the counters and into the middle of the old kitchen, the tires of her wheelchair squeaking on the polished floor, the motor making a hum like a refrigerator. "If we can't do it my way, then," she said, "how shall we kill him?"

"It's not a joke, Merrie. I want to expose him."

"All I have to do is roll into his office, leave a package behind, boom, blow him to bits. Simple." She was smiling lightly, throwing her hands up in the air in mock explosion.

"They wouldn't let you in his office . . . "

"If you are in a wheelchair, you may feel like a freak, but they let you in. He'll see me. You said he still wants to buy our company. How can he not see me?"

"He'd give you the package back."

"I'll wrap it like a present. Tell him it's a cake, something I baked myself."

"They will hang you."

"I'm already dead. And we already said all this. What do you suggest, then? Nothing?"

"Take your lithium and I'll tell you."

"I don't need any pills now. Let's go into the front room and build a fire. Then you can tell me your dazzling scheme."

We went down the passageway from the kitchen, past a row of hooks holding Alistair's faded green raincoat drooping over his green wellies. Next to that his gray sweater, capped by a shapeless rain hat. His umbrella leaned against a corner and an old brown leather jacket I had seen him wear hung with empty sleeves on the last hook.

On the sideboard, in the front room, there was a snapshot of Merrie and Alistair together, students, before the accident, arms around each other; Merrie looking straight ahead, Alistair smiling happily, looking down at his prize, the prettiest and brightest girl at Bristol. The leather sofa pulled in front of the massive walk-in stone fireplace bore the imprint of where he sat. Unfinished magazines he'd been browsing through lay on the floor. There was a stack of seasoned oak logs he had cut and split and stacked on the hearth. A basket held old newspaper, kindling and a box of long matches.

"Come on," Merrie said, "Alistair won't bite you. Pile it on, make it roar."

As I was crumpling the newspaper, breaking the kindling and laying it crisscross, I looked back at Merrie from time to time. She was wearing an old seaweed-green jumper of Alistair's, the stretched and pilling kind that Oxbridge men like to wear at home. There were dark circles under her eyes. Her face was thinner and her hair lay flat on her head. But her eyes were bright. And because she was slender and small, she looked as if she were an unruly child, playing at being in a wheelchair. As if she would stand up at any moment and walk away, bored with the game.

I struck a match on the cold granite hearth, lit the tip of an old *Guardian*, and the flames started slowly at first, then the yellow kindling began to catch and the fire roared into life. Look into the flames and you will see the first stories. Before there were stories, there were fires, with the stories waiting to get out. Look into any fire and there will be a cave glowing deep inside with the heat of an evil idea. Watch it grow, spout blue flames and pulse to its own hot beat before it goes black.

"If you can tear yourself away from admiring your work for a moment, Forrest, Alistair has a nice old brandy in the cupboard on the left. Not the one in front, over to the side."

I stood up. "No thanks, Merrie," I said, "I don't drink."

"I know. But I do."

"I thought you weren't supposed to."

"According to the doctors, a deep breath could kill me. Well I am a doctor of aeronautics. And as a doctor of air, I declare I have a right to take a breath or a drink whenever I want. The snifters are just above, on the second shelf."

I poured a glass of Château Perignon Napoleon Vieux Grand Fine Champagne Cognac, and Merrie swirled the brandy and sniffed, the flames reflected in her glass. She looked up at me as if she had asked a question and were waiting for an answer.

"What did the police say about the black box on Alistair's car?" I said.

She continued to look at me.

"The electronic management system. The microchip you were going to ask them to check."

"Oh yeah. I mean no. I didn't. I didn't do anything for two days after the funeral. I couldn't. It's one of about ten thousand things I didn't do. Is it too late? I mean what was the point?

"I thought maybe a computer expert could tell if the chip had been altered or replaced. Or if they found some receiving unit that would alter the electronic management system, stick its throttle open. Something like that. Something to expose the wizard."

"We're off to see the wizard . . . "

"That one. You remember when Dorothy whips the curtain away and the wizard is a little old man pulling levers to make great roaring sounds and thunder."

"Sure."

"Pull the curtain back and there is Naughton pulling the levers, throwing the switches."

"You're sure?"

"No doubt at all. Naughton killed Alistair and Phil, and he will try to kill me. He thinks I know how he did it."

"Do you?"

"You remember that morning when Susan and I came over from the hospital? What I heard on the earphones has to be what Phil heard—an attack dog that sounded real enough to make me jump. Both times they were Alistair's earphones. The ones he was supposed to wear. And when that didn't work twice, they set up the computer on Alistair's car to floor the throttle, turn out the lights and lock the ignition on."

"You think Naughton did all this?"

"Naughton doesn't have to do anything except wave his hand. One of Naughton's companies is a security agency, and two of their agents are working on our team. I think

Naughton told them to do it. I don't think he told them how.
I think they were also broadcasting interference with my
car's electronics at Silverstone. But I don't know how. It has
that complicated and screwed-up feel of a professional
operation.''

"No KISS."

"Kiss?"

"Keep It Simple, Stupid. The hallmark of all great engineering. You think that's why your car was cutting out at
Silverstone?'' Merrie swirled her brandy glass and took a
long swallow. Her face was no longer pale white with black
and blue under her eyes. In the light of the fire she looked
warm. A kind of red and gold. "Where would they broadcast
from?''

"I don't know. Anywhere.''

"Electronics are a bit outside my field, but I'd guess that to
break into the engine management system with an outside
broadcast, you'd need a lot of power. You couldn't reprogram
it from a distance; all you could do is screw it up with a heavy
electrical field. Or maybe they could rig up a kind of receiver.
Either way you'd need a directional antenna. Did you see anything that looked like an antenna?''

Thinking of Copse, and the engine cutting out, the image
came back to me. The broadcast truck at the end of the
grandstand just before Copse, where my engine had been
breaking up. It had been there for the session. And I'd
thought it strange for the broadcast media to cover tire testing. Usually tire testing gets a couple of paragraphs in the
motor racing mags and that's it.

"It wouldn't hurt to have an antenna for sonic VR either,''
she said, "for your phantom attack dogs. What do you want
to do?''

"I think Naughton is a killer. I think he enjoys it. I've
given him an excuse to kill me.''

"Sounds smart to me. You wait and see if he kills you.
And if he kills you, then you know he's the guy?''

"Then I'll know. I think I can jump out of the way.''

"Suppose he doesn't come after you, though. I mean, if it was Alistair he was after all along. Our poor old wind machine isn't any threat to him now. Maybe he wouldn't want to take the risk?"

"I'm going to rattle his reality cage. Do you know Tom Rayfield?"

She thought for a moment. "The comedian. Does impersonations. Like The Queen, John Major, Jackie Stewart. I've seen him on television, but I've never met him. I never meet anybody."

"He does a convincing impersonation of Murray Walker," I said.

"What are you talking about, Forrest?"

"I want Naughton to think he's watching a different race than the one that's happening in front of him and his senators. If Murray and James Hunt, or what he thinks is Murray and James, say the new aerodynamics of the car come from a virtual reality wind tunnel, he'll panic. He'll try to stop my car, make it crash, something. He'll probably try to talk to Laurel and Hardy, get them to do it. I want him to think that we have aerodynamically changed the car with your virtual reality wind tunnel and that we are winning the race."

"That winning part sounds like it could be tricky," she said, enjoying this.

"If I start the race with just a third of a tank of fuel, I'll have a tremendous weight advantage."

"Until you run out of petrol."

"Sure, we're talking about the first few laps. Can you make some large, obvious change to the look of the car that won't hurt it too much aerodynamically?"

"I don't think we could make noticeable changes to the wings or the underwing and the diffuser if we wanted to, and that's about ninety percent of the aerodynamics."

"Something obvious, visual, like the nose."

"I'm not sure what you want. Paste a lump on the car and call it aerodynamic? We could alter the body, that'd be obvious and wouldn't have much effect."

"Could we take a look at it tomorrow?"

"I guess so. I'm awfully tired." She did look exhausted, her brandy glass drooping from her hand. "I still think a bomb is a better idea. Do you know what software Laurel and Hardy are using?"

"They're plugged into our system, Cyrus, but they could have their own too."

"I'll have a look. Don't look at me like that—it's easy. I was into Alistair's software all the time. I'll give you a floppy disk. All you have to do is put in the disk, turn on his laptop and type GOGET. It'll suss out what the machine is and its operating system and what software they have. If I can get into Laurel and Hardy's software, I might find out how they did it. I might find out all kinds of things. Think you can do it? If you can, I'll make up another disk and you can alter their program with a couple of keystrokes."

"I'll see what I can do," I said. "You look ready for bed."

"Do you mind?" she said, pushing the lever on the wheelchair forward, wheeling out of the room and down the hall. She stopped at her bedroom door. "It's OK," she said. "I have to get undressed and all of that, and I'm getting better at getting into bed myself. A few more days and I'll get it right. All it takes is practice and not caring how stupid you look."

I bent down and gave her a kiss. "Your room's next door," she said, giving me a little peck on the cheek. "Sheets are on the bed. Hope you don't mind making it yourself. Loo's down the hall." She whirred off into her bedroom. I went next door, into a quiet little guest room with an old farmhouse bed and pressed flowers in an oval frame over the washstand. I made up the bed and lay down and went to sleep.

Chapter 28

"Forrest!" Josh hollered, running full tilt across the gravel for the takeoff and, thinking better of it, skidding to a stop. "Hi," he said. Mr. Cool again. "Bummer about Russell knocking you off."

"Yeah, bummer," I agreed, surprising myself at how glad I was to see him. "If I'd been looking in my mirrors, maybe it wouldn't have happened."

"That's what Mum says," he said, looking down at the gravel, walking alongside me. "But he was way out of control. No way was he going to get around that corner. He speared you."

"That's what I say," I said, hearing the stomp of little feet behind me. I turned just in time to catch Sue Two, flying in midair, arms outstretched.

Sue Two squeezed my neck, pressing her hot little face to me, and I gave her a squeeze back. "How come you guys are home this afternoon?" I said.

"Chicken pox," Sue Two said happily in my ear.

"Yick," I said, holding her out at arm's length, "you're all covered in red spots."

"I've got some," Josh said proudly. He did too. "Mum says if a man got it when he was all grown up, his nuts would swell up like footballs."

"I think that's mumps, but I'll keep an eye out. Where is your mum?"

"She's on the phone. She's been on the phone all day. Those lawyers keep calling her up. I had to make sandwiches for lunch,'' Josh said, looking up with a nine-year-old's version of an adult isn't-life-a-bitch look.

"Diss-gusting,'' Sue Two said, snuggling in for another choke hold on my neck.

"Lead me to her,'' I said.

Susan was indeed on the phone, in her office, going, "I quite appreciate, yes, I understand . . . Yes . . . Well, that may be, but . . . '' Another voice was squeaking on the other end. Susan looked up at the three of us with a beleaguered smile and an arch of the eyebrow. She was wearing tennis shoes, an old pair of blue jeans and a loose and faded Team Joyce T-shirt, and she looked terrific. High, clear forehead, soft brown hair. Those brown eyes were glad to see me, I thought. Or was it just me?

I took the phone from her and put it to the ear that didn't have Sue Two in it. A dry woman's voice was going, " . . . to consider our options because Mr. Naughton feels that it is really quite essential to move quickly on this, Mrs. Joyce, and I'm afraid, substantial . . . ''

"This is Elmore Guiness,'' I said in a deep, slow and important voice, taking my time. "Mrs. Joyce's financial counsel. Ring back in a week. Good day.''

"Forrest,'' Susan said, horrified and laughing in spite of herself as I put the phone down, "I'll have to call them back. You'll screw up the whole deal.''

"I certainly hope so. You have anything for lunch?''

The kitchen looked like a nine-year-old had been making mustard, mayonaise, banana, grape jelly, lettuce, ham, cheese and tomato sandwiches in the middle of a bread war. "Want me to make you one?'' Josh said.

"Make us both one, Josh, but skip the banana, grape jelly and ham, and I'll tell your mom about her new car.''

"Ham and cheese for me, Josh. What new car? Hey, no banana for me, Josh. Or Forrest.''

The phone rang in the office. We let it ring until the answering machine picked up.

"I spent the morning with Merrie bent over a hot CAD/CAM computer screen."

"How is she?"

"She looks tired, but she seems better, more relaxed. I guess you know how she is."

"I don't want to think about that. I think I'm almost over Phil and then I stumble across some damn thing. Like his face when he watched me get dressed in the morning. Anyway, what are you two up to?"

"She was working on different shapes and running them through a virtual reality wind tunnel program. We've come up with a new needle nose that rises," I said, shaping the air with my hands, "up steeply to a kind of hump in front of the driver. It has the effect of another small wing. And the vacuum behind it sucks away sixty-five percent of the added drag. If Merrie's VR figures are correct, the new nose will also quiet the air around my helmet so our heads won't get bounced around racing speeds. Are the transporters back yet?"

"Raymond rang me from a café this morning. They're still in France, locked solid in a roundabout outside Fontaine-bleau. Most of the strike is breaking up, so he thinks they could be back before midnight. Josh, stop messing about with that banana. We expect a complete lack of banana on both. What are you talking about, Forrest? You're not changing the shape, are you? What will they look like?"

"They'll look a bit like whooping cranes," I said.

That part, at least, was true.

Chapter 29

"Clarence has got flu. Where were you?"

"Having a ham-and-banana sandwich. Clarence?"

"Your head draftsman, Forrest. Clarence Harmon, and that just leaves Bill Henry and Cathy Bieber. Don't you know your own people? Alistair used to say you never left the ground floor."

"I was just going over there, see how they were getting along."

"You'll find Bill's tied up on fine-tuning the new diffuser."

"I thought that was out of the question."

"It was. But after you left, I was just fooling around, going through Alistair's CAD/CAM files, and I found a drawing he'd done of exactly what we were talking about that was virtually finished, and I think with proper heat treatment, we can make up a new one from your old one. If you know what I mean."

"The one with flexible walls in the venturi, to give me more downforce at lower speed."

"Yeah, that's the good news. All you have to do is take an existing one and modify a couple of dimensions in the exit and heat treat it. I think. The bad news is you can only have one nose and one diffuser because Bill is going to be tied up seeing that one through, and that just leaves Cathy for the nose."

"So I'll have one of each. Perfect."

"Each?"

"The reason Naughton was so pleased about the new engines is they let him off the hook. If the cars are faster, he can always say, 'Yeah, that extra power is really doing it for us.'"

"Is that the way he talks?"

"Surefire, sweetheart."

"Don't mock him, Forrest. You sound like a game show host. I still don't see what you are trying to say."

"If my car looks different from Russell's, and is much faster than Russell's with the same engine, then that swings the lens back to your aerodynamics."

"But it won't be much faster. I mean the new diffuser will give you a half a second a lap. At the most maybe three-quarters of a second, especially a fast track like Silverstone. And that hump in the nose could cost you half of that. Anybody who knows anything about aero will know the thing is a fraud."

"Merrie, the one great rule of racing is the same as the great rule of Hollywood. Nobody knows anything. You know it's an extra drag because you ran it through your VR wind tunnel. But nature gets weird out there on the technological edge. A lot of people thought Ferrari's double floor would work."

"They were all at Ferrari."

"Doesn't matter. The only person I have to fool is Naughton."

"OK, but even if he buys it, they may only have time to lay up one new nose. Once they get the buck right, it's an overnight. But it'll take most of the week getting the dimensions right on a new buck. If you run into anything in practice, or somebody backs into it in the pits, you might have to go back to the old one."

"I'll try to keep my nose clean. You sound better."

"I am. Much. Thanks for staying over last night. And for putting me to bed. I'm really grateful." Her voice sounded fuller, rested.

I wasn't sure what she meant because I hadn't put her in

bed the night before, but she sounded so much better I didn't want to rock the boat. I said, "Sure. Anytime."

"See you at the track," she said.

"You're coming to Silverstone?"

"I wouldn't miss it for anything."

"See you there."

Chapter 30

"Whatcha up to, sweetie?"

"I'm just looking over Cathy's shoulder at a new shape we've run through the VR wind tunnel. Looks promising for Silverstone. You are damn good at tracking me down."

In front of me Cathy was rotating the long needle/humpback nose on her screen, making a sour face to indicate her opinion of Merrie's new bogus aerodynamics.

"Yeah," the phone said, "I could have been a great hunter, zinging those arrows. Zap, take that tyrannosaurus. I miss you."

"Is that Naughton I hear breathing in the background?"

"That is the sound of your paranoia coming out your nostrils. Hey, what's with you, Forrest, he's a friend. He took me to dinner. He's worried about you."

"What's he doing in Hollywood?"

"This is Bel-Air, and it's a long way from Hollywood, which you would know if you came out here. You would also know that he is not here and he doesn't tell me all that much. I still think it's a good idea, your coming out here, I mean."

"Hollywood is crying for another actor."

"There aren't that many male leads. You got Douglas, Gere, Dillon, Willis, Gibson, Cruise, who else? Hoffman is over fifty and anyway he's a dwarf. Paul Newman is sixty-eight years old. There's not that many. Hollywood is short on hunks and you could do it. You have reality, kind of like a young Randolph Scott."

"Who's Randolph Scott?"

"Didn't you ever see any of those old Westerns? Scott was like Robert Stack, you know, always looking off to the horizon, only better looking."

"Robert Stack?"

"Forget it. Anyway, believe me, you have reality and that's scarce out here. You could be really big."

"How many big stars do you know who are happy?"

"Hey, Forrest. You want to be big and famous, don't give me that middle-class happy shit."

"Sounds irresistible, Virg. The British papers were full of you meeting Naughton at the airport."

"Great. That was Sheila's idea, 'cause she found our flights were crisscrossing. She's hooked up to Sam's PR, and they put it together. Whole shoot took around ten minutes. How many papers?"

"I don't know, I just heard about it."

"I'll find out. I'm coming to London in a couple, maybe three, four days. I'm really looking forward to seeing you. Sheila's organizing a shoot after the race. It's you all sweaty and covered with oil and stuff from the race, and me, I'm all pristine white with your dirty hands on me. It'll look really good. You know, when we finally got it on, I thought it was really special. I mean, I really like you, you know?"

"Tell Naughton we have a real breakthrough. We'll be right up front at Silverstone."

"Yeah, I got your message for Sam. You got any for me?"

"I like you Janice. I like you a lot. And when I heard you met Naughton at the airport in Paris, I felt like I'd been stabbed in the back."

"Hey, it was a shoot. I was outa there in fifteen minutes."

"I know. But it bothers me you never mentioned it."

"Forrrrest. If I told you everything I do, you'd die of boredom."

"Maybe, but it got me thinking that I like you, but I can't see us as a couple."

"What, living in a little white house with kiddies and shit? Holding hands in the movies? We could do that."

"You are a great game player, Janice. And it's a ball to play with you. But it doesn't feel real to me. It feels like a game."

"Well, play with yourself, then, if that's the way you feel. You are a real prick, Evers. I'll call you when I get in. If I feel like it."

When I put the phone down, Cathy looked up at me from her screen, rings on all four fingers holding her chin, raised eyebrows over her eyes, dark circles underneath. "Who was that?" she said.

"Alistair asked me the same question," I said.

"Well? What'd you tell him?"

"I told him I have no idea."

"You must be a slow learner."

Later that afternoon I rang Tom Rayfield. "Forrest," he said, "what a delightful surprise." The voice of several "Spitting Image" characters sounded light and relaxed, up-to-date BBC, which is central cultural Britain with just a touch of East London to indicate hip. You'd never guess he came from James Mason's old village in Yorkshire. "Wait'll I tell Harry you rang. He's a great fan of yours."

"Well, tell Harry I'm a fan of his." I was too. At age seven he could do the best imitation of John Major I'd ever heard. His Maggie Thatcher was good too, but his Major was even better than his father's. Another family I no longer saw after my divorce. "Are you busy?" I said.

"Keeping bread on the table."

"I wonder if you could do a Murray Walker for me."

"Sure, what for?"

"I want to fool an old friend."

"I guess so. As long as there's no harm."

"I want to prevent harm. Can you do it for scale?"

"Not for broadcast?"

"Strictly private."

"Sure. When do you need it?"

"Thursday would be good."

"Let me check. You have a studio lined up?"

"How about yours?"

"Glad to. Seventy-five an hour OK?"

"Fine."

"You got an engineer, or you want me to do it?"

"If you can, I'd like you to handle the whole thing."

"Sure, SFX, music?"

"Sound effects but no music. You know anybody does James Hunt?"

"Nick Salaman does a good Hunt. He's expensive, though. One fifty an hour with no buyout."

"No problem. Just don't take the whole package over a grand. You have a fax modem?"

"Sure. Wired to the world."

"I'll fax you tonight."

"Why don't you bring it yourself? Drive down. Come for supper."

"I would if I could, Tom, but there just isn't time."

"Never is, is there?"

"Give Helen a hug for me."

"For God's sake keep your hands to *yourself*," he said in his all-purpose indignant lady voice.

Chapter 31

Tuesday brought us a fine, lingering English summer evening, with the sun hovering on one horizon and the moon on the other. In the villages around Silverstone, men and women stood outside the pubs, looking happy and relaxed in the golden light, holding their pints and gin-and-tonics, flirting, telling stories and making plans, still feeling the warmth and light of the day even though it was almost ten P.M. At Pury End, the newly named Team EFORT were scrabbling like cats in a litter box.

The transporters hadn't got back from France until six P.M. on Monday. They were directed straight into a blockade just north of Fontainebleau and surrounded by angry striking truckers. They could have been stuck there for days if the rain hadn't driven the striking truck drivers into a café. Our ace lorry driver, Morris Hamilton, led the way by backing out. Just as he was about to drive clear, one of the truck drivers looked out the window of their steamy café, saw him, ran out and pounded on his truck with a jack handle. But Morris kept going. At the next roadblock he told the French truckers that "the guys down the road let us through" and they were let through. A police escort led them through the back roads to Boulougne, and they drove flat out up the Motorway and pulled into Pury End at six P.M., putting us just eighteen hours behind schedule. Jeremy Buckingham and the yellowjackets spent Monday at Heathrow, clearing the new Hozuki engines through customs while the mechanics stripped the cars and began rebuilding them for our test session at Brands Hatch on Wednesday. When the new engines finally cleared customs and arrived at five A.M. Tuesday morning, we broke open their crates.

These intricate magnesium, aluminium and carbon fiber lumps may be the true sculpture of the computer age. Just over two feet long and less than twenty-four inches high and wide, they could each let fly with over 750 horses. Or so we thought. Until we started to install the engines in the cars, we didn't realize that their black boxes, the electronic brains without which nothing happens, were missing. Phone calls to Nagoya in Japan at 7:45 A.M Tuesday our time had caught the Hozuki Formula One engineers just before they left for the day. Ah hi. Hi. No, no. Black boxes seplat shipment.

Armed with fresh waybill numbers, Jeremy, Hiro, Minoru and Takao raced back to Heathrow. After another day of wrestling with Her Majesty's Customs and Excise, they roared into the compound at six P.M with two small crates of black boxes wrapped in lead foil. In One Building, the mechanics and technicians were sorting out which box went with which engine, as the black boxes were all, according to Minoru's probing laptop sensor, configured "unsame." Which made me suspect that the engines were in different stages of development. So even if we could match the little computers with their engines, there was no knowing, without more phone calls to Nagoya, which had more staying power and which ones would blow up like grenades after a dozen laps. Nine-forty-five P.M Tuesday was six-forty-five A.M. Wednesday in Nagoya, and we would have to wait two hours before the Hozuki Formula One team arrived to answer our questions. While we waited, the yellowjackets were zinging faxes of serial numbers and urgent requests to get their team in Nagoya off to a running start.

In the meantime, the fabricators had found that Merrie's new nose didn't allow enough room for full suspension movement, and Cathy was busy on her CAD/CAM altering the hump-nose design. I was trying to remember when the last time was I had stood outside a pub on a summer evening when Sam reached out from Los Angeles and grabbed me by the phone.

"Fill me in, will you, Forrest," he said by way of greeting. "I just got back from lunch, and I've got fifteen minutes before I take my next meeting."

"Always a pleasure to hear from you, Sam," I said, and filled him in on the engines and our plans for practice in the morning.

"Well, keep on it. I want EFORT to put on a good show on Sunday. I don't think our friends from the House are going to make it, but I've got Senator Dickerson from the Armed Services Committee on board. We'll drop down at Dulles, refuel, gather the good senator up in our arms and land at Luton around eight A.M. Chopper will have us at the track by nine Sunday morning. Virgin tells me you're jealous. I'm flattered."

"Not jealous, Sam. Suspicious. You inspire suspicion in me."

"No need to be suspicious, Evers. I'd fire you if I could, simple as that. Virgin also tells me you are fucking around with the aerodynamics of the car. What the hell is that about?"

Inside One Building one of the cars fired up, and I had to shout into the phone. "I was hoping she'd tell you," I said. "We're going to put on a hell of a show for you, Sam."

"Jesus. I don't want any surprises. I need to talk to Susan. Can you put me through?"

"No trouble at all, Sam. See you Sunday."

By midnight we had it sorted out. Out of twelve engines, three were for qualifying, six were prototypes from various stages of earlier development and to be used only as backup, and three were for the race on Sunday. More race and qualifying engines would be shipped airfreight in a week, for the German Grand Prix. In the meantime we should use the latest of the development series for testing and work our way down through the deck.

Buckingham hadn't slept in three days. He wasn't going

to sleep tonight until the engines were installed. In the midnight half darkness of early July, he looked as happy as a schoolboy on holiday. I told him we never would have gotten the engines without him.

"Or without Naughton getting Hozuki to step up their schedule. Or God knows, Hiro, Minoru and Takao. They are *men,* Forrest."

"Glad to hear it," I said. Jeremy missed the irony but Jeremy wasn't missing much. Formula One is fueled by money and power, but all the money and power in the world won't win races. Ask Ferrari. The essence of Formula One is detail. Several million bits of information, not all of them important, need to be sorted, weighed and related one to another. In the equation of whether the car turns into the turn or crashes into the wall, you may include how the rebound rate of a shock-absorber bumper relates to the flex of the wall of the tire in the ride height of the underwing platform, which in turn relates to cumulative downforce and its effect on the coefficient of friction between the tire and the asphalt, considering the trajectory of the curve, angle of the tires, ambient temperature and mental state of the driver. Not to mention the infinite variety of several thousand mechanical bits and pieces, each of them with their idiosyncrasies of behavior under stress, deformation from ideal specification and position in or absence from our stockroom. And as Formula One time moves east and west simultaneously by satellite and jet in an intercontinental schedule, the great trick for a team manager lies in having all of this infinite detail come together in order on sixteen Sundays around the world, in a controlled two-hour explosion. With his financial training and Harvard MBA, Jeremy was doing just fine.

There was a crunch crunch of gravel in the soft night, and Susan was speaking before we could clearly see her. "What time do you think you'll be hooked up?" she said to Jeremy, moving into the light, looking tired and relaxed, and brushing her hair away from her forehead.

"Three if they slot in. We're fitting Dev one and two.

Leaving Race one, two, and three and the three Qualies on the shelf for Silverstone." "Dev" "Race" and "Qualies." Jeremy was inventing the jargon as he went along.

"If we're not testing the race engines, what are we testing?" I said. Brands is a narrow, bumpy, up-and-down twisting track. I love it, but it couldn't be more different from Silverstone, so there was no point in testing suspension and wing settings. The setups for the two would be radically different.

"From what Takao says, the major difference between Dev one and two and the Race engines is metallurgy," Jeremy said. "The Devs may not last as long, but their performance characteristics should be similar."

"I think as soon as they are ready," Susan said, "you better load them on the transporters and get on the Motorway. If we wait until morning, it could take three or four hours just to get down there. I've been on the phone to Nicola at Brands. She said she'll leave the gate open."

Jeremy went back to the cars in the building, and Susan said, "What are you doing, Forrest?"

"Doing what every good manager does. Helping out."

"I mean, what are you up to? You've been running around like a mad thing, and I want to know what it is about. What you are about."

Susan's kitchen was half-lit, with the light on over the Aga and the midnight midsummer evening glow coming in through the windows. "Do you have the tape? Could I hear it?" Susan said, pouring herself another glass of gin and tonic. "I suppose if anybody could imitate Murray it would be Tom Rayfield."

"I'd have to get it back from Emmett. He's setting up a tape player in the TV inside Emron's corporate suite with a remote switch so he can turn it on fifteen, ten minutes into the race. Whenever there's a quiet moment, he'll do a fluid interrupt."

"So your idea is that when Sam hears Murray and James

going on about the wonderful new virtual reality wind tunnel, that he is going to ring, radio or whatever Laurel and Hardy and have them arrange to have you crash."

"Right. And when he can't get through to them, he'll have to go to the broadcast truck and push the buttons himself."

"And," Susan said, pausing to take a big sip, "the crowd will see him punching the buttons as you go sailing off the course, because Naughton will be on the Diamond Vision screens."

"Fifty feet tall on five screens around the track."

"And you are serious about this."

"Emmett has already rigged up a race cam for the broadcast truck. He thinks he can patch into the Diamond Vision without them knowing."

"Rube Goldberg, Forrest, was a simpleton compared to you. And all of this is to get the killer on the screen where everybody can see him."

"If he's not a killer, then no real harm done. He won't ring Laurel and Hardy and he won't rush over to the broadcast van. But if he is . . . Naughton is so used to remote control, pushing buttons."

"You may be right about his business dealing, and I'm happy to take another look at my contract with him, but I don't think he's a killer."

"Who else, then?"

"Just because you can't think of anybody else doesn't mean Sam is a killer. He's a businessman for heaven's sake."

"He has several billion dollars at risk and if he doesn't get his wind tunnel contracts approved he's finished. He's desperate."

"What about me?"

"I think he sees a chance to get a Formula One team for nothing, and he'd like to get his hands on Alistair's software."

"I mean suppose I did it."

"Killed Phil?"

"This team which you accuse me of trying to give away is worth a great deal of money. And you know Phil and I didn't have a physical relationship. So there are two motives there. And you know that Alistair was here the night he died. Maybe you don't know that I had ended our affair."

"I didn't know that."

"We met, I guess that is the delicate way to put it, twice after Phil died, and it was awful. Somehow when Phil was alive, I could prop it up, telling myself that it was a way to keep my marriage together. To not resent Phil. That it was just a physical arrangement. All right. Alistair wasn't much to look at, but he was kind. And he adored me. And when you are lonely that can be a very attractive quality in a man. Even if you know you are anything but adorable. Even if you don't love him. After Phil died, all those excuses were blown away, and it was just a small, mean thing without love. And if you are lucky enough not to know, let me tell you, Forrest, that there is nothing like making love without being in love to make you feel empty. So I ended it. Alistair didn't want to, insisted on coming back one more time. So we talked it through again, that night, in this kitchen. He was sitting where you are and I told him I didn't love him. Besides," Susan said, getting up and walking over to the window, not looking at me, "there was something else. I told him I was in love with you. In love with you, Forrest, since the first time you walked in here. As stupid as you are. Isn't that just the best reason you ever heard for smashing Alistair to bits?"

"I didn't know," I said.

"No, you didn't and you still don't. You like to believe in all this damn technical rubbish. Computers and, what was it you said, 'fluid interrupts.' You believe in all that high-tech claptrap because you couldn't find your heart with both hands. Doesn't the thought occur to you that Alistair was upset, was simply driving too fast? I still can't accept that Phil's death was an accident. But there isn't any other explanation, is there? None that makes any sense. I do know how upset Alistair was when he left. If you want to blame someone, blame me.''

Susan had turned around and was looking at me, as cold as a poker player. I stood up and put my arms around her and she cried out with the pain of what she had been holding inside. ''You bastard, Evers,'' she said, crying hard, gasping for breath, ''you are such a hopeless, stupid bastard. Are you sure you don't wear that awful stuff?''

Over her shoulder, through the kitchen window, Jeremy was walking across the gravel toward the kitchen door. Time to go.

Chapter 32

Gregory Peck and Trevor Howard stand on the runway. They wear 1950s business suits with pinstripes and wide lapels and they both need a strong cup of coffee. Grass sprouts out of the cracks in the concrete, the hangars are rusting, with holes in their roofs, and in the background the old NAAFI is boarded up.

The wind is blowing hard across the high dome of land. Just the wind and the two men in suits stand on the deserted airstrip for a minute, listening to the wind.

Then there is a hum in the distance and then a roar, and the ground shakes as squadrons of Lancasters and B-17s fill the sky overhead and we pan back down to earth, where Trevor Howard is a kid with six weeks RAF training, coming in the front gate on a jeep, holding his orders, shouting, "Where the hell is STACS OPS?"

At the end of the movie, after their best friends have died and the war is over, Trevor Howard and Gregory Peck are on the cracked and weathered runway that runs through a farmer's cornfield, the wind blowing their hair and their business suits. Then they are gone, and there is just the runway running through the cornfield, and the wind blowing the corn stalks.

Which was how it must have been when the Royal Automobile Club turned the old bomber field into a racetrack in 1948 for the first postwar British Grand Prix.

The first Silverstone racecourse ran around the edge of the field, on the old airfield perimeter road. Halfway around, it turned down the main runway to the middle of the field and U-turned back out to the perimeter road. Then it ran on around the perimeter road to the other side of the field to turn down the main runway again, only this time from the other direction. It ran down to the middle of the field and U-turned back out to the perimeter road again. The RAC put up canvas screens at the end of the U-turns to save the drivers the distress of seeing another Grand Prix car hurtling head-on at full whack. World's first virtual reality safety device.

Silverstone still looks like an old aerodrome from the air. Down on the ground you have to look hard to find the old airfield underneath what they now call a Formula One facility. The old main runway (In '48 they called it Seagrave Straight and Seaman Straight, depending on whether you entered from north or south.) is still there. And the bomber hangars that haven't been torn down house businesses and a couple of Grand Prix teams. Still, on a quiet day in the middle of the week, something about the open space and the dome of sky reminds you that the home of the British Grand Prix was a war machine.

I love it. Silverstone is my home pitch and the heart of Britain's racing green. It is closer in spirit and in fact to Birmingham than London and layered with history if you know where to look. Hangar Straight, as you would guess, had a row of bomber hangars alongside. Club and Woodcote were named after the RAC's club in Pall Mall and their old Woodcote Country Club in Surrey. Deeper down, in the woods between Becketts Corner and Chapel Curve, there is the rubble of Thomas à Becket chapel. It was bulldozed to make way for the bombers. The chapel was built, they say in the local pubs, to make up for the family ancestors stabbing St. Thomas on the altar of Canterbury Cathedral in 1170 . . . a plot my ancestor, Everard of Norfolk, may have had a bloody hand in, since the King gave him half of Norfolk shortly after the murder.

Stowe is named after the sixteenth-century mansion of the Duke of Buckingham, now Stowe School. Abbey Curve and the double corners of Luffield are the namesakes of the four-teenth-century Luffield Priory. And the Priory's cornerstone, the original "Siler ston," was the altar whereupon the Druids let blood in the light of the moon.

So the old hilltop, scraped off for an airfield, was a fine site for a Formula One track. There always was a touch of blood and magic to the place.

It was early Thursday morning, and the mist was still hanging on the hills. But I was not early enough. Cars and busses, lumbering motor homes, their cupboards tinkling with bottles of booze and crystal, nosed the tails of Europe's most powerful transporters painted with the medallions of their sponsors and crammed with intricate electronic machin-ery. They idled patiently behind wobbling caravans on their annual pilgrimage to the fields outside the course. All inching forward, waiting to turn left off the A-43 toward the old airfield. The space-age circus of Formula One, a procession of marketing execs, promoters, mechanics, physicists, mar-keting managers, electronic engineers, journalists, public re-lations execs, Marlboro girls, TV crews, officials, fans, dogs and cats and at least one driver, was just another traffic jam on an island inching closer to coast-to-coast gridlock.

I looked carefully both ways, checked my seat belt and floored the Aston Virage Ford had loaned me, bounding up the grass verge. The back end slid over the edge of the ditch, and I steered into the skid, keeping my foot down, scrabbling for a little grip. The car straightened out, and there was a concrete culvert twenty yards ahead. No way to stop—I was doing about seventy-five, and going down into the ditch did not look inviting—but there was a wee gap. A caravan just before the culvert was a little slow on the uptake, and I spun the wheel left and right, onto the hard surface for the few available feet and back on the grass again, never letting my foot off the pedal, engine screaming into the redline and clods of green flying behind me, and I was grinning. It was going to be a great day.

At least it would be better than Wednesday. Had to be.

Wednesday we had arrived at Brands at four A.M., slept in hotel rooms by the front gate and woke up at six-thirty to pouring rain. Yes, we had checked the forecasts. Yes, the forecast had been for sunny and warm. No, we didn't have rain tires and we wouldn't have gone out if we had. So we waited, stranded, until the weather cleared at two in the afternoon. At three we ventured out, going around slowly, drying out the track. After five slow laps I came around Clearways onto the main straight, put my foot in it and the crankshaft broke through the engine and out into the countryside, spewing oil and expensive bits of racing machinery all over the track. It took half an hour to clean up the mess. Russell went back out, put his foot down in the back part of the track they call Dingle Dell, and his engine broke its crankshaft, locking his wheels and spinning him into the earth bank.

I was luckier than Russell. I didn't have his bruises and sore shoulder. And I didn't have to sit pinned in my seat while the rain started to fall again and wait for the tow truck and the ambulance to show up.

We got packed up in time for the rush hour, crawled around London on the M-25 and rolled on up that endless parking lot they call the M-1, getting back to Pury End at a quarter after nine P.M. to start stripping the blasted engines out of the cars and put in the new ones, with prayers that they did not have frag bombs for crankshafts. The only good thing about Wednesday, as far as I was concerned, was that while Laurel and Hardy went for coffee on that cold rainy morning, I had time to slip Merrie's floppy disk into their laptops. Although doing it made me feel like a sneak thief.

So even if I only drove through the gates of Silverstone, Thursday had to be a better day. "Drove" gives you the wrong impression. After my charge down the grass verge, I had rejoined the queue, practicing for that unhappy day when I became an adult. Inch by inch, forward toward the hallowed, bloody ground.

As a racecourse, Silverstone has a double nature. She can

be as sunny as the day in 1951 when she hung a laurel wreath around Florian Gonzales's neck for winning Ferrari's first Grand Prix victory. But she has a mean streak too. Like the day Graham Hill started the British Grand Prix on the front row next to Jack Brabham. Or rather didn't start. By the time Hill got his BRM fired up again, he was half a lap behind the whole pack. Graham drove the race of his life, sliding through the corners, passing cars on the inside, on the outside. He passed every car in the race. After seventy-seven laps, flying into Copse, comfortably in the lead with just five laps to go, his brake pedal went to the floor and he went spinning off the track. Some days it doesn't matter how hard you try, the weird gods of Silverstone will take it all away.

This is the track where Keke Rosberg cruised around to qualify for the 1985 British Grand Prix at 160 miles an hour on in the 1,200 horsepower Williams Honda, the fastest Grand Prix lap of all time. That sent the fat ladies back to their Slow-Down-Racing committees. And this is the battle-ground where Nigel Mansell feinted left, right and way left with his wheels on the grass, and then went right at over 200 miles an hour to take the lead from Piquet going into Stowe, to win the '87 British Grand Prix.

I inched forward cautiously. Another six inches closer.

And Stirling Moss. You can't talk about Silverstone without Stirling. In 1954 a hundred thousand fans came out to Silverstone to watch Stirling Moss drive his Maserati 250F. "His" Maserati because Moss had paid five thousand pounds for the car out of his own pocket. Fangio was in the factory Mercedes.

But before Moss could get to Fangio, he had to get past Mike Hawthorne in the factory Ferrari. For an hour they hounded each other, going through corners side by side, changing the lead four times. You never would have known if you were watching, but Stirling was not driving flat out. Stirling, who has always been careful with his money, didn't want to stretch his investment too much. Five thousand pounds was a lot of money. Stirling's mechanic, Alf Francis, put a red marker on his lap board signaling Moss to go for it, take the Maser to the limit. Moss went two whole seconds faster on the next lap, leaving Hawthorne in the dust and setting after Fangio. Moss passed Fangio on lap 55. No question of making up twenty seconds on Gonzales in the rain, so Moss backed off to make sure of second place. Then the Druids of Silverstone decided Moss had had his day and broke his gearbox. (They must have done it, because Maserati 250Fs never broke their gearboxes.) Stirling had to walk in. Mike Hawthorne finished second to Gonzales in the Ferrari, but Stirling's fans didn't care. Moss was the new young lion in Formula One. The next season Mercedes didn't want to take any chances, so they hired Stirling to drive alongside Fangio. And that's when Stirling Moss won his first British Grand Prix.

Media folks peeled off to the hut inside the gate to get their credentials, and the queue began to roll whole feet at a time.

Gonzales and Moss, Fangio, Jimmy Clarke, Peter Collins, Jackie Stewart, Emerson Fittipaldi, James Hunt, Clay Regazzoni, John Watson, Alain Prost, Ayrton Senna and Nigel Mansell all won at Silverstone. Just to drive there in the British Grand Prix is to be a part of history.

But history won't take you very far, and history had nothing to do with my grin. My goofy grin came from being woken up by Susan. I hadn't gone into the house until after midnight, and Susan was already asleep, which was fine by me. I was so tired I couldn't put two words together. I went up the stairs and down the hall to my room, stripped, showered and nose-dived into the pillow. The next thing I knew, Susan was shaking my shoulder, saying, "Wake up, Forrest, you old goat. It's morning."

Susan was wearing her faded blue silk robe, and her face looked rumpled and sleepy, younger than twenty-eight. She might have been a university undergraduate, a roommate. Her hand held a mug of tea for me. I took the tea and set it down on the nightstand, and took Susan's hands and pulled her down to me.

"Hey," she said, "I'm not awake."

"Then go back to sleep."

"Forrest, I'm not ready for this. It's too soon." She was tense, not sure what to do.

"Of course it's too soon," I said. "Just because I've hauled you onto the bed doesn't mean we have to go through the whole movie."

"What *are* you talking about?"

"I'm saying it's OK, Susan. Relax. We have plenty of time. There's a lot of tension around here," I said. "We can wait. But that doesn't mean we can't be good friends."

Susan relaxed and I kissed her on the mouth. She tasted of toothpaste and tea. Like coming home. "Besides, I've heard it's risky to sleep with the boss."

"You are damn right it is," Susan said, kissing me lightly.

"I thought you liked taking risks."

"It's your risk too," I said. "You know I am not a domestic animal. And I don't think I would be good for Josh and Sue Two so soon after Phil. Especially since I'd be away so much, tire testing in Brazil, shaking hands with our sponsors in Quatar."

"We don't have sponsors in Quatar. But yes, I know. I mean, I don't know, either," she said.

So we lay still for a while, our arms around each other, growing warm. And I could feel the tension draining away from her. Both of us feeling at ease and glad to be holding each other.

"I've got to get the kids up," she said, pulling away.

"Give them a hug for me," I said.

"You give them your own hugs," Susan said, bending down to kiss me again. "They deserve the best."

So I was grinning. There was indeed, plenty of time. In the meantime I had more than enough to do. Susan's no-fault theory was lovely and typical of her, but I didn't believe it. I knew in my bones Naughton was responsible for Phil and

Alistair, and I was going to make him famous for it. World famous.

A weathered official leaned inside my car, saw my FISA card and waved me through the gates. Emmett, low cap over his eyes, was waiting just inside the gate. I stopped, opened the door and let him in.

Chapter 33

"Bit dreary without the mo-ahs," Emmett said, looking out the window at the track. Emmett was nineteen, in his second year reading electronic physics at Cambridge, and he pronounced motors as if it had no t. He could also say, "ca coo a or" for "calculator" without breaking his jaw. Anybody who says an East End accent is lazy hasn't tried it.

We were in the Emron suite in the Paddock Club, overlooking the double corners of Priory and Brooklands and their mirror image at Luffield. "Try it," I said.

"I don' feel right abou' it," Emmett said. "I 'preciate it's just a summer security job 'nall, but I could lose it."

"No harm in listening," I said. "And I've already said I'll guarantee your job."

Emmett went over to the TV set and switched it on to BBC1. A breathtaking black woman in a red dress was reading the news with mild concern. "Rioting in Angola today," she said, "followed the shooting . . . "

As Emmett pushed a button in his pocket, a voice on the run like Murray Walker's said, over the whine and scream of racing cars, "Absolutely incredible the change in performance in Evers's Team EFORT car. While teams like Williams have been spending their millions on wind tunnels, would you believe EFORT has built a wind tunnel in their computer for next to nothing? That nose may look out of joint, but by Jove it works."

While the BBC picture switched to the ragged bodies of mortally wounded shoppers in Angola, Hunt's voice chimed in, "I was talking to Forrest before the race, Murray, and he told me their computer program will make the big aircraft wind tunnels as obsolete as dinosaurs."

The picture switched back to the BBC newscaster while Murray's voice said, "I'll believe that when I see it, but Evers will be making an important announcement about it after the race."

The newscaster's voice was back on the air. " . . . in Cairo," she said, "Moslem fundamentalist leader . . . " Emmett switched off the set, swiveled it around and popped off the fiberboard back.

"See, 'ere is the player with the microreceiver," he said, pointing to a small black box. "What it does is when I turn it on by remote, it picks up on the broadcast sound levels so Murray comes in at the same levels as what's on the air, so it's a fluid interrupt." He put the back of the set back in place, tapping it with his fist. "'Specially when you got, you know, racing cars 'n' all on the screen 'stead of the news 'n' shit. Although, I got to say, at the end of the day, it'd be whole lot less no'iceable if them two geezers you got on there didn't go on like they was 'avin a Sunday chat. You are stretching it."

"A little stretch is good for you," I said, picturing Naughton next to his senator, hearing Murray's voice. "Have you got the camera rigged in the CSN broadcast truck?"

"Took abou' ten maybe twelve minutes. I patched it in here so you can see it." He punched buttons on his handheld control panel and the TV screen switched to a fish-eye view of the control panel stacks of computers and blank video monitors inside the CSN broadcast truck. It looked like the inside of a submarine.

"And you've patched that signal into the Diamond Vision screens."

"No, I 'avent," he said. "They ain't even 'ere yet. I'm not sure if I can do 'cause I have no idea what sort of on-line detects they got 'n' all. And if I do get you on, it's not going to be for mor'en a minute or two, because they are going to see that on their monitors and they will find the patch.''

"It won't take long," I said. "Just switch to the signal when Naughton barges into the truck."

"You are really nuts," Emmett said.

Outside, the sun was shining and a small crowd had gathered around the Aston Martin. Kids with their dads, mums, schoolboys who had snuck in from Stowe. They held out their programs for me to sign. "Hi, Forrest." "Good luck, Forrest." I smiled and signed. Shook hands. Sure Hill was the favorite, I said, but we would do what we could. Nice to see you too. I slipped behind the wheel of the Aston and drove over to the main runway and down past the helicopter pads, through the gates and into the drivers' parking lot. I put up the top, got out and walked through the paddock gates and over to our purple-and-gold Team EFORT motor home. Even though it was only Thursday, fans were standing outside the paddock fence, fingers gripping the chain link, hoping for a glimpse of a Senna or a Schumacher. A couple of them waved to me and I waved back.

Gerald Berryman, motor-sports correspondent for the Gannett Newspaper Group, was helping himself to a cup of espresso in our forecourt. "What's new, Forrest?" he said.

"Well," I said, "we've squeezed a wind tunnel into our computer."

Chapter 34

The car rose up and stopped. Over my head a bright blue warm summer sky. I closed my eyes, hot inside my Nomex head and body sock, dressed for Alaska, with gloves, suit and helmet, my feet on the brake and the clutch. Slowly, from a distance, the sounds came back to me. The metallic clatter of the air jacks, as the mechanics swapped tires for a fresh set, the shouts of their voices. The engine giving me a vibro buzz. Somebody, Pat Hutchins, my crew chief, was crouching, leaning over the cockpit, shouting something. I nodded my head as if I were listening, but I didn't hear a word.

I am at Becketts, picturing how it will go, getting down into fourth on the decreasing radius turn and back hard on the power going left, just touching the inside curb, launching the car into the short straight up into fifth . . . running through my perfect lap in my mind.

We have time for one more flyer before the end of qualifying, one more chance to get it right and move up from fifteenth on the grid. Fifteenth is behind nowhere. Fifteenth is where the sponsors start to question their investment and look for escape clauses in their contracts. Where drivers are forgotten before they disappear. Where it is almost impossible to win the race. Where the accidents happen because drivers are trying to overcome the limits of the cars, and the limits can be crossed, but they cannot be overcome. Fifteenth is invisible. Fifteenth is violence and pain in the dark.

I cut short my frustration and concentrate on the track, on

who is out there. Brundle, Senna, Patrese and Cavelli are out there, and the two Jordans, Barrichello and Boutsen, and Fittipaldi, maybe, in the Minardi. The track is too crowded for a good run, but it is not going to get better. Brundle has been out for half an hour and may just stay out. Cavelli and Patrese are warming up for hot laps, and I will let them go by before I go out onto the track. Seven-and-a-half minutes left to the session, time to get two laps in before they close the course. A tap on my helmet and I open my eyes as the car drops down to the ground off the jacks, and I am off the clutch and on the gas, motoring down pit lane, up through the gears, taking my time easing out onto the track on the inside of Copse, checking my mirrors in time to see Senna turn in sharply to the corner, grow large and blow by me with a whoosh of air and an explosion of noise as if I were at the outside of a gun barrel when the bullet emerges followed by hot gas, grit and the vacuum that pulls you along for a moment, urging you to follow.

Senna disappears over the hill, and I am in fourth, hard on the throttle now, picking up speed, tapping the display button temp, oil pressure OK, back to revs.

There is no point in going at partial speed on any lap once the tires are warmed up. There is no point thinking you can turn up your confidence, commitment and concentration for qualifying and the race. These are all learned and practiced as hard as a concert pianist would, or a World tennis champion. A Formula One race is like facing Boris Becker's 115-mile-an-hour, twisting, skidding serve for two hours without a break. Before one ball hits the ground, another is coming off his racket. No taking your time staring into your own racket between points. Coming out of the left-right-left of Becketts, the grandstands are coming toward me, rising up out of the ground like a 160-mile-an-hour steel-and-concrete wave, and the time to deal with it is now, while the track sweeps right, tightens up and goes downhill.

When I am learning a track, I start out by learning a curve as a series of actions and committing it to memory, finding the line, thinking, Get on the brakes at the 150-meter marker, shift down a half a beat later, turn it at the beginning of a black skid mark that looks like a question mark. I learn that in the beginning, then I don't even think about it. If I think about it, I am going too slowly. When I am driving well, my mind is in another state, somewhere above thinking and feeling, where the two are combined and there is an abundance of time and space. When I am driving well, I am wearing the car, feeling through the violence of the noise and the g-forces accelerating, braking and cornering, feeling the adhesion of a tire, the compression of the rock-hard suspension, and my mind is already up at the curve ahead, setting up the car, entering into the perfect arc.

Coming out of Luffield on a flyer now, I am already urging the car up the straight past the start/finish line a quarter of a mile away. The car leans hard with both left tires all the way onto the edge of the corrugated, teeth-shaking concrete rumble strip at the outside of the track, and I stay hard on the power, the force of acceleration jamming my head back. I let up partway on the throttle for a microsecond, and tapping the clutch to shift from second to third to fourth, I turn into Stowe, where the start positions are painted in white on the track, and they blur at the edge of my vision because I am far down the track now, to fifth to sixth, with my vision focusing on the white dot, the little white 100 sign where I will begin to turn into Copse, where Senna, his car a tiny blur of red and white, is just turning in.

In the middle of the pit straight, just vaguely aware of the CSN broadcast truck on the left behind the fence, a Minardi, maybe Fittipaldi, is easing over to the right, letting me go by. Our pit is halfway down the pit wall, and I give them a raised fist as I pass. We are on this lap on the do-or-die of a qualifying lap. And I will give it everything I have. My hand drops back down to the steering wheel, feeling rather than seeing how full the stands are and feeling their attention follow me down the track. I ease the car left to position for Copse, go past the point where I would dab on the brakes with my foot still down, going an extra five yards in five-hundredths of a second, and quicker on the brakes and down to fifth and sharper turn in from the old corner, and I know I am going too fast, that the car will drift too far and hit the curb on the exit. Fine. I am coming in a little early, and I will just shave the inside where they've chopped off the old curb, letting my speed take me out. I am right on the power before the apex, going wide, feeling the front end start to push wide, inviting me to get off the accelerator and stay on the track, but I stay on the power all the way over the blackened curb on the exit, jolting hard against the black-and-white ridge on the edge of the corner.

The tire rides up on the top of the curb, riding up there for a yard, and I will the car on the track, and I stay hard on the power going uphill, getting into sixth before Maggots, which is really part of Becketts now, it's really a fifth-gear chicane and it takes total commitment all the way through. The steering wheel is stuck in cement, and I have to put my shoulder into turning it to move the car across the track and back, and across and back, just touching the inside of the curbs, just enough to reassure myself that I am using all of the track, but not so hard I upset the car, or get off onto the grass. The car is a four-ton 150-mile-an-hour bowling ball rocking from side to side, four g's one way and four g's immediately the other, and I am trying to control it with my fingertips and my foot on the throttle, keeping the power down. I feel the weight drag my blood from one side of my body to the other, and I weigh six hundred pounds sideways. The steering is stiff all the way through, with the car having maximum downforce, and I get down into fourth at the last kink because the car has scrubbed off fifty miles an hour through this double S, which I want back right now because the track is straight and I don't want to wait for it, accelerating hard. This last exit is the most important because it determines my speed down Becketts, and I stay off the curb, drawing out the exit, quick shift up to fifth and sixth, my hand darting out to the little wooden gearshift nob on my right and back to the wheel and back again, the movement faster than a card shark as I launch the car down the half-mile Hangar straight, dipping down under the Shell bridge overhead, the car bottoms hard on a dip in the track, sending a jolt up my spine and a shower of sparks hanging in the air behind me, and I first see a red-and-black car turning into Stowe.

The grandstands at Stowe rise up as massive as the old Berlin Wall, and if you pay attention to them, they lean into you like a wave. My eye is on the apex of the turn as I am easing the car in and braking, as the corner tightens up and I am shifting down from sixth to fourth, quick smooth dabs on the clutch and the corner tightens, drops down into Vale, and I am flat out in fourth, fifth, seeing the black car turning in, maybe a Sauber, then down to second for the left-hander at Club. The car feels cumbersome with no downforce and a rock-hard suspension so it slithers around on the bumps and I want to get on the power right away trying to accelerate but the Sauber's back end kicks out as he tries to pull over right too soon and I see his back wheels spinning, the car arcing out into my path and I feel a surge of panic, not for the almost inevitable crash, but at the thought of losing time, which I cannot do. My foot stays flat down and I let the car unwind, out to the edge of the track and beyond, the left wheels just touching the grass, sending up a cloud of dust and I am away down the track, down the inside of Abbey, having lost maybe a tenth of a second or more as the car takes a while to settle down, fishtailing for a few yards and I get on it hard, flat out through the inside of Abbey, and I don't relax, or think about the Sauber spinning behind me; my mind is down, under the Fosters bridge, banking into that great sweeping turn.

So I am on the hill coming down, from high, and dive down into it like a jet fighter plane. I get into the curve and feel the car compress and I sweep away. Two beats on the brakes and lots of g's going left, into not two but really just one corner. Same for Luffield, two curves really, one only right this time, being careful not to touch the curb and unsettle the car, and out of the corner hard on the rumble strip of concrete, and the long endless wait of time while whole tenths of seconds crawl by, moving me further down the grid, as I sit there, waiting for the car to drag itself through Stowe and past the start/finish line for as good a lap as I am going to get today.

Crossing the start/finish line, I punch the display button four times, and it displays 1:23.804 in cool green, my qualifying time, almost a second faster than I have ever driven before. As I am turning into Copse, the CSN broadcast truck on my left, I become aware of a screaming in my ear. Jeremy is screaming on the radio, *"Tenth Tenth. We're in the top third."*

I kept over to the right coming out of Copse, letting three cars go by. Tenth wasn't fast enough or high enough to stand out, but it would have to do.

Chapter 35

A whop-whop-whoppa-whop of helicopters whopped me out of sleep. Grand Prix Sunday, and Silverstone the airport emerges, reborn. Every helicopter in Britain still able to lift a load of marketing executives off the ground is up there, making Silverstone queen of Europe's airports for a day. Multiply two hundred and fifty pounds for a fifteen-minute round trip by three thousand times the average helicopter seating capacity and maybe you too will run out and buy a helicopter. Most of those three thousand landings and take-offs were scheduled for eight A.M., if the noise was anything to go by. One of them would have Naughton, Virgin and the senator on board. Listen for the bigger whop.

I was losing my nerve. Plenty of time before the race to get it back, bite the bullet. Take one of the mechanics aside and persuade him to fill the tanks a quarter full before the start of the race. Figure out a way to hide that deception from Jeremy and the yellowjackets, who would be looking at computer printouts of my consumption and miles to empty. Find a way to persuade myself to do it.

I couldn't do it. Even though it was my only chance of running with the front runners, it meant throwing the race. Starting with quarter tanks meant I couldn't finish, let alone win. And I just couldn't do that. Somehow it was all right if Naughton tapped a button with his pinkie and that knocked me out of the race. I was ready for that, had practiced in my mind going off at Copse, where it would happen again, in front of the CSN broadcast truck. There was a long, broad gravel pit, plenty of room. It wouldn't be pleasant, but it wouldn't kill me. But if I was going to race, I was going to race to win. Even though I knew I didn't have a reasonable chance. Starting from tenth on the grid, four whole seconds a lap down from Hill and three down from Cavelli, it would take more than a little luck to finish in the points. It would take a miracle to win. Even so, I could not start a race without enough fuel to win.

Could not.

So be it. The voices of bogus Murray and imitation Hunt would have to do the trick.

Along with the Goose Snoot, as the *Daily Mail* had dubbed my car's false nose.

I had slept late because I hadn't gotten to bed until after midnight. The night before, when I had gone into the back of my motor home to go to sleep, coming home from dinner with Susan and our eager sponsors at The Ivy, there was a lump in my bed. I pulled back the blanket and uncovered a small, naked teenage girl. She woke up with a fright, saw who I was, and sat up on the rumpled bed with her knees drawn up.

"Hi, Forrest," she said. "I fell asleep." She had a raw, bony redhead schoolgirl look. Freckles and dabs of pink on her pale and innocent skin. Somebody's little sister.

"How did you get in?" I said. Admission to the track took off at fifty pounds for the day, and access into the paddock required a special pass. The paddock was fenced in with guards at the gate. That would have been difficult enough. Lord knew how she had found my motor home and my bed.

"Easy," she said, drawing the sheet up over her nose like a harem veil and peering out with large green eyes. "I hitched over to Stowe School. And I knew this guy, Sam, we had a dance there, and I went with him and his mates through their special, you know, gate, where they sneak in. Then I walked in the paddock this morning holding this guy Dario's hand. He was really cute, a mechanic for Brabham, he said, but I think he coulda been justa gopher. Then I hung out for a while this morning, until you were all out practicing, and I just walked into your motor home. I hid in the loo most of the time. I'm not sure when I got into bed. Maybe like about six?''

"So you haven't had anything to eat for a while," I said.

"Not since a roll for breakfast. I'm starving. I mean I'm Linda," she said, smiling for the first time. "Come here, big guy," she said, letting the sheet drop. "Let's do it." The line she had been rehearsing.

I'll admit I felt a twinge of desire. And maybe even more than a twinge, but Good Grief. What I said was "Put your clothes on, Linda, and I'll get you something to eat out of the fridge. Then I want you out of the paddock."

She looked disappointed for a moment. Then, weighing the situation, she shrugged her shoulders and relaxed. "You won't tell anybody?" she said, reaching under the bed and pulling out a pair of blue jeans with her knickers stuffed in them.

"Not unless I see you in the paddock again."

"I mean that we didn't do it. This means a lot to me. I bet fifty quid."

"Get dressed," I said.

She told me between bites of cheese and leftover potato salad that she went to Langover School, fifteen miles away toward Banbury. "No way I can go back there tonight," she said.

I took her over to Marlboro, and Veronica, one of Marlboro's PR assistants, offered to drive Linda back to her school. I went to sleep with my sheets smelling of too much perfume and the musty and slightly acid smell of schoolgirl.

Eight A.M. was late for coffee, but I wanted a cup, so I threw on a pair of oat linen trousers (every Grand Prix driver should have a pair of oat linen trousers) and a purple-and-gold Team EFORT T-shirt, slipped into a pair of loafers and went out across the paddock to the Team EFORT motor home for a wee jolt before getting suited up. No food for we who bulk large in the cockpit. There's always the chance of a violent accident spilling open the contents of your stomach. I've heard Nannini used to drink forty cups of espresso a day before he quit. I think if I have just one, two, or at the most five, I won't have to quit.

The paddock of the Silverstone Grand Prix is one of the last of the great European esplanades. A grassy avenue thirty yards wide and a hundred yards long runs between rows of sidewalk cafés and the ornate two-storey motor homes, with awnings attached, of the Formula One teams of Williams, Ferrari, Benetton, Ligier, Marlboro MacLaren, Ligier and EFORT. And the corporate motor homes of Ford, Renault, Honda, Marlboro, ELF and Goodyear. The cafés serve breakfast and lunch to the teams and their wives, to sponsors, to journalists and to whoever the team or company feels like buying lunch. Entrance, apart from little Linda, is by invitation only.

Walking down the middle of the grass avenue, to the Team EFORT purple-and-gold awning, I passed Keke Rosberg in his new little round shades and his day-old cigarette. Jack Brabham and his son Geoff waved from the Ford forecourt. Two stunning brunettes in leather miniskirts gave me identical brilliant smiles from the arm of an Italian motor manufacturer who really was their father. Several rumpled journalists were parading up and down, trying to look as if they were heading for someplace while hoping for an invitation into one of the inner circles. David Hobbs, who broadcasts for ESPN, was talking to two journalists from *Autosport*. Eddie Jordan and John Watson were chatting to Williams Chief Designer Patrick Head. And Martin Brundle and his beautiful wife, Chris, were heading for the Benetton awning. Around the outside, at a distance, fingers pressed through the chain-link fence, the fans were already two and three deep, hoping for a glimpse of a hero.

Halfway to the little picket fence surrounding the clutter of tables and chairs and the spread of fruit rolls and hot plates of breakfast at Team EFORT, I was stopped by Alton Barker, motoring correspondent for the *Adelaide Express*.

"Morning, Forrest," he said. "What do you make of the 'Fuck Yourself, Forrest' banners?"

"Love 'em," I said, going past him into the EFORT breakfast, where he could not follow. I had seen the banner, draped over the side of the grandstand at Becketts. It was part of what Panaguian called "marketing backlash." Whatever you called it, there were definitely signs of a growing resistance to Formula One, the "sexual attractor." Several of the women's pages had denounced Formula One as "manipulative," "sexist," "male chauvinist" and "the lowest common denominator in a bullshit male attempt to subjugate, humiliate, dominate and impregnate women." That last, quoted in *Private Eye*, first appeared in the radical feminist weekly *Trenches*.

The Guardian had run a test on the stuff and come to the conclusion that far from being an attractor, Formula One was a "repellent." "If Chantal's stand-up dummy Forrest Evers can win women wearing the stuff," *The Guardian* concluded, "maybe Chantal should consider bottling him." Being a sex symbol was wearing thin.

At eight-fifteen on race morning EFORT's tables under the purple-and-gold awning were nearly full. I waited in line, thinking coffee while Rennie MacAlister, a round and balding journalist from *Trackside*, helped himself to eggs, bacon, beans, mushrooms, tomato, sausages, fried potatoes and toast. "Tough day?" I said in his ear as he speared a third sausage.

"Oh hi, Forrest," he said. "Not as tough as yours. When's Virgin coming in?"

"She's not going to like it when she gets here and sees you've wolfed down her breakfast."

MacAlister looked back at me and speared a fourth sausage. "You must tell me about your new nose."

We sat down, and I said, "My new nose is a way of getting more downforce on the front wheels and less buffeting for the driver."

"No, really," MacAlister said through a mouthful of sausage, eggs and potatoes. "What's it all about? I mean, obviously it's not cosmetic. Do you think it's made the half second difference between you and Russell?"

"More than that, Mac," I said. "Russell has a habit of qualifying a half to a full second faster than me," I said. "So the difference could be as much as a second and a half."

MacAlister paused for a moment, pulled a small, flat leather-covered notebook out of his shirt pocket and scribbled down the figures. "Why isn't Russell driving it then?"

"Because I am the team manager," I said, finishing my cup of espresso and getting up. Across the lawn a blaze of flashing lights was headed in our direction. "Mac," I said, "just out of curiosity, what would it be worth to you for an hour alone with Virgin?"

"Exclusive?" he said, his eyes brightening with hope, dreaming of covering fields beyond motor racing.

"You'd have to be naked so she could be sure you weren't carrying a microphone or a camera. Just pen and paper."

"I could do that," he said.

"I'll see what I can arrange," I said. A flash of light made me turn around. Naughton's silver head was above the moving swirl of photographers and journalists. The photographers were jumping in the air, holding their cameras straight up over their heads, to take flash shots of Virgin and Naughton. Their acrobatics gave the moving crowd an air of a circus coming to town.

Virgin broke free, running toward me. "Forrest," she cried, arms flailing, trying to run in the soft grass in silver-leather sling-back platform spike heels and a pin-striped business suit with a tight short skirt, all buttoned up with a dark silk tie, her hair still short, close cropped, but jet black now. Her face was translucent, pale, with dark circles under her eyes. Virgin running toward you is like being at the focal point of a searchlight. All the faces turn toward you. She almost tripped over her flopping sling-back heels, and I jumped over the fence to catch her. It can't have been an easy flight, I thought, all the way from Los Angeles with a stop at Washington for the senator.

As the cameras flashed behind her, she did fall, reaching out with dark red fingernails. I caught her under her arms to keep her from going face-first into the wet grass.

"Why the hell didn't you call me, you dumb fuck?" she said as I pulled her up. Then she threw her arms around me and gave me a big smacker, smearing my mouth with fresh lipstick as the cameras flashed. She pulled back to face the flashing lights, grinning wildly. Then she sniffed. And sniffed again, and whispered in my ear, "Give the bimbo you're sleeping with a tip for me, will you, sweetie. Tell her to spend more money on less perfume."

Chapter 36

It may be that the real stars, like Virgin, sparkle in their own eyes. I can tell you that the bright life loses some of its luster when you see it from behind the footlights. On the one hand we had photojournalists flashing away and three TV cameras rolling while the soundmen pointed their directional mikes at us, hoping to pick up a key phrase. Something the gilded people said. Which was wonderful for Team EFORT and our sponsors. Your modern Formula One car is an upside-down wing doubling as a marketing platform. So the hotter the glare of publicity the better.

On the other hand I was sitting in front of a plate of rubber eggs and bacon, watching the grease congeal, out of my element with a woman who was clearly in hers, facing a man I despised and a United States senator who was trying to ask intelligent questions. To which I was trying to give intelligent answers while I ignored sharp kicks from Virgin's pointed shoes under the table. The noise from the helicopters taking off and landing, punctuated by the scream of a Formula One engine from the pits, meant we had to shout. To the cameras and the faces peering at us we may have looked like we were having the time of our lives. I don't know what anybody else at that table thought, but I could not wait to get out of there, have a shower and get into my driving suit and my race car.

"What," Senator Dickerson wanted to know, "are you doing about the environmental issues?" The senator had, as people who live in the middle of nonstop demand for their attention do, a limited focus. Blinders evolve with the power. I didn't blame him; he represented interests. It was his job to be informed on "the issues." The Environment was the hot one, no doubt, in his home state. Soon to be the hot one in Britain. And he'd had a rough trip. I imagined him coming out of some senate subcommittee on revenue enhancement, crawling across the hot smog of Washington in rush hour, to the airport, cooped up in a small jet overnight, with no sleep to speak of and spit out of a helicopter into a foreign spectacle he didn't understand.

"We're talking about them," I shouted across the table. He looked puzzled. "The environmental issues. I think we'll all use pump gas pretty soon," I said.

"What the hell do you use now?" he said.

"They use the same stuff," Virgin said, "that makes Evers irresistible to women. It smells like cat's piss." She gave me a tender kick under the table to emphasize her point.

"Yeah, but does it work?" said the senator. "And can you get me a bottle?" His face was young, on the verge of sagging around the jowls, with a blurred copy of Jack Kennedy's cresting wave of hair over his low forehead.

"You better believe it works for Forrest," Virgin said, sliding her shoe behind my leg.

"I'll get you a bottle, Senator," Sam said, looking at the photographers and squinting at their flash guns. "Maybe it'll work better for you than for me."

"You don't need it, sweetie," Virgin said.

I wondered what she was doing under the table with her other foot.

"What interests me is the technology," the senator said over his coffee cup, slipping into his sound-bite mode with ease, his voice rising enough to be overheard. "Nations arm themselves with the weapons of the past. While wars are won with the weapons of the future. I think the great battle of the future will be for the environment, and I was hoping your sport might be evolving some relevant technology. I read about automatic transmissions, traction control, active suspensions. You Emron guys don't seem to have any of that.''

"We have a wonder of an aerodynamics program," I said.

"I expect you do," the senator said, putting down his coffee. "Although I hope you don't charge yourselves what Sam here wants to charge us for his wind tunnels." He gave Sam a big confident one-up look. Just sticking the needle in.

"We don't use wind tunnels, Senator. Wind tunnels are out of date," I said. I got up to go. "You'll have to excuse me," I said. "I've got to get into my costume."

"What do you wear?" the senator said, breaking into his big vote-getter grin. "A cape?"

"Layers of fireproof Nomex," I said. "So I don't end up looking like the bacon on your plate." I shouldn't be allowed out before a race. I become irritable, distracted and heavily unfun to be around. My ex-wife, Susan, called it my PRTs: Pre-Race Tension.

"You'll have to excuse me for a moment," Sam said, standing up as I left the table. "I want to talk to my driver."

Sam walked alongside me across the grass until he was sure we were out of the senator's range, and then he put his hand on my arm to stop me. "What the hell is all this business with the new nose?" he said. "It looks like a joke. And I don't want you talking to any media types about it. Wait a couple of weeks and you can say whatever the hell you like. Right now I want you to keep your mouth shut. And for Christ's sake stay off of wind tunnels. You are way over your head."

"Oh hi, Forrest." Merrie's bright, clear voice rang out over the noise of the helicopters. She had rolled up behind Sam, and he stepped aside. She had on a soft, clingy white dress and white shoes with heels. She had traced on bright red lipstick. With her dark hair and pale skin and those eyes too large for her tiny face, she looked vulnerable and beautiful and exhausted.

"Hi," she said, holding out her hand, her other hand holding onto her laptop computer. "You must be Sam Naughton. Alistair used to talk about you all the time. If I knew you were coming, I'd have baked a cake.''

"Glad to meet you Mrs. uh . . . "

"Benkins, Merrie Benkins. Maybe you don't remember, I'm Alistair's wife. Or was. You know what I mean. So pleased to meet you.''

"The pleasure is all mine," Sam said with a cold face. "I didn't expect to see you here.''

"Alistair got me a permanent pass, so I managed to get to most of the European races," she said. "Are you ready to see Forrest amaze the world?" Then she turned to me, barely drawing breath. "Where's Susan? I thought she'd be wrapping herself around you by now, Forrest.''

"We do expect great things from our new Hozuki engines," Naughton said, trying to change the subject, giving Merrie his official corporate line.

"Oh well, the engines," she said, waving her hand in the air. "They are Japanese. Any extra performance we get comes from our aerodynamics.''

"Merrie, if your 'aero' can give us half the eighty horse-power the Hozuki folks have given to us, we have a lot to talk about. I've always had a lot of time for your company. Was even interested in acquiring it at one time. What do you call it, Soft Air? Why don't you come watch the race with us at the Emron suite?''

"Thank you, Sam," she said, nodding primly. "I'm afraid I already have a wonderful spot down on the track for the race. And I've still got masses to do," she said, turning her chair to me. "Give me a kiss, Forrest. I haven't had my good-morning kiss yet.''

I bent down and kissed her on the cheek. She looked up at me, her eyes bright and her mouth set. "Wow, that was sure sexy, Forrest. I don't know who gave you the lipstick, but you ought to give me a chance sometime. Don't you hate it when people kiss you like you're a cripple?" she said to Naughton. She started to wheel away, then whirled back to face us. "Don't you worry your pretty head, Evers. I'll have it all set up. Nice to meet you, face-to-face, Mr. Naughton.''

"Is she all right?" Naughton said, watching her roll down the grass and between the Jordan and Minardi motor homes, toward the pits.

"There are days when she forgets her lithium," I said. "And she's thinks Alistair was murdered."

Sam winced at that. "Where is Susan? I need to see her. I need to be sure we are giving the same message to the media."

"Keep your eyes open, Sam. She'll be here."

Susan, I was glad to see, was already there. Waiting for me in my motor home. She slid out from behind the table opposite the fridge, wearing loose silk shorts and a short creamy top with a scoop neck, and stretched up to put her arms around my neck to kiss me but stopped. "If you are going to wear lipstick, Evers, put it on straight."

"Virgin put this on me," I said. "I don't think she cared about her aim."

"Well, I was going to give you a doozer from Sue Two. But I think I will wait until you clean up the skid marks. Virgin?" she said, taking a step back. "What are you doing kissing that pop reject? God, I hate following in somebody else's lip-prints."

"It's in my contract," I said, grinning, glad to see Susan.

"Hi, Forrest." It was Russell. I had been so intent on Susan I hadn't seen him sitting on the sofa in the gloom. "You guys go ahead. I'll just sit here and get sick on the carpet."

"I'm sorry you don't approve. We were just warming up," Susan said.

"It's not you guys. I just feel terrible. Like I'm going to barf or something."

"Don't worry about it," I said. "It's Silverstone Fever. Every Brit gets it before their first British Grand Prix."

"That's great, Forrest, but I think I'm really sick."

"That's because you have about a half gallon of adrenaline sloshing around in your veins. It feels like fear, but you'll feel fine once you get out there on the track. Just take it one corner at a time. Naughton is looking for you," I said to Susan. "He says he wants to talk to you."

"I know. He has a list. Sign the contract, sign the contract, sign the contract. Then he goes, how do we get rid of Evers?"

"He's got Virgin and Senator Dickerson with him."

"I'll try and keep a straight face. I did promise I'd see the race with him."

I started back toward the bedroom to shower and change. "Just don't believe everything you see on television," I said before I shut the door.

Chapter 37

Phil Bullmore, who has been with the RAC for thirty years, holds up the "One Minute" sign. One minute stretches out over the horizon and disappears into the gray English sky. It will be forever before the race begins. I am concentrating on the left rear tire of Capelli's Ferrari in front of me. It is a way of passing the stalled time, staring into the black sticky surface with the grit of small stones and a piece of gum wrapper imbedded into the rubber.

There was a time, it seemed like years ago, although it could only have been a half an hour back in real time, when we went around the track for a parade lap. I passed the CSN broadcast truck as I turned into Copse, and I thought of my far too complicated plan: the BBC broadcast with the bogus announcers, and Naughton, unable to raise Laurel and Hardy on the radio, charging into the CSN truck, and pressing the code into the computer, sending me off into Copse as his guilty image loomed on the giant TV screens around the track. And I had thought, as we cruised around the track, that if I were smarter, I would have thought of a simpler scheme. But it would have to do. It was the best I could do and it would have to work.

For Phil and for Alistair.

That was gone now. My mind was as empty as a cup, waiting for the green light, engine buzzing at 2,500 rpm, clutch in, just waiting. Overhead a small flock of birds flutter in the cloudy sky and I sense the urgency of their flight, in a hurry to get across the noisy open space before all hell

breaks loose and I bring my eyes down to rest on the red
light. I watch the dark red light, waiting for it to come on,
aware of the cells in the lens, the red tint of the glass and
the dirt on the surface of the lens. The light bulb behind the
lens illuminates and I bring my eyes down to the darkened
lens of the green light, waiting for it to go on in two to seven
seconds. Around me twenty-five cars join the scream of
mine. My right foot is on the brake and the accelerator, and
the side of my foot has the revs up to eight thousand, as I
watch the darkened green glass for the light to go on. Patient
as a cat waiting for a bird to drop down one more branch.

No hurry. It will come. I concentrate on the bulb behind
the glass. I can't see the bulb, but I know it is there, and
when it first begins to glow as it warms up to full illumi-
nation, I am lifting off the clutch and getting my whole foot
down on the accelerator, bringing my eyes down to ground
level, to the spinning tires throwing grit and smoke along
with the rage of hot gas and the smell of burning dry-
cleaning fluid.

Cavelli in the Ferrari in front of me has begun to move,
spinning his wide wheels and the back end starting to slide
out to the left, too much power too soon. I move right, my
wheels getting more grip, and move alongside him as the
back end of his car swings back toward me, keeps on coming, and I edge over next to the concrete wall of pit lane,
shifting up from second to third, accelerating now as hard
as the car will go, doubling my weight, forcing me back
against the car. We are too close for comfort. If I touch the
wall, the wall will grab my wheels and pull me into it. Or
worse, bounce me back into this insane charge of power,
noise and wheels going a hundred miles an hour and accelerating hard. But there is a gap, clear to the front of the field,
which is moving over to the left, lining up for the entry into
Copse. I keep my foot down.

An inch now from the wall but clear of Cavelli, and I
move away from the wall and in front of the Ferrari, shifting

into fourth about 140 miles an hour, still accelerating hard when one of the Lotuses six feet in front of me suddenly slows and I am on the brake, not hard, but enough. My nose just touches the gearbox of the Lotus.

No damage that I can see. I don't know what made him slow. Traffic.

Back on the accelerator again, and I want to get over, to the left to line up for Copse, but we are three across. The car on the far left, on the outside of the track, is blue, a Ligier, half a car in front of the car in the middle, French blue, must be a Ligier who just has his front wheels in front of mine, so they could both drive right over my new nose turning into the first turn in the race. I am accelerating as hard as I can, two feet behind the car in front. I want more track. I want to get in front of the Ligier alongside. At the same time I am watching the exhaust pipes of the Lotus in front. They are buried deep behind the horizontal suspension arms, but I need to see them to give me the first alert that the car in front is slowing down. I want his space. Everybody is in everybody's way, and we are all slowing one another down, looking for an extra inch.

Up front, the lead cars are already around Copse, soaring uphill into Becketts, flat out. I am in the middle of the herd, still trundling into Copse. You can't win the race in the first corner, the old saying goes, but you can lose it. And I almost do. The Ligier and the Lotus alongside me touch, and the Ligier goes airborne for a moment. But I am already turning in, keeping the power down and looking for a way around the Lotus, must be Herbert, in front.

Herbert pulls away from me going up the little rise into Becketts. He has the new Ford V-8, and it looks like he has more horses than my Hozuki.

By the time we cross the start/finish line at the end of the first lap, Herbert has a half-second lead on me and my pit sign reads, ''7.'' So I have moved up three places. (I passed Cavelli at the start, and the Ligier and the March went off at Copse.)

The race settles into a single file. I am a second to two seconds behind Herbert; Cavelli is two seconds behind me. By the tenth lap I am more relaxed, falling into a rhythm, taking time to glance up at the big Diamond Vision screen, looking for Naughton's face. Thinking it should be any moment. It depends how long it takes Naughton to get to the CSN truck.

And I am ready, every time I turn into Copse, for the engine to cut and lose downforce. Thinking I will not try to hold the line but let the car run wide onto the generous run-off on the other side of the curb on the exit.

Twelve laps go by. Nothing happens.

I try to make up time on Herbert through Stowe, turning in faster and running wider on the exit, and find that it works. I can gain five yards on him there. But he seems to be able to get on the power sooner than I can coming out of Club, and by the time we are coming across the start/finish line, he still has two seconds on me. Almost two hundred yards.

Fifteen laps. Still nothing on the big screen.

On lap 18, as I was committing to Copse, just a dab on the brakes and down to fifth, turning in and starting to roll on the power, two things happened. Just as I caught sight of a marshal on the inside of the corner, waving a yellow flag, my motor coughed and died. That quick. Then turned on again with a vengeance, full roar and would not let up.

The other was a wheelchair, coming toward me. A white figure in a dark chair rolling. White dress fluttering in the wind.

I would like to think that I had some control. That I stood on the brake and turned away. I didn't. I was traveling at almost ninety yards a second. Merrie was coming toward me at whatever the speed of that device was, forty miles an hour maybe. So we were approaching each other at something over two hundred miles an hour. I started to lift off and put my foot on the brake and the clutch and turned the wheels and there wasn't time. And there was the distraction of the engine soaring on, screaming up into the redline, over 14,500 rpm, though I had started to lift. One second I was turning into the corner, committing myself to the arc all the way through to the curb on the exit, and then, within that same moment, she was there, coming toward me, one hand on the control box at the end of the right arm of her wheelchair and the other on her laptop computer.

Merrie reached out to me with both hands, and I would say her mouth was open, half smile and half kiss, inviting. But that must be my imagination, as the nose of the car struck her feet, pitching her face-first into the nose of the car just in front of me, shattering the fiberglass and throwing her up overhead into the sky. The nose of the car slid under her chair and plowed into the six 12-volt car batteries, exploding them, sending a heavy shock through the car and jerking me hard forward through the pieces of fiberglass and wheelchair suspended in the air.

I felt the car start to spin, and I caught just a glimpse of the big blue TV screen, where there was not Naughton's face but a white-and-red rag doll tumbling through a sky littered with the wreckage of her wheelchair, my car and, just behind her, her laptop computer open, sailing through the air. By then my car was out of control, self-destructing. My feet were standing on the clutch and the brake, and I remember hearing the engine blow up with a bang, as the car struck the curb, rose up into the air then plunged into the pebbles, sending them up like spray. I lost consciousness so I didn't see Merrie rise high up into the air, tumbling like an acrobat, and dive in a long arc headfirst onto the black track. Or the three cars swerve and go off the track and into the gravel pit in the few seconds before they waved the red flag and stopped the race. That spectacle I saw later, when they played the tapes over and over before they determined that it was not really my fault.

Chapter 38

As I was coming to in my car, I saw Merrie's face again, looming up out of her wheelchair to greet me. She was flying, her hair streaming in the wind, her eyes wide and bulging and her mouth red with lipstick and open for a kiss before bowing down and into the nose of my car. It was an image that would come to be an old friend, and I expect the shock of seeing her, of seeing me hit her, must have struck me with as much force as the impact of six 12-volt car batteries at over two hundred miles an hour. Later I would find that my body was crisscrossed with cuts and bruises from my safety harness.

The fire marshals were quick to realize that the fizzing on the fiberglass and exposed carbon fiber of my car was battery acid. And that if the acid was on my car, it was probably on me. So they were soaking me with water when I came to. Someone had taken my helmet off, and cold water was splashing on my face and my feet. I was too tired to unbuckle my seat belt. And I thought how good it would be to just lie there, in the cool water, and not have to face the wreckage outside. Not have to face what I had done.

It was so blindingly obvious now. Poor, sad, ferocious girl. Alistair had crippled her, cheated her and hidden her. She had tried to kill him twice. And she kept trying. Killing Phil and almost killing me that day when Humpty-Dumpty fell off the wall. Plenty of power in those six 12-volts to broadcast to Alistair's headphones. Plenty of chances to program Alistair's car. And mine. I had even helped her do that. I had even helped her to kill herself. I wondered if she had designed the nose of my car to throw her up in the air and out of my way. Poor sad damaged woman. Deluded wrong-way Forrest. Chasing after Naughton. Don Quixote had charged the windmills and stuck his lance in the air. And killed her.

Voices were coming through to me. "Are you OK?" "Can you move your feet?" "Do you feel any pain?" They had red-flagged the race, and anxious faces were peering over me. One of them was saying, "I'm really sorry, Forrest. I should have stopped her. She had a track pass, so I thought she was OK, Forrest, and she just rolled right past me out to where the photographers were on the inside of the turn. I thought that was OK, she had the pass. But she didn't stop. I tried to catch her, Forrest, but that thing was fast as hell."

I did a slow mental cruise through my body like an airline captain going through his preflight checks. My feet could move, calves, knees, thighs, hands and on through to my neck and head. I was dripping wet but no more than bruised.

The doctor was leaning over me, asking if I was OK. A moon face with a mustache and a red shirt. "I'm all right. How is she?"

"She is dead, Forrest. Before she hit the ground, I expect." His face was as white as milk, and he was shaking. He had seen her. "Can you walk?" he said, standing up. I unbuckled my harness, put my hands on the side of the car and pushed myself up. Wobbly but OK. Fifty yards away, they were closing the door of an ambulance, shut. No blue light going. No need to hurry. What was she like, I wondered, when she was a student? I walked across the track.

By the time I got to the other side, I was surrounded by track workers and marshals, by fans and reporters who had run out to the scene, and yet I had this peculiar feeling of space around me, as if I were walking in silence toward the row of cars that had pulled into the pits. Toward the popping of flashbulbs.

Merrie's ballooning face rising up to greet me. Kiss me.

Virgin was running down pit lane, in those hopeless sling-back heels, setting off flashbulbs. I had the totally irrelevant thought that she was in fine shape for thirty-eight, running over a hundred yards in those shoes and a tight business skirt.

"Jesus," she said, stopping in front of me, then putting her arm around me and walking alongside, breathing heavily. "Are you OK?"

"Fine," I said. My voice sounded hollow, distant.

"I saw it on the big screen," she said. "God, it was awful. Horrible. What was she, some kook?"

"No, she wasn't . . . ," I started to say. Then I realized that I didn't know. She couldn't have been sane. I liked her. A friend of mine. "I knew her," I said. "Her name was Merrie, Alistair's wife."

"Alistair," Virgin said, stopping. "You mentioned that name before."

"He was my friend. The man who was killed the night before I met you in Paris."

"And she was his wife?"

"I think she killed him."

"She almost killed you. You knew her?" Virgin was staring at me intently, wanting more. We were surrounded by photographers, and yet they seemed miles away.

"She and Alistair were sweethearts at university. They had an accident on his motorcycle, and she was paralyzed. She told me she was in the hospital for months, and while she was there, he had an affair with Susan."

"Susan? Who's—"

"Never mind. Anyway, it wasn't a secret; he told Merrie about it. Then he asked her to marry him."

"And she did? She married him? That is very strange, Evers."

"I thought she must have loved him very much, after all that, to marry him."

"Loved him? He cripples her. She is lying in the hospital, what did you say, for months, while he is bonking this other woman? You can't be serious. I mean, you are such a romantic. Ask any woman. If she married him she didn't do it for love."

"What for then?"

"For what every woman wants. Revenge."

The reporters were thrusting their little cassette recorders at us, shouting questions. Maybe Virgin was right, that Merrie had wanted to kill Alistair for years. We started walking again. "How's Sam?"

"Sam? Sam's fine." She smiled happily.

"How'd he react to the TV?"

"What TV? You sure you're OK?"

"The race broadcast," I said, "when Murray Walker and James Hunt talked about our new aerodynamics."

"I don't know those guys or what you are talking about. We never turned on the TV."

Maybe it was just relief, but I had to laugh. The grand scheme and they never turned it on. The best laid plans. "OK, tell me this straight, Virgin. Why are you here, walking down pit lane with me?"

"For the pictures, dummo," she said, smiling, then trying a more serious, concerned look, looking into a flashing camera. "Panny called me this morning. He says Chantal's cutting way back on their budget for Formula One. I guess they are gonna go with that foot picture."

I looked blank.

"You know, the one they took in Canada, my feet point up and yours in between point down. They like that one. So he said, 'Get a couple more shots with Forrest in the pits after the race and that's it. We'll use the stuff we've got for the rest of the year.' So this is, like, it. Sad, huh? You are a real prick when you want to be, Forrest, but I like you. We were good together."

"I don't have any regrets about us. Except it was Sam, wasn't it, way back in Montreal, who sent you after me."

"Sure. So what? He thought it would be good for my career, give me a little boost, and he was right. Hey, you had your shot. I thought about it, you know, and Sam can be a mean prick too when he wants to be. But there is one big difference between you and Sam.'' We had reached the EFORT garage, and Virgin stood on tiptoe to whisper in my ear. ''He needs me.''

''You're sure he's not after your money?''

''Of course he is. It's part of my attraction,'' she said with her big show-biz smile. ''Look, I gotta go. Just wanted to be sure you're OK. You come to LA, give me a call, maybe we can get together.''

If Virgin had been looking into the garage she would have seen Susan coming through the back door. But Virgin was looking the other way to make sure the cameras were pointing at her from pit lane and give them a wink. I turned to smile at Susan, let her know I was OK, so I didn't see Virgin reach out and grab a handful of driving suit and driver's cock.

''No hard feelings?'' she said.